Frances Whiting is an award-winning Australian author, journalist and columnist. She is a senior feature writer for *QWeekend* magazine in the *Courier-Mail*, and her Sunday News Limited column has been delighting readers for twenty-three years. Words have been delighting her for much longer than that.

Also by Frances Whiting

Fiction
Walking on Trampolines

Non-Fiction
That's a Home Run, Tiger!
Oh, To Be a Marching Girl

FRANCES WHITING

THE BEST KIND OF BEAUTIFUL

MACMILLAN
Pan Macmillan Australia

First published 2019 in Macmillan by Pan Macmillan Australia Pty Ltd
1 Market Street, Sydney, New South Wales, Australia, 2000

Reprinted 2020

Cataloguing-in-Publication entry is available
from the National Library of Australia
http://catalogue.nla.gov.au

Typeset in 12.5/17.5 Adobe Garamond LT by Midland Typesetters, Australia
Printed in Australia by IVE Group Australia Pty Ltd

The paper in this book is FSC® certified.
FSC® promotes environmentally responsible,
socially beneficial and economically viable
management of the world's forests.

To John, Max and Tallulah
and my mother, Shirley Whiting

To be alive: not just the carcass
But the spark.
That's crudely put, but...

If we're not supposed to dance,
Why all this music?

Gregory Orr, from *Concerning the Book That Is the Body Of the Beloved* (Copper Canyon Press, 2005).

1

He looked, Florence thought, like a glazed Christmas ham. His face was a burnt shade of orange beneath the party lights as he shouted: 'You're one of Amanda's children, aren't you? Now what was the name of that song you all had . . .'

Florence pulled the corners of her mouth towards her ears like curtains.

She did not want to be here, at her cousin Samantha's eighteenth birthday party, with a potpourri of relatives who'd known her for twenty-seven years but kept telling her how much she'd grown. Florence longed to say to them, 'Well yes, because that's what people *do*, isn't it, grow?' She didn't much care for cousin Samantha either who she felt was determinedly pouty and had once bitten Florence on the leg when she was babysitting.

Florence's eyes narrowed, looking over the man's shoulder to the birthday girl and the black and white photographs of her in various poses dotted around the walls.

'Like soft porn,' her sister Isolde had whispered in passing earlier.

'What was it again?' the man shouted, his breath like a warm wet curry in her ear. 'Don't tell me, it's on the tip of my tongue.'

Florence shifted her attention back to him. 'All right I won't,' she said mutinously.

'Something about a cat . . .'

Florence sighed. '"Santa Was A Jazz Cat",' she said, giving in, because she could see he would not be giving up.

'That's it,' he said, slapping his thigh. 'Now, what was the chorus? Something about purring . . . Could you do that bit for me?'

'No,' she answered, thinking that if she did not get away from him this instant, she would find an apple, shove it in his stupid, piggy little mouth and ram it down his stupid, piggy little throat.

For a moment she felt a spark of shame at her thought, the *violence* of it.

But it had been a long night of flying the Saint Claire flag, as her mother Amanda insisted on calling any gathering of her clan in public, and Florence was exhausted.

'I'm going now,' she told the man, and then added, 'but ask my mother to sing it for you, she'd love that.'

Aunt Margo would be annoyed at her younger sister Amanda nabbing the limelight yet again, but Margo had irritated Florence earlier by poking at her ribs and saying she looked 'peaky', so Florence decided to poke back.

Then she left, before the man could say another word, before she could hear her mother oblige, purring at the piano keys.

Because Amanda would.

She always did.

*

'I can't believe you left the party without saying goodbye,' Isolde said the next morning. 'Lamanda is not happy with your trapdoor exit.'

High Notes music magazine had recently featured Amanda Saint Claire on its cover – half-closed glittered eyes, and curling white smoke straying from her lips, her head tilted, like a cat waiting to be stroked. *LA AMANDA*, its headline had read, which Puck, Florence's younger brother, had changed to 'Lamanda', a contraction Amanda Saint Claire did not care for. But the name had stuck, if only among her three children, who used it when she was out of earshot, or when they wanted to burrow a little bit beneath their mother's scented skin.

Florence considered her younger sister, Isolde's black-clad long arms and legs folded about her, giving her the appearance of a migratory crane that had somehow unexpectedly found itself in the kitchen. It was certainly unexpected for Florence. When she had moved out of Kinsey, their family home, three years earlier, Florence had thought she'd be living in the small worker's cottage alone, away from the constant thrumming within Kinsey's walls.

'It's only one bedroom, with a sleep-out, but it does have a rather lovely garden,' the rental agent had said, and Florence had thought, *Perfect*.

The cottage was only a few streets away from Kinsey, close enough to walk between the two homes but far enough to live your own, particular sort of life, and Florence had very much wanted to live her own, particular sort of life. But as she had begun to empty out her drawers and cupboards, filling and lining up cardboard boxes in the hallway, Florence had noticed that the boxes were multiplying, her neat rows joined by a jumble of boxes in various states of falling apart, and all of them marked *Issy*.

Isolde, being Isolde, had not said anything at all to Florence about the growing pile, except to once ask if Florence had any spare packing tape.

Florence had seen her moment. 'Isolde,' she'd said, 'do you think you're coming with me when I move out?'

Isolde had looked at her with the same eyes that had followed her out the gate when Florence had started primary school, a three-year-old Isolde sitting on Kinsey's front step calling, 'Where you going, Florrie?' Now Isolde had answered, 'Of course I'm coming with you, Florence,' untangling a jumble of coathangers dangling from her hand, then added, 'I always come with you.'

Florence had capitulated, as she had known she would from the moment the first box marked *Issy* had appeared. Isolde was like a cat that followed you around, rubbing itself against your legs and tripping you over in doorways. It was exasperating but when it slunk away you found yourself looking for it under the beds.

'Fine,' Florence had told her, 'but you're not getting the main bedroom.'

Florence looked at her younger sister in the kitchen of their cottage, which Florence mostly paid the rent for, and was mostly glad Isolde was there.

If only she would sit still for a minute.

Isolde, Florence thought, did not actually know how to sit, how to relax into a chair, instead she constantly folded her limbs into complicated shapes, like human origami. 'The Stork', 'The Crane', 'The Lily' – her sister could do a whole series.

She was doing it now, tucking her knees beneath her on the window seat and folding and unfolding her arms into a V shape, her hands clasped around the back of her neck.

'I know I should have said goodbye, Issy,' she told her shifting sister, 'but it was so hot, and some man with an orange face was annoying me.'

'Oh, that's Margo's boss, Adrian. Completely overdoes the self-tanning thing, but he's harmless – anyway, Mum is angry with you,' Isolde replied.

'Full-blown tempest or just scattered showers?'

'I'd say cloudy with a chance of thunder. Anyway, where were you?'

'I just needed to go home, Issy, I was tired.'

'Mum said you threw your glass at Adrian and stormed out.'

'What?'

'She said you had a fit over something he said, tossed your champagne in his face and left,' Isolde grinned.

Florence frowned at her mother's need to wrest every last drop of drama out of a situation, to make a thing – anything – bigger than it was. Amanda Saint Claire's latest album was called *Stories I Could Tell You*, and she and Puck had subtitled it, *And Not One Of Them True*.

'Well I didn't,' Florence said, 'and you should get going, Issy, if you don't want to be late for your voice lesson.'

Isolde and Puck were both in Mercy Jones, a five-piece jazz ensemble Florence had repeatedly refused to join, the notes of their previous family group, the Saint Claire Swingers, still sharp as glass shards in her ears.

The name – which all the children had hated – had been her parents' long-time agent, Richard Miller's idea. Richard, Florence often thought, was worse than that man in *The Sound of Music* who was always forcing the Von Trapp children to sing in public and wear Lederhosen.

What was his name?

Uncle Max, that was it – well, 'Uncle Richard' made Uncle Max look like a two-bit carnival hawker.

The Saint Claire Swingers was an unfortunate name in what Florence had come to think of as a particularly unfortunate period of her life, and never more so than each December when their gargantuan hit, 'Santa Was A Jazz Cat' came back to rake her with its claws.

The song had topped the 1988 Christmas chart, and had – the odd novelty song about drunken tradesmen notwithstanding – repeated the feat most years since. When it had first reached number one, Amanda and Florence's father, Lucas Saint Claire, had been thrilled, Isolde had been hysterical, Puck had been quietly pleased, and Florence had been fifteen, and mortified. But there was no getting away from it, Jazz Cat, as the family called it, had a thumping bass line, a swooning clarinet solo played by Lucas's nimble hands, and a chorus which featured Amanda felinely breathing 'purr, Santa, purr'.

Florence had hated cats ever since.

She was particularly dreading this year's Christmas, just a few months away and the last Christmas before an entirely new century began. 'Santa Was A Jazz Cat', she knew, was set to *erupt* in a wave of nostalgia, when everyone was caught between hoping that the year 2000 would herald some sort of new world, and already looking over their shoulders and pining for the old one.

Not that it mattered. She would never perform it, or any other song, with her family again.

The last time Puck had asked, she had told him, truthfully, she would rather eat the damn cat.

After Isolde left for rehearsal, automatically ducking her head beneath the front door – 'Freakishly tall,' a man had once commented to Florence about her sister. 'Statuesque,' she had corrected him – Florence put the coffee cups in the sink and called her mother.

'Hello,' Amanda Saint Claire's answering machine message began, her voice deep and low against a clarinet solo in the background ('So obvious, Mum,' Puck had said), 'it's Amanda speaking, if you are calling regarding either the Saint Claires or Mercy Jones, please contact Richard Miller at Miller's Music . . . Ciao!'

Florence hung up without leaving a message; her mother pretended not to know how to use the machine and would probably not return her call even if she did.

Besides, she could imagine the conversation . . .

'Mum, I did not throw my glass at that orange-faced man.'

'Didn't you, darling?' – Amanda, distracted – 'Well that's a shame, I rather wish you had. Do you know he made me sing Jazz Cat in front of everyone? So tiresome . . . Margo was a bit put out, I think . . .'

Florence shook her head at her imaginary mother and went into the laundry to iron her uniform: khaki shorts, and shirt with *The Green Team* emblazoned across the back and beneath that, in looping letters, *We Plant Dreams*.

Florence often thought how absurd the slogan was.

The Green Team did not plant dreams, but they did plant hundreds of native saplings in the Mount Bell State Forest, the huge tract of bushland that nudged part of her own East Elm neighbourhood, casting its grey shadows at its edges. Florence and the other members of the team also spent a good deal of their day making sure the forest never actually crossed the line into the manicured lawns of East Elm, hacking away at the lantana and cat's claw like an advancing artillery unit.

No, Florence reflected, pressing the iron down hard on the raised lettering, there was nothing dreamy about it. Mostly it was hard work that left her flesh knotted and her bones aching and Florence rubbing her neck at night with her sore, sorry hands.

Once a little girl had asked Florence in that reedy voice children have, 'Do you really plant dreams?'

'No,' Florence had answered, 'of course not. We plant native fauna,' and the girl had spun away, her voice trailing behind her, 'I was just asking . . .'

Florence turned the shirt over to its front with her own name embroidered across its right-hand pocket. *Flo*, it said. She was not a Flo, although Isolde had persisted in calling her that for a brief time in their teens, until Florence had given her a Chinese burn to make her stop.

But she was not, she thought, particularly a Florence either. Florences were winsome creatures, like that girl Miranda who vanished into thin air in *Picnic at Hanging Rock*, disappearing between the looming grey boulders with those irritating panpipes playing in the background.

'I am more of a Ruth,' she decided, picking up her uniform and taking it into the bathroom. 'Someone to be taken seriously.'

Not an easy thing to pull off in her family.

As she changed her clothes in the bathroom, Florence took in her reflection in the mirror, a crack in one of its corners where Isolde had once thrown an electric toothbrush. Her skin was a deep, nut brown; her body, angular and, her last lover had whispered, prodding at her ribs, 'too thin'. 'Just right,' she'd answered, and shown him the door.

Florence ran her hands along her arms and felt the slight bump of her muscles on her forearm, pleased by their contours – useful arms, she thought, *worker's* arms.

Who'd have thought it? She grinned at her reflection, pulling her long hair – dark like her eyes; 'Honestly, you're like a *crow*, darling,' she heard her mother say – into a tight ponytail at the nape of her neck.

The woman who looked back at her was not beautiful, as Amanda sometimes felt compelled to point out. 'You, darling,' her mother would say, extending her index finger to tuck beneath Florence's chin, tilting her face this way and that, 'are not one of those horrible little pretty girls with faces like Pekinese who age so badly, no, you are far more interesting looking,' and Florence remained unsure whether or not it was a compliment.

But she's right, Florence thought, staring hard at her face. *I am interesting looking. More of a dragon flower than a rose.*

Better than looking like that drippy Miranda, she decided, and headed out the door to walk to work.

*

'Morning Flo,' Victor Babieri called out from behind his fence, sagging under the weight of the passionfruit strung along it like strands of popcorn. 'I've got some snow pea cuttings for you, if you like.'

'I do like,' she answered, 'thanks Victor,' bristling a little, as she always did, at the 'Flo'.

But Victor was harmless, and a man taken to endlessly hanging around his front fence casting for conversation since his partner Leon had died a year ago. So Florence decided not to bristle and instead smiled, giving him the Saint Claire 'maximum wattage', blinding in both its span and delivery, the whole, open horseshoe of teeth. All the Saint Claire children could do it, a smile that flicked on like a switch when the house lights eased down and the stage ones crept up.

'I'll pick them up later, Victor,' she said, and continued to the end of the street where she passed through the two lampposts that guarded the entrance to Rushton Park and always made Florence think of the entrance to Narnia.

Florence followed the park's main path through its avenue of Hill's Figs, lifting her eyes as she always did to their light grey branches clasped in prayer above her. *People shouldn't bother going to cathedrals, they should just look up*, Florence thought, *if it's grace they're looking for.*

Then she walked through the children's playground, the usual scatter of yesterday's forgotten balls and water bottles on the ground, its swings riderless and slightly swaying. Although she was not especially fond of children, she thought there was something particularly grim about a playground without them in it.

Florence stopped to pick up a lone sparkly shoe and put it on a post, knowing that the tiny Cinderella who owned it, or more likely the tiny Cinderella's mother, might come back later to claim it. *Quicker than waiting for a prince*, she thought, then took the small curved path from the playground to the East Elm Library, with its jaunty sign welcoming visitors in eighteen different languages. Florence, although sorely tempted at times, didn't have the heart to tell Monty Rollins, the head librarian, that at least two of them were spelt incorrectly.

The Green Team had their small, shambolic office in the library and their banner was draped hopefully, if somewhat limply, across its entrance. Last year some local kids had spray-painted over its jaunty *We Plant Dreams* slogan, so it proclaimed: *The Green Team: We Plant Pot!* and Florence laughed out loud at the memory.

She had supervised the sign's original creation, working with the children from the nearby East Elm Primary School. They had painted its calico letters outside on the lawn, and the students in their hot-pink art smocks had looked like chattering flamingos on the grass.

In return for their space at the library, granted by the long-standing local member Barry Piccolo, the Green Team was required to teach the children of East Elm about the wonders of nature – but not, Barry had warned, wagging his finger at them and wriggling his eyebrows, 'the birds and the bees'.

Florence found Barry Piccolo to be a very tiresome man.

He gave out bumper stickers that said: 'Need to Know? Call Piccolo', sported a comb-over that stretched like cling wrap across his skull, and went to every single public event East Elm had on offer.

Barry Piccolo, it was said, would go to the opening of a barn door.

Nevertheless Florence and the other members of the Green Team voted for him at every election, worried that if he were turfed out, so would they be.

Florence usually did one or two school sessions a week, sitting on a hard chair in the children's section amid a flurry of five-year-olds clutching kidney-shaped beans in their soft, sweaty hands.

'Are these Jack and the Beanstalk beans?' a little boy had asked one morning, opening his fingers like a starfish.

'No,' Florence had answered truthfully, 'that's a fairy tale, it never happened,' later earning a sharp rebuke from Monty Rollins, who explained to her the importance of magic and wonder, and Florence had explained to him the importance of reality.

But the truth was, Florence didn't need Monty to remind her of the earth's magic. She felt it every time it cracked beneath her spade, the moment it yielded to release its strange scent of otherness. Florence loved watching the first trembles of the saplings she had planted, or the silent unfolding of a flower's throat; when the earth's skin broke and gave up its secrets, Florence felt like she was witnessing the real entrance into Narnia.

Florence passed beneath the welcome sign and through the library to the Green Team's office, where a man with a messy thatch of fair hair leant back in an armchair in the corner, the broadsheet paper in his hands, his work boots unlaced on his feet. He looked up and smiled at her.

'Good morning, Florence.'

Albert Flowers, who had his own particular scent of otherness.

Albert was the first co-worker Florence had met when she'd joined the Green Team a year earlier. He'd pointed to his own embroidered name, before saying it aloud, and she'd echoed the gesture and said, 'Flo,' and then added, 'Actually it's Florence, I don't know why they shortened it.' Isolde's face had flashed before her: 'Probably to make you seem friendlier.'

Albert had smiled at her. 'They asked me if I wanted Bertie.'

'The horror,' she'd replied.

In the days and weeks that followed, she'd come to realise that just as she was not a Flo, Albert was most certainly not a Bertie. Berties, she thought, were men who laughed like braying donkeys and drank beer from their tennis shoes.

No, despite his rigorous social life, Albert was an Albert, no matter how many parties he went to.

He was also attractive, if you liked, as Isolde said when she met him at Florence's twenty-sixth birthday lunch, a man who looked like a garden shed.

Looking at Albert now, his legs set like pylons on the floor, his arms hunkered around the paper and his thick jaw tilted towards her, she could see Isolde's point.

Albert was a giant – not Isolde giant, not all gangly limbs and sharp corners, but solid and sturdy, able, she supposed, to withstand strong winds.

Exactly like a well-built garden shed.

If you liked that sort of thing.

That first morning he had led her into the Green Team's office, saying, 'This is Florence, everyone, be kind.'

Because Albert Flowers was kind, not just to Florence, but also to Monty who was pompous and ridiculous in his spotted bow ties, and who constantly fussed around the library shelves like a moth caught in a bell jar. He was kind to the children of East Elm Primary who tumbled into the library like acrobats and blew their noses on their sleeves and didn't care who saw them. Once she had seen him scoop up Mrs Trenton, an elderly sparrow of a woman, as she struggled to reach the slot outside the library to return her books. 'Alley-oop,' he had said, lifting her deftly off her feet and then returning her gently to the ground, where she'd stood rosy-cheeked and twittering.

'Hello Albert,' Florence smiled back. 'It's going to be hot out there today,' adding, 'I'll think of you in the thirty-five-degree heat while I'm in here in the set-at-a-very-comfortable twenty-four degrees air conditioning.'

Albert got up from his desk and plucked his daypack off the hook, tossing a water bottle in it.

'Some of us, Florence,' he said as he walked out the door, 'have dreams to plant.'

'Really, because I thought it was salt wattle today?'

Albert grinned at her. 'That too,' he said, closing the office door behind him.

Her family, she thought, would be shocked to see her like this, *bantering.*

There were very few moments when Florence felt truly relaxed. She remembered being at one of those awful university balls when she was studying horticulture, and a boy from her class had passed her a joint saying, 'Here you go, Flo, this will loosen you up,' and Florence had refused, without telling him that was exactly what she was afraid of.

But when she and Albert tramped into the park's fold, with the flashing blurs of lorikeets swooping overhead, Florence felt herself settle. While she scattered seeds on the forest floor, or felt the satisfying tug beneath her fingers as a recalcitrant weed gave way, Albert would tell her his stories that began when the automated doors of the library closed quietly behind him at the end of each day. Then life would rush at Albert Flowers, taking him in cabs to parties, or drinks at rooftop bars in the city, or weekends on houseboats, and Florence would listen and sometimes imagine herself on the boat, or at the party, or gazing at the wash of city lights beneath her with a salt-lipped glass in her hand.

Life did not rush at Florence when the East Elm Library's door slid shut. It did not call to her or shout across dance floors. The siren song that Florence mostly answered to was the whistle of the kettle on her stove's blue-lipped flames. Unless of course you counted being trotted out at various events as a paid-up member of the Saint Claire clan, or occasionally joining Isolde and her friends for dinner, or being dragged to gigs by Puck or . . . the other thing.

Florence blinked and a faint colour rose to her cheeks, as if just by thinking about it her own particular cat would be out of the bag.

The Green Team's office door opened and Monty Rollins appeared.

'Florence,' he said in his rich, fruity voice, 'your public awaits.'

Florence went out into the library as a jumble of red and green checked tunics came tumbling in, smelling like wet sandwiches.

God, thought Florence, *it's like being trapped inside a lunchbox.*

'Good morning, Miss Saint Claire,' the children chorused, their voices like birds.

'Good morning,' she answered them. 'I hope you're all going to at least try to sit still today . . . Now,' she asked brightly, 'who would like to hear the story of *The Very Hungry Caterpillar*?'

'I wouldn't,' answered Pedro Perkins, five years old, dark hair, strands of it permanently dangling over his left eye.

'Tough luck, Pedro,' she said. 'We don't always get what we want,' earning a raised eyebrow from Monty hovering at the shelves nearby.

Well we don't, she wanted to tell him.

'Right,' she said, pulling herself back to the cluster of children at her feet, '*In the still of the night an egg lay* . . .'

After the last school group had left for the day, Florence stacked the beanbags in the corner, plucked the odd empty chip packet from the floor and returned the books she had read aloud to the shelves.

She sat at her desk looking up plant species in the library's bright red reference books, waiting for Albert to come in and say, 'Still here, Florence? Fancy a coffee on the way home?'

If he had somewhere to go, and Albert Flowers was a man who often had somewhere to go, they would part ways at the gate to her cottage, and she would stand by her pink-tipped camellia bushes and wave him off.

Isolde, witnessing the goodbye from the upstairs window, once said, 'Honestly, Florence, it's like he's going to *war*.'

Florence would watch him wander down her street, stopping to chat to Victor, lying in wait behind the fence to ask Albert about his butter pumpkins. Then Albert would continue on his way to dinner or drinks with his band of friends, who he sometimes referred to as 'the usual suspects', a phrase that made Florence bristle, and feel momentarily glad she wasn't one of them.

Every now and again Albert would come inside the cottage, stamping his work boots on the mat outside the door, and hang his hat on the hook in the hallway, filling her house with his frame and smelling vaguely like damp forest leaves. They would sit at her kitchen table and he would fill her in on what he and his friends were up to that night, and she would smile and nod as if she too had a band of usual suspects, girls, she supposed, with names like Tilly and Flick who would take their shoes off to dance.

Albert's friends seemed to be mostly someone called Jeremy, and a girl called Lydia – whom Florence suspected was irritating.

Florence found the name Lydia irritating all by itself.

Somewhere in his telling, Florence would close her eyes for a moment and enter the story, elbowing her way in amongst the semicircles laughing at something Jeremy or Lydia – no, not Lydia – said.

She would find herself walking home barefoot beside him, her feet damp from the grass, the thin strap of her shoes hooked on the tips of her fingers, the cool night air on her cool, dark skin.

Sometimes Albert would tilt his head back and laugh at something one of his friends had done. He had so many friends, she'd thought once, panicking, and she only really had Isolde and Puck – and Victor, if you counted a man who said good morning to you from behind his runner beans every day.

As a child Florence had never been the sort of girl to have a knot of other girls to link arms with; her ears had not been the ones secrets were whispered into; and in the migratory paths of mothers dropping their daughters off at homes around the neighbourhood on weekends, Kinsey had not been on the route.

Florence knew why, she had always known why, and hadn't much cared for the most part.

The Saint Claires were not like the other families who lived in the streets around Kinsey, and the Saint Claire children were not like the other children who rode their bikes and skateboards along those streets. Sometimes Florence would watch them through the rear window as Richard's van pulled away to take the Saint Claires to gigs, and she'd splay her hand against the glass. She wondered what might happen if she curled her hand into a fist and rapped loudly on the windscreen, so they would all look up from the bikes strewn on the footpath and see that she was there. Florence thought that Albert never really looked up and saw that she was there either, or if he did that he didn't suppose she was the sort of person who would enjoy his nocturnal wanderings.

Perhaps he thought she was not at all the type of girl who would find it fun – a lark, Lamanda would say – to swim all the way home by climbing over fences into people's swimming pools.

Scowling, she thought, *I could have a lark, I could be larkish.*

Except she couldn't, because she was prickly.

Everyone said so.

*

When Florence was nineteen, she had overheard her mother and her best friends Leticia Pepsi and Nancy Adams through the lounge-room door left slightly ajar.

'The problem with Florence,' Leticia had announced, 'is that she's prickly.'

'Like a cactus,' her mother had agreed.

'What's that desert cactus?' Nancy had asked. 'You know the one like a big flat hand with all those great thorns jutting out of it?'

'A prickly pear,' Leticia had answered.

'Well that's her then,' Nancy had continued. 'Lovely but spikey.'

Florence had blushed, mostly because Nancy had called her lovely, but also because she felt uncomfortable being discussed in this way, in any way.

'And talented,' Leticia had added. 'It kills me that she won't sing.'

'I wish Lucas was here,' Amanda said, 'he'd know what to do with her,' and Leticia and Nancy had murmured their agreement.

Florence had padded past the door and into her father's studio, where his music scores lay on top of the piano and his newspapers sat beside his wing-backed armchair, books stacked on top of them, scattered crumbs caught beneath one of their jackets.

Photos of her father and Amanda, flattened like insects behind glass, stared from the walls: as Bonnie and Clyde on their way to a fancy dress party; of Amanda looking past her father's shoulder on a boat, both of them laughing in the wind. In a cluster around them, photos of Florence and Isolde and Puck: Puck's impish face smiling from behind the wheel of his pedal car; a tiny Isolde enveloped in her mother's fur and high heels; and one of Florence on stage, holding a microphone bigger than her hand.

Her favourite photo was one of the whole family at the beach beneath a red and white striped umbrella, Amanda's hair tucked into a terry-towelling turban, and Florence wrapped in a towel in her father's arms.

It was like being inside a conch shell.

Lucas Saint Claire's 'lucky' clarinet leant against the wall, waiting for his lips to settle against the mouthpiece. He always moved his head just slightly to one side before he began to play, followed by a sharp and deep intake of a breath. When she was younger, Florence liked to sit with her back against the hallway wall, her legs straight out in front of her, listening. Her father's music always soothed her, whether she'd been fighting with Isolde, or later if some boy she'd liked had met her blinking, eager glances with shrugging indifference. She would sit with her head tipped back against the smooth walls and blot out everything except the notes escaping under the door and dancing down the hallway. After a while, her father would poke his head around the studio door, sensing her presence in the hallway. 'Come on in, Florence,' he'd say. 'Come and make some music with your old man.'

The music room's bay window looked out onto the street below and the enormous pine that stood sentry in the front yard of Kinsey with its three tyres still dangling hopefully from its branches, even though the children were long past swinging. Florence liked to sit at the window seat, chin resting against her cupped hands on the sill, and look out through the branches to the people below carrying groceries and holding children's hands, sometimes looking up to the house where her family lived.

When her family had started to become well known, people had stopped walking past Kinsey's green and white gables and started pausing in front of it. They would crane their necks to the music room's window, where a seven-year-old Isolde had once flashed her bare bottom against the glass, and Florence had been both horrified and full of admiration.

Waiting for Albert in the Green Team's office, Florence laughed, picturing Issy's pale white cheeks pressed against the window, her dress hitched up around her waist. She could see Lucas striding across the music room floor to lift a wriggling Issy off the seat, but now Florence couldn't recall whether he was shouting or laughing at her.

Either was possible, but either way she couldn't ask him.

Because Lucas Saint Claire was dead, killed in the very ordinary, un-Lucas Saint Claire manner of crossing a road without looking both ways and being mowed down by a milk truck.

Had he looked one particular way, he would have seen the van bearing down on him and felt its low growl in time to neatly sidestep it, wink and smile at the person nearest to him and say, sucking in his breath to form a long, low whistle, 'That was a close one.' But he had not looked, and he had died – Lucas Saint Claire, 'famous jazzman, sometime actor, writer, husband, and father' – 'in a motor vehicle accident', the obituary in the *Argus* had read. This was in deference to Amanda's wishes that the unfortunate detail of Lucas being taken out by a Packers Dairy milk truck be omitted.

The obituary spoke of his talent, his artistry, his break-out album *Love Walked In*, his mainstream hit 'Santa Was A Jazz Cat', his marriage to Amanda – 'one of jazz's most enduring professional, and personal, collaborations' – and his three talented children, each named, it noted, 'with trademark Saint Claire flair'.

Amanda, in head to toe black, with a net cobwebbed over her face, had been inconsolable at the funeral, sobbing at her husband's demise, mostly, it seemed, at the way in which he had met his end. 'A milk truck!' she had kept saying, 'A milk truck!' It was exactly, Florence thought, like Lady Bracknell shrieking, 'A handbag!'

Isolde, of course, had gone into fourteen-year-old histrionics at the wake, flapping around in complicated layers and getting in everyone's way until Leticia had taken Florence aside and said, 'For God's sake, do something about your sister, she's like a March fly in there.'

And Puck?

Puck had been Puck, in a deep blue velvet suit with a shiny blue tie, his pork-pie hat pulled down almost to his eyebrows, sitting on the grass outside the hall, drumming his fingers against his thighs.

Puck, Lucas always said, was a born drummer, emerging from the womb with rhythm in his veins.

Puck drummed when he was happy, he drummed when he was sad, and he drummed when he didn't know what he was, a twelve-year-old boy at his father's funeral, wearing a suit of velvet armour.

Florence had sat stony-faced through the service and scowled her sixteen-year-old scowl when anyone approached her at the wake.

Prickly, everyone said afterwards.

*

The door to the office opened and Albert walked in, smiling at Florence as he took his daypack from his shoulder.

'Still here, Florence?' he said.

'Obviously,' she replied and instantly regretted it.

It had sounded sarcastic when she had meant it to sound fun, flippant, *larkish*, and Albert had dipped his head the way he did when he was unsure of what to say next.

'How's the lantana in the east section?' she asked, altering her tone to a lighter *dolcissimo.*

'Unruly,' he smiled at her. 'How was our little friend Pedro?'

'Also unruly,' she smiled back.

'Coffee?' he asked.

'Absolutely,' she answered, standing to grab her bag off the hook.

They walked home the usual way, ducking the odd East Elm third grader whizzing past on their BMX – 'Hello Miss Saint Claire, hello Mr Flowers' – and through the park, but today Albert suggested a diversion from their path.

'Let's just sit, Florence,' he said, 'if you have time?'

He looked tired, leaning back on the park bench to close his eyes against the sky. 'So I went to this wedding on the weekend . . .'

2

'I'm not in love with her.'

'What?'

'I said I don't love her, mate.'

Albert and Simon Bishop looked across the lawn to where Simon's bride was twirling underneath her father Tom's outstretched arm on the dance floor.

Siobhan Peters – now Bishop – looked, Albert thought, like spinning fairy floss, her white gown taking on a lolly-pink hue beneath the party lights.

'Oh,' he replied, watching her dance, joyfully, cluelessly, in her father's arms. Tom Peters held his daughter close. He would hold her closer still, Albert thought, if he could hear this conversation by the lake.

'Don't just say "oh", say something helpful, mate,' Simon Bishop demanded, his face too close to Albert's.

'All right,' Albert replied. 'Stop drinking' – *and stop calling me mate*, he added to himself.

'Fuck you,' Simon answered, throwing a stone into the ornamental lake, its small weight immediately sinking into the inky blackness.

Albert had wandered down to the wooden landing to take a break from the party and the conga line that was about to inevitably break out on the dance floor.

He had been thinking about what he would tell Florence later if she asked him to describe the wedding dress – frothy, he had decided – when Simon had lurched up in the darkness beside him, a beer in his hand.

'Got a smoke?' he'd asked.

'No, sorry,' Albert had answered, wishing Simon would lurch away again, back to his leering mates who had cheered his leering speech, while Siobhan had smiled wanly beside him.

Siobhan, Albert thought, probably had a life of smiling wanly ahead of her.

Lucky she had a sense of humour – earlier when Albert had complimented her on her wedding dress she had laughed. 'I know, I know, I look like the wedding cake,' and laughed harder when he'd said, 'Only the first tier.'

There was something endearing about Siobhan Peters, something about her face that was slightly off kilter, making her, he thought, the best kind of beautiful, the almost kind.

Albert had met Siobhan a year or so earlier at his local watering hole, World's End, where she had insisted on paying for their drinks and had pretended to be interested in his ongoing struggles with the African boxthorn weeds. He'd gone to World's End after work, still in his uniform, and she had introduced herself at the bar, the two of them chatting easily for a couple of rounds before Simon had turned up, kissing her on the cheek and raising his eyebrows just slightly at Albert.

'Hi sweetheart,' he'd said, then looking at the name embroidered across Albert's chest: 'and Albert I presume – either that or you've nicked someone else's shirt.'

It was a funny line, Albert had conceded, but there was something in the delivery of it, something in the way Simon had sat back and waited for the laugh, that had rankled. Men like Simon Bishop, he thought, always waited for the laughs, knowing they would come, knowing as they tossed their throwaway lines into the air that someone would always reach out to catch them.

Listening to Simon order a drink, Albert had realised he knew Simon's younger brother, Douglas. They had the same deep, clipped inflections – to Albert's ears, all the Bishop boys sounded like Malcolm Fraser. Douglas had been in the same year at the grammar school Albert had left a decade earlier, loosening his tie on his way out through Farrow's grey, whorled gates, never to put one on again.

Douglas, he remembered, had once been knocked out during a rugby match, not getting off the ground, not getting up while it seemed the sky held its breath, and his teammates had shifted on their feet, biting at their lips.

When Douglas did get up, groggy, empty-eyed, the boys in his team had been held back from touching him, while the medical staff ran onto the field.

'I was there,' he told Simon, 'the day your brother got knocked out at rugby.'

Simon's brow had furrowed, trying to place Albert in amongst all the old school ties.

'Were you one of Dougie's mates, did you come up to the house?' Simon asked, and Albert had noted the 'up'.

Once a year the Bishops threw open the doors of their home, Avalon, to the public, its pale salmon brickwork sitting atop East Elm's only hill like a pale glacé cherry on a dessert. Natalie Bishop would welcome people from just behind its elaborate front gates with their curling wrought-iron inlays, while her children – there was a younger sister as well, Sadie, who had flirted with him earlier at the reception – would serve iced tea from jugs to people who would never ordinarily be wandering about their garden. The Bishop boys – and they would be called the Bishop boys even as they turned into old men – would be stationed behind the bar, serving flutes of champagne and orange juice to women in a swathe of bright dresses fluttering like Monarch butterflies about the cabbage roses.

Albert wasn't sure how many Bishop boys there were – he thought perhaps three, but it was hard to tell. They were indistinguishable from one another, and from most of the other Farrow boys, always travelling in small packs, and looking, Albert thought, like striped rugby jerseys caught together in a dryer.

Albert had never attended an open day at Avalon, but his mother Georgina once went with a friend, returning to their family home with a sigh etched on her face. 'It's such a beautiful house,' she kept saying, and somewhere in it he heard the reproach to his father Laurence that they themselves did not live in it. They lived quite near it, their back fence actually met once of its boundaries, but near enough, it seemed, really wasn't good enough.

Now he looked at Simon, who had grown up within those walls, who had, it seemed, everything, including the almost beautiful Siobhan, and still was not satisfied.

Albert tilted his head towards the underbelly of the sky, the clouds slung low above them.

'We should probably get back in,' he said, 'they'll be waiting for you – Siobhan will be waiting for you.'

The music from the marquee drifted down to them, carrying with it the sounds of laughter and music, drifting bubbles of happiness.

Simon suddenly sat up straighter and slung an arm around Albert's shoulders.

Aaah, Albert thought, *the pally stage.*

'The thing is, mate,' Simon said, 'you've got the right idea – no ties, birds lined up to meet you, no fucking worries, no bloody dinner dates with the parents . . .'

'So why do it?' Albert asked, looking into Simon's face in the semi-darkness.

'Because it's the right thing to do, isn't it? Three years we've been together . . . she's put in the time.'

She's put in the time?

Albert shifted, causing Simon's hand to drop from his shoulder.

What was it, he thought, that made perfectly sane women like Siobhan Peters fall for men like Simon Bishop?

Did her mother, Olivia, whom Albert knew vaguely through the library's garden club, look at her daughter when she was extending her shapely leg so Simon could remove a frilly garter with his teeth, and think, *Twelve years of school, five years of debating, four years of architecture at uni, a Rotary scholarship to study in Germany and she ends up with this . . .* ? Or did she look at Simon Bishop and see no further than the salmon-pink bricks of Avalon, its gates opening to let her in?

He had, of course, no idea what Olivia Peters thought of her new son-in-law, but he knew what he did.

Albert felt the rush of words come to him, too late to stem the flow from his lips. It always happened this way, when he was riled up, when he was dealing with people like Simon Bishop.

They tumbled from him in free fall before he could catch them and slow them down, part of him, if he was truthful, not really caring where they fell.

'Simon,' he said, 'you are a fucking idiot, and you've probably always been a fucking idiot, but by some complete freak of nature Siobhan has decided that you're her fucking idiot, and if you do not go back in there and take the miracle that is Siobhan Peters in your arms and love and honour and cherish her for the rest of your days, and get down on your knees and thank the Lord that she sees something in you that fuck knows I can't, then you are even more of a fucking idiot than even I give you credit for.'

The lake lapped beneath them.

Simon swayed unsteadily, his body tipping to one side before he righted himself by placing his hands on Albert's shoulders.

He stared at him, eyes pulling into focus then narrowing as he tightened his grip on Albert's shoulders.

'Bloody hell mate,' he said, 'you're right,' and walked unsteadily back up the hill, making a beeline for his bride who was joining the conga line that had just broken out.

*

'So, what was the bride's dress like?' Florence asked.

'Frothy,' Albert said, 'decidedly frothy.'

'Did you stay long?'

'Right,' Albert told her, 'to the bitter end,' and then he told her about the food and the dancing and the conga line, which had snaked, eventually, all the way down to the lake, where Simon Bishop's mates had thrown him in.

'What a lark,' Florence found herself saying, and then immediately wished she hadn't.

'Actually, it was the highlight of the evening,' Albert said, 'Simon Bishop being tossed in the drink.'

'You don't like him?' Florence asked, and Albert told her about his conversation with the runaway groom, Florence visibly prickling at Simon's 'she's put in the time' remark.

There were some circles in Albert's social life that Florence had no desire to elbow her way into at all, and the Bishop clan sounded like one of them. They reminded her of her parents' late-night crowd, men and women who romped and caroused at afterparties and occasionally spent the night at Kinsey, sleeping off the evening before on one of its couches, a man once shouting at Puck to 'shut up with the fucking drumming'. Florence had flown at him. 'You shut up!' she had shouted back. 'And get off my mother's tartan couch.'

Florence smiled, she had always liked to be specific. Now, listening to Albert, she thought it was a good thing she hadn't elbowed her way into that particular conversation. She would have been specific with Simon Bishop too.

'So what did you tell him?' Florence asked.

Albert smiled at her. 'I told him he was a fucking idiot.'

He stretched his arms wide along the bench, his arm nudging Florence's back as he asked, 'What about you? What did you get up to on the weekend, Florence?'

'Oh just pottering around,' she said, which was largely true.

Largely.

Florence felt the lights from her own Saturday night on her skin.

*

She pulled the netted cap tightly to her skull, wriggling it a little at her ears as she always did.

It was a ritual, the linking of her hands beneath her chin, elbows propped on the dressing table, as she studied her bare face in the mirror.

Dipping her fingers into the cold crème she massaged it into her skin, eyes closed, then patted her hands against her cheeks and ran the tips of her fingers along her eyebrows. She applied her base with a sponge, turning her face one way, then the other, considering. Then she reached for her brushes and began applying her eye shadows – Bayou Blue, Pot Black, Chartreuse Shimmer – brushing each shade across her lids, before painting on the thick black eyeliner, turning her wrist to apply the perfect flick at the corners.

The mirror made the pupils of her eyes look strangely iridescent, which was, she thought, exactly how she felt: strangely iridescent, burning bright, like the light bulbs that danced around the mirror's frame.

Reaching for her lip pencil, she outlined its red tip along her lips, drawing a cupid bow where there was none, then filled it in with Cardinal Red lipstick.

Finally she dipped her biggest brush into the pot of powder blush, blowing on it as she raised it to her cheeks, tiny pink particles dancing in the light, and swept it along her cheekbones.

Lastly the wig, a short, cherry-red bob, its long fringe sweeping across the side of her face, almost covering her left eye.

She raised her head slightly and stared at the woman in the mirror.

'We're ready for you, Miss Suki,' the stage manager called from the dressing room door.

Florence stood up and considered herself one last time in the mirror, while beside her the Nightshades wriggled out of their makeup chairs to join her.

'This place is a dump,' Veronica Allen said.

Orla O'Loan rolled her eyes. 'Like you're normally at the Opera 'Ouse.'

'Let's leave the banter for the show, ladies,' Florence said, clicking out of the door in her kitten heels.

*

'So you didn't get up to much?' Albert was asking, his voice bringing her back to the jacaranda branches dipping above them.

'No,' she answered, the last strains of Miss Suki and her Nightshades fading away. 'Puck came over and I helped him with some of his music theory, he's got his final exams coming up.'

'How's he going, is he all right?'

Albert was one of the few people outside of the Saint Claire circle who knew about Puck's habit of disappearing, dropping out of their lives as if a trapdoor had sprung beneath him, so that one of the most repeated phrases uttered at family gatherings or gigs was, 'Where the fuck is Puck?' through gritted teeth.

Florence smiled at him. 'Well, he hasn't disappeared in a puff of smoke for a while, so that's a plus.'

'A Puck of smoke,' Albert smiled, then added, 'Sorry, that was truly appalling. So where does he go, Florence, do you know?'

'I don't think he goes anywhere in particular, he just sort of hits the road. My father used to say that Puck has so much rhythm in him, he has to count it out with his feet.'

Puck's wanderings had long been accepted by his family, although when he was very little – five or six, Florence remembered – Amanda would sit fidgeting, watching the door and going up to the music room to look out the window, until Lucas, if he was home, would finally say 'Go', and she would jump in her car to drive around the neighbourhood, Florence often riding shotgun beside her.

But later, when he was older, around nine or ten, they all – even Amanda – just let him go.

Florence was watching Albert's face closely, the way he was digesting this particular branch of her family tree.

He had already met Amanda, who had flirted with him and said something vaguely suggestive about the size of his feet, and Isolde who had flapped around him like a magpie pecking at an insect, and Puck who had nodded at him, jerking his head down in what she supposed was meant to be a hello before ducking out the door. Just once, Florence had thought, it would be lovely if she brought someone home and her family just said 'Hello', without putting on a display of all their particular tics. The Saint Claires had always been like peacocks among pigeons, and Florence had often longed to be a pigeon.

When she was eight years old a family had moved in next door to Kinsey for about a year, renting the Prentices' house while Professor Prentice was on secondment to an interstate university. Florence had stared, round-eyed, from the music room's window as a car had pulled up behind the removal van and a man and a woman had got out, followed by two boys and a girl she thought looked about her age.

'Please let her be my friend,' Florence had prayed, screwing up her eyes with the effort. 'Please let her be my friend, and let her be . . . normal.'

And Amy Burton was normal, Florence remembered, gloriously so.

She and Florence had quickly formed a friendship, one Amy's mother, Caroline, kept a watchful eye on, the Saint Claires perhaps not quite what the Burtons had in mind for their daughter.

Still, Amy and Florence had flourished, Florence spending every spare minute at the Burtons' for the whole year they had lived next door, both girls weeping the day the removal truck returned.

The first time they had played together Florence had asked Amy if she'd like to go down to the local creek with her.

'I don't think I'm allowed,' Amy had answered. 'I'm not really allowed to do anything.' And Florence, who was allowed to do everything, thought that sounded wonderful.

Lucas had found her infatuation with Amy and her family hilarious.

He'd called it her 'Year of Living Not Very Dangerously'.

A single, purple flower fell on Florence's shoulder, and she felt the soft shock of Albert's hand plucking it off.

'The first of the season,' he was saying. 'You know it's good luck if a jacaranda flower falls on you.'

'I thought it meant if you hadn't started studying for your exams you were in trouble,' she answered.

'That too,' Albert grinned. 'Anyway, you were saying about Puck's travels, do you worry about him when he takes off?'

Florence shook her head. 'No,' she said, 'although I think my mother did when he was smaller. I used to too, probably more than anybody, because I was the eldest and thought it was my job to take care of him. But Puck has always known how to take care of himself. He got teased a lot at school, mostly because of his name; you can't imagine how awful it was for him.'

'Oh, I can,' Albert answered. 'I know how cruel kids can be.'

Florence felt the rush of words to her lips before she had a chance to catch them. 'No, you don't Albert,' she said. 'You actually have absolutely no idea at all.'

Albert had been twirling the jacaranda between his thumb and index finger; now he stood up and released it, the purple trumpet falling slowly to the ground.

'Actually, I better get going,' he said, 'I've got some seeds I want to catalogue from the north end of the gully . . .'

Florence saw the slight rising flush on his cheeks and across his neck as he picked up his daypack and slung it across his shoulder.

'Sure. I'm going to stay for a bit,' she said as she watched him walk away, probably off to join the usual suspects who, she suspected, didn't bite his head off for expressing an opinion.

Florence wasn't entirely sure why she had, except, she supposed, that there were just so many times you could hear about parties you weren't invited to with people you suspected you wouldn't like anyway. And because nobody, least of all Albert Flowers, with his doughy mates Jeremy and Lydia and Siobhan Peters skipping about cluelessly in her wedding cake dress, had any idea how brutal children could be.

Florence lifted her foot and slowly ground the flower to a sticky purple pulp beneath it.

But Puck did. They all did, one way or another.

*

'It's the song that gets beneath your skin,' Jonathan 'The Chart King' Hammond was saying in his oozy, liquid voice.

Florence felt her cheek against a dark green velvet curtain, her father's hand pressed into the small of her back, Isolde somewhere behind jiggling every part of her body, and Amanda beside her with Puck, tapping his sticks together.

'Tipped to be number one on the 1988 Christmas charts, let's all put our paws together for the Saint Claire Swingers with "Santa Was A Jazz Cat"!' shouted Jonathan, who had earlier pawed both Amanda and Lucas in the dressing room.

They ran out onto the stage to take their positions, first Puck, then Isolde, Florence, Amanda, and then finally Lucas smiling in his corduroy jacket and running a hand through his greying hair while all of the women, and some of the men in the audience, looked straight through his wife and children to try to catch his eye.

Lucas swept his arms out to each side, acknowledging his family, then drew Amanda to his side, curling his arm around her waist and kissing her on the cheek, before counting in the beat.

It was a signature move, orchestrated at the start of every Saint Claire show, and the audience loved it. They lapped it up, Lucas once said, 'like cats let loose in the Colosseum'.

When Florence was younger, she had loved it too. She'd fizzed like a can of shaken lemonade when she ran out to take her spot and looked over to where her parents stood, bathed in their tungsten glamour.

She had even loved the matching outfits the Saint Claire

Swingers wore, each one dreamt up by Richard, and all with an embarrassment of sequins.

Sometimes, people – Florence couldn't bring herself to call them fans – would wait outside stage doors to meet the Saint Claires, among them, occasionally, girls her own age. The sort of teenage girls who followed Florence were not at all like the girls at Florence's school, not the cool ones at least, who redid their lip gloss in the playgrounds at lunchtime, holding compact mirrors in their hands, snapping them shut when boys walked by. No, Florence's groupies were usually girls who played viola or oboe in their school bands, girls who almost always had two long plaits draping over their shoulders. Once, a teenage boy had asked Florence for her autograph, and she, flustered, had obliged, writing her name in looping letters with, she later recalled with horror, little stars over the i's.

As Florence grew older, walking with her head down towards her teens, she came to like these moments less and less. She grew uncomfortable on behalf of the girls who hung around stage doors, embarrassed for them as she ducked past their outstretched autograph books into Richard's van. 'Don't you have somewhere better to go?' she wanted to shout at them. 'Or someone better to look at?'

On stage, she found herself increasingly envying Puck his position at the back, head down and half hidden by his drum kit.

Isolde, being Isolde, never seemed to notice, or care, about the way the audience looked at them, the way their eyes flicked around her family, always settling on her father. Isolde would be

Isolde, flapping around the microphone, doing her short, jerky little dance moves, just as she did at home when no eyes were upon her.

Sometime around her fourteenth birthday, Florence began to resist, not in an overt way, but in a choreographed series of rolled eyes and long audible sighs whenever Richard arrived at their house with his bags of costumes and news of upcoming performances.

Once, he had booked them to play at a country music festival and Florence had shouted at Richard that she hated the country, and its music, and that he'd be driving to Boondella, or whatever its stupid country name was, without her.

She had gone, of course, overruled by Lucas and Amanda, Lucas annoying her by throwing in a lecture on the commonalities between jazz and country, Florence rolling her eyes as far back as she could get them.

In the van she had sighed and shifted constantly in her seat all the way to the large paddock where the festival was being held, which Lucas insisted on calling a natural amphitheatre. She complained that Isolde's knees were pressing into her back, and that Puck was drumming his fingers on the book in his lap too loudly, until Amanda had leant forward and turned the music up so that none of them could hear her at all.

At the festival site they had been directed to the dressing rooms, four trailers at the back of the catering vans, and Florence had been going to roll her eyes about that too, but Amanda had said, 'Just leave it, Florence, your father is very tired,' while Florence simmered inside.

Richard had arrived in the dressing rooms just before the performance and had pulled five pairs of white denim overalls and five differently coloured scarves from his bag.

'Quickly everyone,' he'd said, clapping his hands and speaking in what Florence supposed was meant to be a prairie drawl, 'get these overalls on, and then pop one of these here kerchiefs around your neck so they can tell y'all apart!'

Florence had taken her scarf then dropped it on the floor.

'So they can tell I'm the one that's not a dickhead,' she'd said.

Her father had laughed his full-bodied laugh and drawn her onto his lap, 'She's right, Richard, we do look a little hokey.'

She had won that round, but not this one, and now here she was, standing on the *Jonathan Hammond Christmas Show* set, dressed from head to toe as an elf.

She was in a red and green felt tunic that flattened and pulled at her breasts, red and white candy-striped leggings, and a hat with a little silver bell at its peak.

Beneath the stage lights damp patches of sweat pooled beneath her arms like those ink blots they made people look at, then say if they thought it was a dog or the Eiffel Tower.

'Maximum wattage, Saint Claires!' her mother had prompted just before they'd run on, but reaching her mark, Florence suddenly found herself to be an entirely different person.

Although she knew what was expected of her, she found herself strangely unable to smile.

Florence found herself unable to hear the count-in beat.

Florence found herself removed from all that was around her.

Florence Saint Claire, nearly sixteen years old, found herself set in stone.

Florence Saint Claire had to be escorted off the stage like a marble statue being carried out of a museum exhibit.

Afterwards, when she had sat looking at herself in the dressing-room mirror while her family performed 'Jazz Cat' without her, Florence wondered which was worse. Sitting here looking at the stranger in the mirror, or being out there where the strangers were looking at her. As she was being led from the stage by a woman who put her arm around her back and said into a headset, 'I'm bringing her down now,' the adults in the audience had shuffled quietly in their sets, and the teenagers who stood at the front had whistled and stamped their feet. One of them, a boy in a yellow jacket, had called out, 'What's the matter, kitty cat?' as she passed.

Florence sat in the dressing room with the door shut knowing she had just lowered the Saint Claire flag to half-mast, and had done it in front of, as Jonathan Hammond kept calling them, 'a live audience'.

Stupid man, as if they'd be doing it in front of a dead one.

Florence stared hard at the mirror, its curved white globes giving off heat to her flushed cheeks, making them feel sunburnt.

Stage fright, they'd say, they talked about it often enough at home, her mother and father recounting the horrors of other performers who felt the rushing in their ears and the words somewhere they couldn't get at them, while their mouths hung slack and open. There was the 'British Nightingale', Gloria Shaw, who had simply walked on stage then turned and walked straight off again, or Sammy Stratford, from Sammy Stratford and the

Straight Talkers, who had stood mute at the mic for an entire song while the Straight Talkers kept right on playing.

Now, she supposed, the name Florence Saint Claire would be joining those who had stared at the dressing room mirror and known that the person who stared back at them had not let the show go on.

It was the boy in the yellow jacket.

As she had run on, she had looked at him and their eyes had locked for just one second. Then he had raised his hand and put it to his forehead, his thumb and index finger forming the letter L, the universally acknowledged teenage sign for Loser, his lips forming the word at the same time.

Florence had felt herself falter, her face aflame.

She had felt herself immobilise, her limbs stilling, her chest pulling itself in, her breath disappearing, felt herself climbing deep into her own bones.

She had heard her father's voice: 'Florence is not feeling well, she's going to have a sit-down and a glass of water and I'm sure she'll be back for the next number.'

Afterwards, the discussions swirled around the house for days, rising up to her on her bed, snatches of sentences wafting from beneath her door. 'Just a teenager . . .' 'Do you think she should see somebody?' 'It's never been a problem before.' 'I don't know how this will affect the Christmas charts.' 'Fuck the Christmas charts, Richard.'

Richard came to visit, bringing chocolates then eating them all himself as he sat on the end of her bed and explained to her why she needed to start pedalling again.

'Sweetheart,' he said with a mouthful of Turkish delight, 'it's like falling off a bike – you graze a knee, then you get back on the bike and you keep going . . . Want a peppermint cream? I hate those, like eating *dentures.*'

Florence told him it was not like falling off a bike at all – not unless you fell off it in front of a live television audience and a boy in a yellow jacket let you see what everyone else saw when they looked at you.

It was not like falling off a bike, unless you fell off it while wearing striped tights and a bell on your head.

Richard kissed her on the forehead and said, 'You're right, Florence, I can see it's not like careening off a bicycle and I apologise for not knowing better.'

Then he'd blown her a kiss and left the room, taking the last of the chocolates with him.

Her father came in to play his clarinet for her and said that if she felt ridiculous in her elf outfit, imagine how her old man felt. 'I looked like a giant gnome,' he told her. 'I'm going to have a word with Richard, tell him to pull back on the theme costumes – would that help?'

Florence shook her head, no it wouldn't.

Isolde buzzed around the house and said, 'What's the big deal?' a lot. 'So she froze like Frosty the Snowman, who cares?' and not for the first time Florence thought how nice it would be to be Isolde, who somehow, in the midst of all her freneticism, saw everything in sharp relief and nothing at all in muddied shades.

Puck said nothing but did put a pair of drumsticks inside a shoebox with *Open in case of emergency* written on its lid.

Amanda wafted in on waves of Shalimar to say goodnight, and Florence waited for her to say she was not angry at her, but she was disappointed. This would be, Florence knew in the way all children do when they have let their parents down, so much worse.

But instead Amanda passed her a mug of hot chocolate and slipped her hand beneath the covers, her sharp, curled nails making a slight indent on her palm.

'It's all right, darling, you know,' Amanda Saint Claire said. 'It's all perfectly all right. So you missed your count-in, who cares? I once forgot to put knickers on before a show, and only remembered just in time before the high kicks.'

'God Mum, that's disgusting . . .'

Amanda laughed. 'My point is, darling, that to be a performer, to make art, you have to move past these things, you have to shrug it off, or laugh it off . . .' She smiled at her daughter. 'You have to pick yourself up, dust yourself off and start all over again.'

Florence looked at her mother, wanting to head off at the pass what she felt was just one beat away. 'Please don't start singing, Mum.'

They both laughed, and Amanda patted her cheek.

'I can't help it,' she said, and it was only years later that Florence would come to understand that Amanda Saint Claire really couldn't.

Not long after the *Jonathan Hammond Christmas Show* went to air, Florence returned to school, reluctantly.

'Why can't you just homeschool me, Mum, or get me a tutor when we're on the road?' she'd asked Amanda, who had laughed and said they were not the Partridge Family.

'It will be fine, Florence,' she had continued. 'You get out there, look them in the eye, and knock 'em dead,' and Florence had wished that her mother would understand, just once, that high school was nothing, *nothing* like Carols by Candlelight.

Instead Hilda Park, the co-ed college the Saint Claires had chosen for their children because of its music program, and other parents chose because it was like grammar school for well-off hippies, was, for Florence at least, hell.

The catcalling began as soon as she walked through the school's bottom gates.

A huddle of students let her pass, and then as she did, a rising chorus of meows reached her ears. Florence kept moving, head down.

In French, Lucy Venables stood up from behind her desk and then posed like a statue. 'Who am I?' she asked as her cohort fell about laughing.

For the rest of the week Florence was on the lookout.

For snatches of Jazz Cat in classrooms, for laughter, for any opening so she could quickly close it by hurrying by, pretending not to hear, or getting in first.

Puck would get beaten up by Scobie Andrews when Scobie called Florence 'The Choker' and Puck hit him, balled fist, straight in his face.

Puck would get a detention, sitting behind the desk drumming his fingers instead of writing an essay on why violence is never the answer, and when he got home Isolde would whisper he should have hit Scobie harder.

Florence would finish high school without ever coming back, as Lucas had promised, 'for the next number'.

There was no next number for Florence and the Saint Claire Swingers; the *Jonathan Hammond Christmas Show* was the last time she shared a stage with her family.

Over the years, Isolde, Puck and Amanda sometimes performed in a depleted version of the Swingers, usually at events where Lucas was being remembered one way or another, as if everyone was terrified that if they stopped invoking the Lucas Saint Claire name it would fade like lettering on curling posters.

If anyone asked Florence why she had stopped performing, and there had been plenty of askers over the years, she would smile and say, 'I guess I just didn't have the music in me.'

But that was not the truth.

Music pulsed and played in her blood always; quivering strings and joyous doo-whops, Florence heard them all. But she had found ways to quieten its call, reading in her room while her family rehearsed in Lucas's studio, concentrating on her schoolwork, then later at university tussling with the Latin words for plants and the occasional boy in her dorm room.

The idea that she didn't 'have the music in her' was laughable, Florence herself felt like laughing every time she said it.

It was a throwaway line, casual in delivery, and designed to move the conversation on briskly.

It also helped widen the space between her and the notes.

Because Florence Saint Claire didn't only have the music in her, she had the whole bloody symphony in there.

Florence stood up from the park bench, picked up her daypack and headed down the path towards her home.

Why had she snapped at Albert like that?

He was not to know about kids who stood like statues when you passed, or beat up your little brother, or asked if your sister had epilepsy or did she always dance like that? Albert had no idea what it was like to have Lucy Venables and her crew sing 'Santa Was A Jazz Cat' loudly every time you passed, until, when you finally had enough and walked straight over to them and said, 'Don't you think it's time you had a new song, Lucy?', seeing too late that it was an open door for her to sail through and shoot back, 'Don't you think it's time *you* did?' and watch Lucy's friends fall apart like bowling pins around her. He was not to know what it was like to have the first boy you liked whisper in your ear, his tongue at its lobe, 'Can you get your dad's autograph for my mum?'

She would apologise to Albert tomorrow, and explain that she was just tired.

She wasn't tired at all, but she was exhausted by her surname.

One day she would like to tell Albert why she had stopped singing with her family, and explain that at least part of it had been the way she had to show all of herself, all of her skin, before she'd had the time to grow into it.

It was not easy being a child star, she would tell him, and sometimes it was harder still being a former one.

*

When Florence woke up the next morning, it was to find Isolde asleep next to her, her sister's limbs folded into hers, one arm flung over her stomach.

Isolde had done this all their lives, when she was small, padding across the floor of their shared bedroom to fold herself in beside her, then settling back to sleep, her breath against Florence's cheek.

She didn't mind, she never had.

She had loved Issy since the day Amanda brought her home, cradling her in her arms, Isolde's dark hair peeping out from the swaddling, Lucas smiling and laughing and saying, 'Another member of the band!'

She had watched her grow – and grow – into someone whose head towered over everyone else's, even the boys in each year's school photograph. She had watched her half folded in the back of vans travelling to gigs, or being told by photographers to 'get to the back' so they could all fit in the frame, and she had watched in wonder at how Issy seemed to notice none of it. She walked into doorways, then reversed her body vaguely back out again; she hit her head on overhanging branches and kept walking; she came in and out of conversations haphazardly; 'What are we talking about?' she'd suddenly say, looking around her family as if she had just that moment been teleported there.

Isolde lived in a world inhabited by herself and those she vaguely let wander into it, and not everyone she allowed in was kind.

Florence kept an eye on her, at kindy, at bus stops, in the playground, in the shops, and later in the clubs where her sister would jerk around the dance floor and people would step back from her flailing limbs.

Men liked Isolde, but it always seemed to be a certain sort of man, the sort who said to Florence, 'Your sister's pretty wild, isn't she?'

And Isolde was wild, but not in the way they thought.

Isolde's wildness was only in the way there was nothing about her that could be contained, her body, her laughter, her way of never looking around a room first to see who was in it.

She looked at her sleeping sister, her body still at last.

If I could paint, Florence thought, *I'd paint this and call it* Isolde in Repose – Finally.

Florence smiled as Isolde opened her eyes.

'Sorry, couldn't sleep again.'

'It's okay, how was the gig?'

'Good, there was one idiot who kept heckling and shouting at us to play some "real music", but Lance sorted him out.'

Florence wondered when Isolde would stay still long enough to see that Lance Bueller, Mercy Jones's long-term roadie and Puck's only friend at high school, was in love with her.

Florence liked Lance, but when she had mentioned to Isolde that she thought he liked her, Isolde had said, 'Lance? I don't think so. How old is he, seventeen?'

That was Isolde, not noticing that Lance had left seventeen behind years ago. She didn't notice dates, didn't notice times; sometimes, Florence thought, Isolde didn't notice bloody *anything.*

*

Walking to work on Monday, Florence was resolved.

Resolved, she told herself.

She would not let her own strangeness – and Florence knew she was strange in the particular way that only a former child star in a band whose leader had been mowed down by a milk truck could be – affect her relationship with Albert.

Albert's family, she was certain, was nothing like hers.

She hadn't met them formally but she had seen them at the library from time to time, his mother Georgina perennially wrapped in a floral dress, and his younger sister Addie wrapped in a similar version. Adelaide Flowers was part of a book club that met at the library once a month, clutching books and coffees and looking disproportionately relieved to be there, as if they'd all just escaped from prison.

Albert had introduced them once, and Adelaide Flowers had nodded, distracted, then mistaken Florence for a librarian and asked if she could put a copy of *She's Come Undone* on hold.

'No, I can't,' Florence had answered. Well, she couldn't.

Georgina Flowers looked like many of the other mothers Florence saw around East Elm; they were like variegations on plants, she thought, only with a silk scarf here, a charm bracelet there. In the summer it was all shift dresses and slides; in the winter it was chambray shirts and dark blue jeans tucked into boots.

'I see its gymkhana season again,' Isolde said to Florence walking into school one morning, passing through a cluster of the mothers at the gates of Hilda Park.

Her own mother was never among them, and Florence never minded because Amanda Saint Claire did not even attempt to blend in. She entered the schoolyard in long silk caftans and jewelled combs in her hair, earrings like glittering chandeliers swinging from her ears. Once, Florence shuddered, her mother had worn a red satin turban. On the rare occasions Amanda Saint Claire did enter the Hilda Park grounds, it was like a cruise ship arriving in the harbour with all its party lights on.

Florence had met Albert's father Laurence once at a service station, he and Albert entering as she was leaving, Florence feeling a strange jolt at seeing Albert out of his Green Team khakis and not in some sort of foliage.

Laurence Flowers had held out his hand and Florence had shaken it, surprised at its smoothness, nothing like his son's. Albert's hands were rough, calluses on their pads, his fingers misshapen from years of mishaps with shovels, patterns of tiny red cuts and welts on his skin, brown from the sun. His father's hands were white and oddly slippery, like river stones shaped by water.

What did he do? Florence tried to remember: some sort of property developer, or real estate agent? Something to do with nothing his son did in any case.

Laurence Flowers had given Florence a quick smile, then said, 'We better get going, son, your mother's Sunday roast waits for no man.'

No, Albert's family was nothing like her own.

Lucas Saint Claire had never called Puck 'son' in his life, and Amanda Saint Claire had never made a Sunday roast, or on any other day of the week. Good for her, Florence thought.

Albert was already making tea in the kitchen when she walked into the Green Team's office, she could hear him chuckling at something Monty was saying, Monty's hiccupping laugh beside it.

Right, she thought to herself, digging the clipping out of her bag.

When Albert walked in carrying his mug of tea, he smiled at her and Amanda's voice slipped through: 'Maximum wattage.'

'Good morning, Albert,' she smiled back, the two of them settling in behind their desks, Albert to read the paper, Florence to stare at the clipping, its contents a key part of her resolution.

'I was reading this on the weekend,' she said, holding it up, 'about the Amorphophallus titanum flower, the one that only flowers once every two to three years . . .'

Albert looked up from his paper.

'The corpse flower,' she continued. 'You know, the one that stinks to high heaven, like rotting meat. Anyway, it's supposed to flower this weekend at the Botanic Gardens, it's a once every few years thing and I thought I'd go along and have a . . .'

'Sniff?' Albert smiled.

'Yes, although they do say the smell is so disgusting that some people need to wear face masks, and the last time the Amorphophallus flowered at the Adelaide Botanic, one woman actually passed out. Would you like to come?'

Oh yes, Florence said to herself, *could you be any more enticing, luring him into your lair with the putrid scents of the corpse flower?*

'I'd like to, Florence,' Albert said, 'but I've got to go to a funeral.'

3

It was not strictly true, Albert thought, walking beneath the jasmine arch at the entrance of Bougainvillea Gardens, listening to the low hum of the bees that danced within it.

He wasn't going to the funeral, thank God, he really couldn't face that at all, but he was going to the wake.

He hated these things, the family with faces caught in tightness, receiving guests who shook their hands, or embraced them, or the more dramatic ones lurching like felled trees into their arms.

Later, as the drinks flowed, the stories would come out, and sometimes the singing. There would be laughter and crying and sometimes shouting, and it never felt to Albert that anyone ever got it right, this sending-off business.

Albert squinted in the sunlight.

What needed to be said, he thought, was none of that 'I am only in another room' stuff, nothing about being kissed by a snowflake on the cheek, or some other fucking palaver.

People, Albert thought, kicking a pebble on the drive, should be let alone to howl.

Walking into the Hibiscus Room, Albert saw that the trestle tables had been set up, and women – always the women – were putting down platters of sandwiches and cake, and that coffee and tea stations had been set up.

This was not really a coffee and tea situation, Albert thought. No, sooner or later people would be requiring something a bit stronger.

Eleanor would, for one.

What to say to Eleanor Markson, mother of Charlotte 'Charlie' Markson, eleven years old and sharp as a paper cut, bright red freckles across the bridge of her nose, legs like sticks and hair like fire.

Charlie Markson, a nice kid with a big future as a water polo player, if she did well at the state trials and if, Eleanor joked to her friends, her mother could keep up with the 5 am starts.

What to say to Eleanor Markson when Charlie was now somewhere her mother couldn't find her?

What to say to Greg Markson, always in the stands to cheer his daughter on, to cup his mouth in his hands and yell, 'Go Charlie!' when she leapt out of the water, arm outstretched to block the ball, rising like a slippery mermaid shooting water from the sea.

Eleanor had once told Albert that Charlie had dyslexia, not that she ever let it stop her. She still managed to get Cs in

English, which just showed you what kind of girl Charlie was, Eleanor said.

Eleanor also told Albert that Charlie sang in the choir, and had been best friends with a boy called Ollie since kindy and didn't care what people thought about that. Eleanor thought Charlie maybe had a little crush on Ollie, and that maybe Ollie had a little crush on her.

The last time they had met, Eleanor had told Albert everything she could think of about Charlie, except for the part when Charlie had gone out for a walk with their dog Beppo and a concrete wall under construction had collapsed as she passed.

Everyone said it happened so fast she wouldn't have known what had hit her.

People actually said that to Eleanor Markson, that at least Charlotte Markson – sharp as a paper cut with legs like sticks who could have made the state team, who stared at the letters in her books hard until they made some sort of sense, who sang in the choir, and had a best friend called Ollie – wouldn't have known what had hit her.

Albert cleared his throat.

This fucking world.

People had started to enter the Hibiscus Room, men and women and children and babies, and a cluster of girls in navy blue West District Dolphins water polo shirts. They moved in a shifting blue rank around the room, a colony of floating bluebottles.

Albert spoke to a few people here and there, surface stuff, the odd 'How are you?' and 'Are you right for a drink?' but mostly he kept to himself, finding he just didn't have the stomach for it, to take on so much sadness.

He had not seen the Marksons and wondered if they had come at all, and thought he wouldn't blame them if they hadn't.

There were too many rules in death, he thought.

Needing a break, he slipped outside through a back room off the main reception area and sat down on some steps, feeling the hot stillness of the air around him, his head in his hands.

When he looked up, Eleanor and Greg Markson were standing just a few metres away, under a poinciana tree, Eleanor's hands on her husband's shoulders.

Albert stood up quickly to turn back inside – whatever was happening beneath those green-lipped branches was not his to witness – but as he did Greg Markson motioned for him to come over.

Albert walked over, the heat beating on his neck.

'We can't go back in there,' Greg said simply.

Albert nodded.

'Eleanor is feeling the heat and she doesn't want to go inside.'

Albert looked at Eleanor Markson, head drooping like a bluebell's.

'Righto.' Albert nodded. 'You go where you need to, and I'll make your excuses for you.'

'We don't have a car,' Eleanor said, throwing up her hands. 'We didn't bring ours, people brought us, because everyone has been so kind, you see. People have been so kind,' she repeated.

Albert looked at the Marksons, pressing into each other.

He reached into his pocket.

'Take my van,' he said. 'It's that one, just there.'

They all looked at his work van, the logo on its side, a few metres away.

'Go on,' Albert said, giving Greg the keys. 'I'll sort everything out inside.'

He smiled at Eleanor. 'It's air conditioned,' he said, then to Greg, 'You okay with a manual?'

Greg Markson nodded, then slipped his arm around the small of his wife's back, but neither of them moved.

'I'll walk you over,' Albert said, realising that the Marksons had become stuck and needed to be set in motion.

He put his arm across the back of Greg Markson's shoulders and guided them both towards the van.

He opened the passenger door for Eleanor, then the driver's side for Greg.

'I can drive if you like,' Albert offered, but Greg put the key in the ignition and shook his head.

'I'll be right,' he said. 'You go back inside – and thank you.'

Albert nodded, then turned back towards the Hibiscus Room as the Marksons slipped away from their daughter's wake, Greg Markson spinning the van's wheels on the gravelled driveway as they left, a bat out of what was surely hell.

Walking home later, after he'd gone back inside and explained that the Marksons had left the wake to a man who seemed loosely in charge (Greg's brother, he thought, who looked only mildly surprised at the information), it occurred to Albert that the Marksons probably didn't know where he lived.

Albert shrugged, they'd work it out. They were hardly going to flee the state in his van, although he wouldn't blame them if they did.

It also occurred to him that the gardens were much further out of town than the drive there had suggested, the walk seeming to take forever in the early November heat, the soles of his shoes sticking to the hot paths.

He also realised he had never been inside the Bougainvillea Gardens' faux Spanish walls before, despite countless dances and weddings and parties being held there.

For a time, before its stucco walls had begun to peel and its bright pink and orange bougainvillea flowers had begun to sink the front fence under their weight, it had been the place to go.

His own high school formal had been held there, but he hadn't gone to that either.

He had driven there that night, though, taking the car all the way up the driveway where he could see the girls in their taffeta dresses with enormous bows at their shoulders, and the boys in their hired suits dancing past the open windows. Then he'd turned around and driven straight back down again.

Why had he done that, Albert thought, remembering the seventeen-year-old boy in a T-shirt and jeans, sitting low in the front seat, the thump of a bass line vibrating through the car's windows. *Why did you do that, mate?*

Why would you get in the car and drive past a school dance you had no intention of going to, no desire to go to, and where it was entirely possible that no-one would notice that you weren't there?

Why would you do that, mate? he asked again, and the answer shimmered in his steps in the heat.

So he could feel the satisfaction of spraying the gravel in the driveway and taking off, like Greg Markson, like a bat out of hell.

The Marksons would find him, or he would find them later, he was sure, when they had got enough of the howl out.

They had much harder things to look for than his house.

*

Florence hadn't gone to see the corpse flower, finding she didn't have the stomach for it, and not just because of its infamous stench. Instead she had gone for a hike in the hills behind East Elm, striding up the Kingfisher Track and scowling at anybody coming down.

Why did hikers have to smile so much, she thought, jabbing her stick into the ground with each step, they were so . . . jaunty. She preferred the runners, who ran past with their hydration backpacks and their wrap-around sunglasses, their mouths set in lines of grim determination. Florence liked them because they left her alone and sped by completely uninterested, whereas the hikers felt compelled to say something to every person they encountered on the track. 'Morning,' they'd say in their checked shirts and khaki shorts. 'Beautiful day', or 'Hot enough for you?' and sometimes Florence would answer, and sometimes

Florence would scowl, depending on how prickly she was feeling in the heat.

Florence kept up her pace until she rounded the last bend and then ran all the way up to the lookout, thinking that somewhere down there Albert Flowers was probably telling Jeremy and Lydia about the woman he worked with who asked him to go and smell a cadaver flower.

Florence ducked under the lookout fence and its sign saying *Do not pass*, and passed it, going down the back spine of the hill where she would see nobody except the odd mountain biker flying out of nowhere to shoot past and shout 'Sorry' through a dirt-spattered helmet.

She felt better with each step, breathing in the sharp smell of eucalypt and the occasional honeyed waft of wattle, much nicer, she giggled, than the old Amorphophallus titanum.

The heat gathered under the trees, settling on her back and shoulders as she strode through the bush, listening to the crackling march of her boots on the path.

Florence walked for a couple of hours, cutting through the marked paths until she rejoined the main track to the car park. She felt much more relaxed, and when a hiker got into his car beside hers, she smiled at him.

Not the full horseshoe, but at least half.

She had picked a little of the wattle for Isolde and a small clump of wood sorrel she could use for dinner, finding a nest of its heart-shaped leaves between some rocks.

It would have to be only a couple of tiny shreds, the plant's oxalic acid deadly in large quantities but delicious in smaller ones.

Amanda and Puck were both coming over. It was one of those rare nights when none of them was performing – *at least officially*, Florence smiled to herself.

Amanda would probably put on some sort of show during the evening.

She got into her car and put on some Gloria Shaw, with whom Florence felt a fond affinity as a fellow choker.

Then she put down all the windows and swung out of the car park.

Driving down the curving road, she felt much lighter than she had driving up. It didn't really matter if Albert had told Lydia et al about the corpse flower. Perhaps one day she could make them a nice wood sorrel salad, with plenty of leaves. Florence smiled as Gloria played to the breeze.

*

'Why didn't you just ask him to the movies?' Isolde asked that night as Florence filled her glass of wine.

'You could have taken him to *Night of the Living Dead*, darling,' Amanda said.

'Or the morgue,' Puck offered.

'Well you three aren't doing much better,' Florence said. 'I don't see any of you out on a date tonight – now why do you think that might be?'

'I'm too tall,' Isolde said, raising her glass.

Florence leaned over and clinked it. 'I'm too prickly,' she said.

'I'm too unreliable,' Puck said, shrugging.

They all looked at their mother.

'And I'm too . . . expensive,' Amanda Saint Claire said.

Everyone laughed, and drew their glasses together in a toast.

'To us,' Florence said. 'The Too Tall, Too Prickly, Too Unreliable and Too Expensive Saint Claire Swingers.'

'Without the swinging,' Isolde said, as a thought struck Florence.

'What would Dad have been?' she asked.

'Oh, that's easy, darling,' Amanda answered. 'Too Much.'

They ate dinner together, sitting cross-legged on the floor, their backs against the couches, except Amanda who sat at the table, by herself, setting out a placemat and drinks coasters.

'Mum, that's ridiculous, come and sit with us,' Isolde said, and Amanda answered, not unreasonably, Florence thought, 'Or you could all get off your bottoms and come and sit with me.'

But none of them moved, Amanda's three children all schooled in small acts of rebellion.

Puck stayed the night, sleeping on the couch, and was gone by the time Florence got up the next morning. Where he had gone, she was not sure. Puck lived in a triangular circuit, sometimes at her place, sometimes at their mother's and sometimes at Lance Bueller's, and always in a place no one else inhabited.

Florence wished she could know her brother better, but Puck's world was solitary, and unlike Isolde, she couldn't accept he was happy there. 'He's fine,' Issy told her. 'He's fine.' Amanda said the same thing, and once when she had approached Lucas about his son's mostly nocturnal wanderings, he had patted her shoulder and said, 'He's Puck,' as if that answered everything.

'Shouldn't we try to get him seen by a doctor or something?' she'd once asked both her parents when Puck had been living in a tent in the backyard for weeks on end.

'No.' Amanda Saint Claire had surprised her with the swiftness of her answer. 'No, we should not. I will not have anyone prodding at him like some dairy cow,' and Florence resigned herself to asking, 'Where the fuck is Puck?' for the rest of her life.

Isolde appeared in the kitchen, where Florence was making some tea, and kissed her on the cheek.

'Morning,' she said, 'that was fun, last night, all of us together.'

Florence nodded, it had been fun, and as the evening had wound down to half-empty wineglasses, Amanda had finally descended from the table to sit and sing with her children on the floor. Puck had sung with his eyes closed, his head against the couch, Isolde beside him, her legs swung over his, and Amanda's and Florence's voices met somewhere in the middle. It had always been this way, her mother's voice and her own finding each other across rooms and stages, their voices so similar it was hard to tell where one began and the other ended.

'You're really good,' Isolde said. 'I wish you'd sing more.'

Florence headed her off at the pass, knowing that what Issy really meant was, 'I wish you'd sing more with us.'

'Tea?' Florence asked, but Isolde, now doing some sort of complicated stretching movement, ignored her.

'You've got the best voice out of all of us, even Lamanda, we sound so much better with you, it feels so much better with you, why can't you just get over whatever it is you need to get over and sing with us again?'

'I sang with you last night, Issy.'

'I mean on stage and you know it,' Isolde snapped, swinging her arms up to the ceiling and sending the low-hanging kitchen lights swaying.

Florence reached up and steadied them.

'Not now, Issy. I've just got up, my head is sore, I've got to clean up from last night – you can help – and I'm just not in the mood to talk about it.'

'You never are.'

'Well take the hint,' Florence said, half shouting, although it could be that the words just sounded a lot louder in her aching head.

'I'm not interested in joining the Swingers again, and you are doing perfectly well without me. This constant carping by you and Mum drives me crazy, so just stop, Issy, just stop.'

Issy paused mid-stretch. 'The thing is, Florence, it's all about you. You never think about us. We'd do much better with you in the group, you know it, you heard us last night. When you sing with us all the pieces come together, it's like leaving an ingredient out of a . . .'

Florence waited. Isolde did not cook, she would have no idea what ingredients went into the meals Florence made her.

'Out of a what, Isolde?' she asked.

'Out of a sandwich,' Isolde shouted. 'Out of a sandwich, Florence, it's like leaving the bread out of a tomato and lettuce sandwich.'

'Well then you'd have a salad, wouldn't you, and you'd have to make do with that.'

The sisters tracked each other beneath the still swaying lights.

'I hate salad,' Isolde said finally. 'And I will have some tea, thank you, with the teabag and the water and the milk and the sugar . . . See Florence, I do know how to make something.'

Florence felt the stirrings of a pulse at the base of her skull . . .

'Look, Issy, it's too early to fight. Can we just put this away for another time?'

But Isolde, grumpy and hungry, kept tugging at the thread between them, determined to unravel it.

'Actually no, Florence, we can't put it away for another time, there's never another time with you, you're always stomping around that forest in your stupid workman's boots trying to pretend you're not a singer. Well, you are a fucking singer, Florence, and you fucking know it.'

Miss Suki shimmered in front of Florence's eyes, wearing a full-length emerald gown with silver stilettos peeping out from the hem, twin stars uncloaked behind a cloud.

'You're throwing away your life out there, Florence. You're a star just like Lamanda's a star, more than me, more than Puck, you've got it. I have to work at it, so does Puck, hours of bloody rehearsal and breathing exercises, and then last night you just open your mouth and you're better than all of us . . . even Dad.

'And that's another thing,' Isolde now in full, flapping flight, 'what about helping us to keep his name out there, don't you think you should think of him? What about his musical legacy, Florence? Don't you think Dad would just love to see us all together again? Do you ever stop to think about more than fucking edible plants, and think about how much your singing meant to him?'

Isolde looked at Florence, Issy's face tilted upwards, her head shaking a little.

'Enough, Isolde,' Florence said, and walked out of the kitchen, up the narrow stairs to her room.

Then she changed quickly, grabbed her bag and keys and headed to the library, ignoring Isolde still pacing in the kitchen.

'I'm sorry, Florence,' she said, but Florence kept on walking, slamming the door behind her.

So childish, Florence thought, all this shouting in kitchens and slamming doors, but that was the way her family was.

The Saint Claire children could unsettle each other with words that, if someone else said them, they would not even notice. But said by a sister, or a brother, or a mother, they arched in the air and took aim wherever they might hurt the most.

What was that? Florence thought, then supposed it must be family. Were other families like her own? She thought of Laurence and Georgina Flowers with their Sunday dinners and thought that no, they probably were not.

It was Sunday, the library would be shut, but she had a key to the side entrance, and the passcode to the alarm system, and the less Monty Rollins knew about that, the better.

Florence liked going to the library on a Sunday, parking her car a couple of streets away then strolling towards it and ducking in the side door when she was certain the coast was clear. She wasn't sure what would happen if Monty caught her, probably nothing except a long lecture about security and insurance and the need for all of them to follow the rules, but Florence wasn't sure whether she was actually breaking any and had decided it was easier not to find out.

She walked to the library's entrance then around the side and quickly let herself in, punching in the security code for the alarm. Then she walked through the Green Team's office and out into the main library itself, settling herself into one of the big armchairs tucked away behind the biographies.

Usually Florence came to the library to work on the set list for the Nightshades, or to talk with Veronica or Orla without anyone listening in.

I am like a spy, Florence thought to herself, not displeased with the idea. *I am like an espionage agent with her own secret hideout.*

But today Florence just wanted the library to do its job, to do the job that all libraries did beneath the surface business of lending out books and photocopying pages for assignments. Florence wanted the library, as it did for generations of quirky kids who found the playground with all it rules and mini regimes overwhelming, or all the mothers who fled their homes with their small children to sit in one of its armchairs beside the picture books, to comfort her.

Florence sat in the chair and closed her eyes, breathing the books in.

It was quiet, no chattering, no teenagers giggling against the shelves, no Monty shushing them with his finger to his mouth, no hum of the photocopier, no mother and toddler groups singing 'The Wheels on the Bus' in one of the activity rooms – and no air conditioning unit creaking into life. Florence never turned it on, sure that Monty would somehow notice a spike in usage on Sundays and launch a full-scale investigation. Instead there was silence, just Florence and the books, keeping all their secrets bound up together.

Florence's eyes flicked to the pictures hanging in a row at the windows. Pegged to red string, the white sheets of paper looked like prayer flags with their crayoned sentences in waxy, bright colours. Across the top of each was written – in varying degrees of penmanship – *What people don't know about me is . . .* and each child had answered in their wonky, going-up-the-page writing.

What people don't know about me is . . .

I am good at drawing.

I am a fairy.

I hate the library – Pedro Perkins, she smiled.

I like to play soccer.

I can make pancakes.

Florence came to the end of the line, and then hung her own, imaginary picture along the red string.

Then she wrote her own secret, her finger tracing the words in the air.

I killed my father.

Bit dramatic, thought Florence, but there it is.

*

'I've been thinking, Florence,' Lucas Saint Claire said from one end of the window seat, while she sat at the other, their outstretched legs somehow fitting on the narrow green cushion.

'Oh don't do that, Dad,' she teased, 'that way leads to madness.'

They were in the music room, where Florence had brought up a cup of tea for Lucas after his practice.

Lucas smiled. 'I've been thinking about you not wanting to be in the band any more.'

Florence looked out the window at the tree and wished she could climb out onto it, down to the street, and pedal away on someone's BMX. That way, she thought, she wouldn't have to disappoint her father.

'I'm sorry, Dad, I just can't do it.'

'It's okay, I understand that. I wish you would, but I can't force you, no one can force you . . . except maybe Richard,' he smiled, and Florence giggled. 'But I was also thinking that there's always a lot of noise here, isn't there? Lots going on.'

Florence nodded.

'So I was thinking . . .'

'So much thinking, Dad!' Florence smiled.

'Don't interrupt me, Florence, all this thinking is quite hard, you know – I was thinking that maybe you felt a bit lost.

'I don't spend as much time with you as I should. When you were little, before Isolde and Puck came along, before I went away so much with work, we spent a lot of time together, do you remember?'

Florence remembered, not so much the detail, but the feeling of walking with her father with her hand in his, or riding high on his shoulders, bobbing up and down streets with Lucas theatrically yelling out, 'Tree!' whenever she had to duck her head beneath a branch.

'So, I was wondering if you'd like to spend a bit of time with your old man, just the two of us.'

Florence grinned.

'I would love that,' she answered, 'although I'm probably a bit old now to ride on your shoulders.'

'Never!' Lucas smiled at her. 'So here's the plan. I'm meant to be going to a recording session in town next week, on Wednesday afternoon, but I'm going to wag it.'

'Wag it?'

'You know, skive off, don't show up. Don't tell me you've never wagged before.'

Florence shook her head.

'Well you should, everyone should, at least once. Have I taught you nothing? So, what I am proposing is that I wag recording and you wag your singing lesson, and you meet me after school in town at the Java Lounge where I buy you an obscenely large milkshake.'

Florence was thrilled; she loved the Java Lounge with its deep booth seats and picture windows out onto the street. It was the place they went for family celebrations – birthdays, shows that had sold out, the time Isolde got her braces off. Florence remembered Isolde walking in, holding Amanda's hand, and looking, for the first and last time that Florence could remember, shy. 'Come on, Issy, show us your choppers,' Lucas had called, and Issy had broken into a smile, the clunky train lines gone.

The family always sat by the front window if they could get it, and they usually could, particularly if Lucas was there, hovering by the table until someone on it recognised him and gave up their seat. 'No, mate, really we were just leaving,' they'd say, and Lucas would smile, 'That's really spectacularly kind of you,' and they would feel the warmth of him long after they had gone home and told the story to all of their friends.

But the family hadn't gone there for months, missing both Puck's and Amanda's birthdays. Lucas had been away touring, and even if they nabbed the booth by the front window, it didn't feel the same without him sliding in beside them and saying, 'What shall we have? I know, let's order one of everything!'

Now Florence was going with Lucas by herself, and she thought she really didn't care where they sat, or that at sixteen she also considered herself a bit too old for milkshakes. Lucy Venables, she knew, was already drinking Bacardi Breezers.

'You're on, Dad . . . What time?'

'Well, I figure if we meet there at four, we can stay for about an hour and walk home together.' He winked. 'As far as anyone else knows I've been to my recording, you've been to your lesson and we just happened to meet outside the gate.'

'What about your recording?'

'I'll tell them I can't make it.'

'What about my lesson?'

'I'll write a note – Oh and Florence?'

'Yep.'

'I'll be wearing a blue feather in my hat.'

'Why?'

'That way you'll know it's me.'

Florence laughed. 'And I'll wear . . . well I'll be in my school uniform, but I'll wear one sock up and one sock down.'

'Genius. I always said you were a very talented girl.'

Florence put out her hand.

'Deal.'

'Deal.'

They both leant forward to shake hands, and Florence felt the giddiness of secret-keeping.

'Dad?'

'Yes, my darling girl.'

'You don't need to wear a feather . . . I'd know your face anywhere.'

'Oh but I must, Florence. Adds to the mystery, you see.'

On Wednesday morning Florence came down to breakfast whistling, gave her mother a kiss, offered to make Isolde a cup of tea, and told Puck she would wash up his plate.

'My, someone's in a good mood today,' Amanda said, and Florence smiled at her, the full, blinding, maximum wattage.

When she passed her father in the hall, Lucas whispered to her, 'Four pm, Java Lounge, blue feather, odd socks.'

Florence spent the school day willing it to go faster, and when the bell rang at three o'clock, she grabbed her bag and ran to catch the early bus, passing Lucy Venables and her henchmen on the footpath.

'Hey Florence, you're in a hurry, do you need to use the kitty litter?' Lucy called after her.

Florence refused to prickle, kept running, and sang Jazz Cat on the bus all the way into town, throwing her hand out the window to give Lucy one glorious finger as it passed her.

She hadn't sung Jazz Cat in a long time, but she settled into its notes and allowed herself to enjoy it, gazing out the window at all the people who weren't lucky enough to be taken out by their father with a blue feather in his grey felt hat.

'*Purr, baby, purr,*' she sang as she got off at her stop, where she paused to pull one sock up and tug the other one down.

Walking into the Java Lounge, she saw her father hadn't arrived yet but their favourite booth was empty, so she quickly slipped into it. Then she settled by the window to watch out for his bobbing step, hands in pockets, lips pursed in a whistle.

She waited while the waiter kept asking her if she wanted anything, and Florence answered grandly, 'I will order when my friend arrives, thank you.'

She waited when the same waiter asked if she really needed the booth seat as other customers wanted it, and she answered yes, she really did.

She waited while she slowly reached down to pull her sock back up again.

Florence checked her watch every few minutes, until it reached a quarter to five, then she slowly got up from the booth and said to the hovering waiter, 'My friend has been detained,' and wondered why she was trying so hard to speak like a grown-up, only in a way no grown-up she knew ever actually spoke.

Her father must have forgotten, she thought, and was not particularly perturbed by it. Lucas often missed things, he was often absent-minded, often late, and it drove her mother mad. When he did show up, striding through the door holding his clarinet case, apologising and running a hand through his wavy hair, it was like the sun had just crept across a shadow.

'Sorry, sorry, everyone,' he'd say, setting his instrument down. 'I apologise for keeping you waiting,' and then he would smile and people who five minutes earlier had been pursing their lips and saying, 'I've paid for a babysitter,' would find themselves saying, 'Oh that's perfectly all right, Lucas, we're all here now.'

Amanda called it his charm offensive. 'I do believe your father could murder someone in this orchestra right now,' she said to her children once as they watched Lucas circle the room, 'and they would say, "Oh that's perfectly all right, Lucas, what's one less second violin?"'

People didn't mind when Lucas Saint Claire let them down, and Florence didn't really mind now, other than the fact she never got to have her milkshake. It was enough that he had wanted to wag with her, she thought, smiling at both the word and the idea. He was probably in the studio now, or at home, and when Amanda said, 'Florence will be back soon,' he would slap his palm against his forehead and curse himself for his forgetfulness.

When she got home, Florence thought, she would pull her sock down again to show him she didn't mind.

Florence left the café and picked up her pace as she started the walk home.

The sun had dipped a little and she felt the evening's promise on her skin.

'Have you got any money, sweetheart?' said a man sitting on a small blanket, an open guitar case in front of him, a few coins scattered in its flattened velvet. 'Just to buy a pie?'

He had startled her and Florence shook her head and kept walking, feeling the man's eyes on her.

She wished she hadn't reacted like that, it was something to do with walking through the day turning into night.

Florence was sure that if it was bright and sunny, and if she had someone with her, she would have given the man some money from her purse.

Lucas would have. Lucas would have given the man all the money he had on him, and the man's eyes would widen at the notes in his hand, and then Lucas would give him something else. Lucas would chat with him, asking the man to show him the guitar, exclaiming over its make or praising its strings, and then he would say, 'I wish you well, brother,' and the man would feel the warmth of Lucas Saint Claire's smile bestowed on him. In that moment, Florence knew, the man would feel loved, and understood.

That was her father's magic, the real reason his concerts sold out and chat show hosts always had a seat for Lucas Saint Claire on their couches.

Sometimes, Florence thought, it was almost like a trick.

She shivered a little and kept walking, wanting to get home, to open the silver handle of Kinsey's front door, put down her bag and yell up the stairs, 'I'm home,' and watch her father hurry down them, his face an apology.

She ran down the last two streets before her own, her thumbs beneath the front straps of her backpack as it bumped against her shoulders. When she rounded the corner of her street, she saw the red and blue wash of the police lights before she saw the cars themselves, one of them parked on the footpath as if in some television police drama.

Florence slowed her steps, and when she came to the Prentices' house she sat down beneath the tree that hung like loose arms over its fence. She still called it the Prentices', they all did, even though they were long gone, Professor Prentice accepting a position at Cambridge University, shaking her hand gravely in the driveway on the morning they left and saying to her, 'Good luck, Florence.'

He was a nice man, Professor Prentice, she thought, leaning her back against the fence. *I wonder what his first name was.*

Florence watched her house from where she sat, her back curled into the fence, hands clasped around her drawn knees. She watched people she knew arriving with flowers in their hands, and people she didn't know arriving with nothing in their hands at all.

She watched as the shadows from the tree's branches grew longer and thinner, and as her mother came out from the house, Leticia and Nancy behind her.

Amanda Saint Claire was looking up the street, scanning it, Florence knew, for her eldest daughter.

Amanda stepped out onto the middle of the road and looked up and down it until her eyes settled on Florence. She said something to Nancy, then patted Leticia's arm and the two women turned and walked back into the house.

Florence knew with every step her mother took towards her what Amanda was going to say, she just wondered how she would say it.

She had known it the moment she had seen the light of the police cars.

Maybe she had known it before then too, all the way home, as the sun dipped and she felt the quickening behind her.

Florence thought that if she could just sit here beside the Prentices' fence, she could hold the moment still, so that everything she knew was coming could go right back into the house with Leticia and Nancy.

She pressed her back further into the fence, feeling its coarse hardness, willing her mother to stop walking towards her.

'Florence,' her mother said, kneeling down in front of her. 'There's been an accident.'

Florence looked at her mother's toes, painted in coral nail polish.

'Your father is dead.'

Florence closed her eyes, and Amanda shifted from her knees to sit beside her.

Florence was glad her mother had delivered the news with such directness and no fuss.

She couldn't have stood it if Amanda had gone into hysterics, wailing at her daughter's feet and sobbing into her skin.

They sat still and silent as the darkness swallowed the evening, and then her mother began to sing.

Florence could never remember the song, if it was a song at all or just some sort of keening, and years later, when Amanda was telling her the story of that afternoon, she had asked her, 'What did you sing to me, Mum?'

'A song of lament, it was all I had left in me, darling.'

After Amanda had walked Florence inside, somewhere in the sounds of Isolde's high-pitched wails from her room, and Puck's drumming from his, and Leticia insisting on helping Florence into her pyjamas, the older woman too close and smelling sharply of wine, a policewoman had appeared at her bedroom door and asked Florence if there was anything she could get her.

'I would like an obscenely large milkshake,' Florence had answered.

'Prickly one,' the policewoman had told her friends afterwards.

*

'Florence?'

Florence, half dreaming, half awake, pressed her entire body deeply into the back of the chair. God, was it Monty?

'What are you doing here?'

Florence looked up at Albert Flowers standing in front of her, a key in his hand.

'I could ask you the same thing.'

'Well, Miss Marple, I've come to do a bit of work.'

'Me too.'

Albert glanced at the armchair.

'Yes, I can see,' he smiled. 'So . . . do you come here often?'

Florence straightened her back. 'All the time actually, but I haven't seen you here before.'

'Ah, that's because I have only recently come into possession of a key.'

'Handy,' Florence said.

'What about you, do you also have a key, or do you just break in through a window?'

'No, I too have a key,' she smiled, 'although do not ask me where I got it.'

She'd got it from a drawer labelled *Spare Keys* in Monty's neat, precise hand, in the staff kitchen – probably where Albert had pilfered his from too.

'All right, I won't. Mind if I join you?'

Florence said, 'Please do,' then 'Not at all,' then 'Pull up a pew,' then she told herself to stop talking.

Albert sat in the other armchair in the corner and took a book out of his backpack.

Florence smiled. 'Is that what you're working on?'

Albert smiled back. 'Yes, now if you don't mind, I really do need to get cracking.'

Florence leant back in her chair, feeling the lids of her eyes close, as if someone had placed a small pebble on them. She would have liked to talk to Albert, they were so rarely alone in this quiet space, but the weight on her eyes was too heavy, keeping her lids firmly shut.

'Goodnight Florence.'

'Goodnight Albert,' she said, giving in to the waves of sleep that beckoned from the shore to pull her and her hangover in.

When Florence woke up an hour or so later, Albert was putting the book into his backpack.

'Was I asleep?'

'Yes.'

'Did I dribble?'

'Copiously.'

Florence nodded.

Perfect.

She stood up and stretched a little.

'Well, that was a very productive afternoon,' she said.

'Yes,' Albert agreed, 'I can see why you like working here, you get so much done.'

'As do you,' Florence smiled as they walked into the Green Team's office together.

'After you,' Albert said at the side door, and she slipped through it.

'Florence,' Albert said, 'I meant to ask, did you go to see the Amorphophallus titanum?'

'No, my family ended up coming over and I had a bit to do to get ready for them.'

'Ah . . . that's a shame. Is it still on?'

'It's not like a Broadway show, Albert, but if you're asking if it's still blooming, then no.'

Florence realised that once again she sounded sharp, when she had meant only to tease. *I am like a violin's strings that won't tune*, she thought.

Albert nodded. 'So, we've missed our chance then, have we?'

Florence thought about the afternoon, how the two of them had been held in the library's hollows, witnessed only by rows of silent authors still lurking, she believed, in the pages of their books. Surely if anything was going to happen, that would have been the moment, under the watchful eyes of all those writers, urging them to begin. Mary Wesley, for one, would have been shouting her head off.

Florence nodded. 'Looks like it,' she said. 'But not to worry, I'm sure it will smell just as repulsive next year.'

4

That night Florence met up with Orla and Veronica for dinner, an invitation she had accepted after their last gig, the Nightshades launching a two-pronged assault on her from either side of the mirror.

'Come on, Florence, come, it will be fun.'

'You never come out with us.'

'We only ever see you on stage.'

'It's actually kind of insulting.'

'It's actually *very* insulting, it's like you don't want to know us.'

I don't, thought Florence, *not really.*

Orla was taking her makeup off, her sweet, pinched face surprising Florence, as it always did, with its girlishness. On stage Orla was all knowing eyes and teasing banter. 'I like your suit, honey,' she'd toss to a man in the audience. 'Does your mama buy all your clothes?' But off stage she was a twenty-three-year-old part-time hairdresser from the Isle of Dogs in the East End of London who'd moved to Australia to be with her boyfriend Gav, who had unceremoniously dumped her shortly after they'd arrived, because, Orla said, he was a 'right tosser'.

Orla had no desire to go back to the East End and her mother Carol-Lea's hair salon, and the council flat her father Seamus, a drummer, blew in and out of in between gigs and greasy breakfasts. She did not want to return to join the ranks of the girls she'd grown up with and marry 'some chav in a shiny suit 'oo finks he's one of the Kray Brothers'.

The girls had laughed, Veronica had said, 'Fair enough,' and Florence had thought, not for the first time, that she loved Orla's East End lilt, which vanished the moment Orla stood in front of the microphone; her flat East End vowels replaced by something far more, as Orla said, 'Kensington Gardens'.

'It makes the act sound classier,' she said to the girls. 'Punters don't want to see three old slappers up there.'

Florence didn't agree with Orla's vocal disguise on stage, she found her true voice far more charming, but who was she to argue? She slipped on an elaborately embroidered cloak every time she became Miss Suki, a woman who never gave out her real name, not even to the Nightshades. They knew her as Florence Jones, a lamentable choice of surname, almost transparent in its commonness, the sort of name a bumbling criminal might choose for his alias. But she had chosen it on the fly when she'd made her first tentative steps back into the footlights, wanting a professional name as far away from Saint Claire as possible.

She'd written down *Jones* in a scratching hurry on the first audition form she'd filled out since leaving the Swingers, deciding in the moment to change her last name. She had toyed with changing her first name too, but decided it would be too complicated to answer to not one but two false names, when she was already wading knee deep into the waters of deception.

Florence hadn't told anyone she was auditioning – she had hardly known it herself.

Her self-imposed exile from singing had ended abruptly one Saturday morning when she was flicking through the copy of *High Notes* Isolde had left on the kitchen table. *High Notes* was the music profession's bible and Florence, despite her self-imposed exile from its ranks, still pored over its listings and reviews and passionate letters to the editor . . . *Really? Only two stars for 'Blue Rondo à la Turk'?*

Mercy Jones, Isolde and Puck's band, sometimes appeared within its pages, as did Amanda, usually smouldering like a dying fire on the cover. And in a box beneath Florence's bed was the *High Notes* edition of 16 September 1989.

Its cover was edged in black, the coda from 'Love Walked In' rising and falling across its pages.

Florence had felt a rush of gratitude to whoever had chosen not to mark Lucas Saint Claire's passing with the last plaintive mews of 'Santa Was A Jazz Cat'.

She had remained loyal to *High Notes,* and on the morning she found herself auditioning to sing again, a small advertisement in its 'musicians wanted' section caught her eye.

Back-up singer wanted. Rock outfit. Good pipes. No try-hards.

Its directness appealed to Florence.

She certainly wasn't a rock singer, but she did have a good set of pipes, and she had spent the last several years not trying at all.

In her kitchen, holding her cup of coffee in one hand and *High Notes* in the other, all the songs that Florence had held to her chest started to sing at once.

It wouldn't hurt, she told herself, to give them a short airing.

Florence Saint Claire drove her car to the address listed in *High Notes*, where Florence Jones filled out the audition form, a somewhat ambitious name for the scrap of paper she was handed, and sang from the song sheets.

She had decided that if she got the gig, she wanted to be sure it was because of her voice, not who she was, or had been.

It didn't matter. Florence Jones did not get the gig as back-up singer for Christian Altman's Furies – Christian Altman telling her after her audition that she was too 'show-tuney'.

'Nice work,' he said, 'but we're looking for someone with a bit more grunt, you know?'

Florence knew, and thanked Christian and the Furies (pale boys with slouched shoulders, who, Florence smiled to herself, had no idea that in Greek mythology the Furies were three vengeful female spirits, Alecto, Tisiphone and Megaera, who had snakes for hair).

'That's okay,' said Florence, 'I enjoyed it.'

And she had. Curling her hand around the microphone in one of the Furies' mother's garages (Florence didn't think Alecto lived with her mother), she'd felt its silvery curve almost leap into the hollow of her palm.

'One, two, three, four,' the drummer had counted in the band and Florence had felt a surge of dizzy joy as she opened her mouth to sing.

She might have overdone it, startling the band with the force of her voice, and the surprising, rolling trill of her contralto.

Christian was right, she was too 'show-tuney', years of performing with The Saint Claires had burnished her delivery with all sorts of flourishes she had learnt at her parents' feet. The slight pause before a beat drop, the casual finger click, the sudden, intense stare deep into the eyes of one audience member who felt the jolt and thought, 'I am here, I matter.' And then there was the invitation.

She heard her father's voice. 'And now let's go on a road trip together, let's go back, Amanda. You coming, Florence? How about you, Isolde? Puck, way at the back, yes? Then let's go down to Hollow's Road.'

It was shameless, Florence thought, the way her father had played the crowd, the way they swayed beneath his almost touch, their hands raised in mirror images of whatever Lucas Saint Claire was doing.

But it was also easy, and she could do it too.

They all could, even Puck if he could be coaxed from behind the drum kit, a wave of his dark hair low on his face, a shy grin beneath it.

The Saint Claire children had inherited their parents' starry threads of DNA, and Florence knew by the end of her first audition with the Furies that she was not a back-up singer.

She was like her father. Too much.

The next time she auditioned, she decided, she would move to the front.

Florence was twenty-five years old, and she had not sung professionally since she was sixteen – almost a decade of biting her own lip.

She was not sure which song had pulled her to her feet that morning and sent her to Christian Altman's door, but it was not done with her yet.

A month or so later she found herself in a freezing basement bar, its walls patched with peeling band posters, with the two slightly hungover women who would become the Nightshades.

Orla, in a ribbed black and white sweater, was tiny with short blonde hair and eyes ringed in smudged mascara, making her look like a slightly pissed raccoon, and Veronica, in some sort of complicated trench coat and boots, was so beautiful, it made Florence want to laugh out loud.

What must it be like, she wondered, to just walk around like that?

Veronica was tall, with a waterfall of red hair, and she spoke with a slight American lilt, leaning, Florence thought, towards the South by way of Brooklyn. It was a hybrid of an accent, and in all the years Florence knew her, she would never find out exactly which United State Veronica Allen came from. Glamazonia, Orla said.

The Nightshades' advertisement in *High Notes* had read: *Working Girl Needed. We are a jazz standards/cabaret vocals duo looking for a front woman. Must have professional experience. Must be available for regular rehearsals and gigs. Own car preferable. No Swiggers/Smokers/Shrinking Violets.*

Florence liked that it was all business. Whoever wrote the ad was looking for a working girl, not a nightingale, and Florence, despite her name, was never one of those.

Florence guessed Swiggers meant drinkers, and also liked that whoever wrote it went in for a little alliteration. She didn't smoke, but she supposed some people might consider her a violet of the shrinking variety. *But I'm not*, Florence thought, *not the Viola odorata kind anyway.* Odorata were the woodland variety of violets, beloved of poets and forever peeking out coyly from beneath clumps of clover. No, she was much more of a Viola hederacea, the Australian native violet, not as pretty, she thought, but hardy, and given the right conditions, a thriver.

In the freezing basement, Florence looked at Orla and Veronica and decided to thrive.

'So, wot experience 'ave you 'ad?' Orla asked.

'I've actually done quite a lot of singing, mostly back-up,' Florence answered her.

Orla nodded, narrowed her eyes.

'Done any lead?'

'No, I haven't.'

'We need someone who can cover all bases. We're a straight cabaret outfit, with sprinkles of jazz and blues. Let's hear you then,' Veronica said crisply. 'Only one way to find out . . .'

Florence nodded and stepped towards the mic, this time cradling it in her hands as she stood still behind it.

'"Stars in your eyes, love takes me by surprise . . ."' Orla and Veronica sat on bar stools as Florence sang the old jazz standard, Orla's eyes wet and shiny by the time Florence finished.

'Well,' she said, 'that was not wot I was expecting,' while Veronica stood up and said, 'The job is yours if you want it, Florence Jones,' and the way she said Jones, as if there was an underline beneath it, told Florence that Veronica knew it was fake.

But Veronica Allen didn't care, she was going to insist on all cash payments anyway, paid on the night by the owner, with a deposit up front, just in case.

'I've been burnt before,' she told Orla and Florence, 'although the last guy who tried is at the bottom of the Hudson River.'

Florence laughed, but Orla didn't, and for a moment Florence wondered if it might be true.

Veronica Allen looked like she was capable of anything.

As far as Veronica and Orla were concerned, Florence could call herself anything she liked, the three of them in it together now, this business of make-believe. Orla, she would find out, had learnt it at the foot of her father's drum kit, her teenage years spent singing with him at jazz clubs around the East End when Carol-Lea was working late and Seamus O'Loan was meant to be babysitting. And Veronica? Somewhere in the Bible Belt of America, Veronica Allen had grown up singing gospel music in a church where her father was a preacher and her mother did the flowers. She had graduated to jazz and blues by way of marriage to a saxophonist she never spoke about, then graduated from him by way of a plane ticket to Australia.

That Veronica Allen was the daughter of a preacher seemed incongruous to Florence, like an azure kingfisher being the progeny of a house sparrow, but Orla swore it was true. As for the husband, the only time Florence asked Veronica about her marriage, Veronica had replied, 'You know when you buy a new a pair of boots and you love them so much that you wear them out? Well it was like that, Florence,' and left it at that.

Florence didn't press her any further. Not doing so was an arrangement that suited them all. It suited her that Veronica and Orla, having both grown up overseas, may never have heard of the Saint Claire Swingers. But if they had, and Florence was fairly sure they would have heard of Lucas at least, they did not prod or push her.

They all left it at that, one way or another.

After that first audition, Florence became Miss Suki easily, just as Orla and Veronica slipped into their roles as the Nightshades as smoothly as their silk dressing gowns slid onto their shoulders.

They began rehearsing at Orla's flat, watched by the flickering and, Florence felt, slightly judgemental eyes of Orla's cat Thomas.

Veronica choreographed each song in the set, adding in the hand claps and clicks handed down from one generation of girl group to another, women who wore go-go boots or cropped leather jackets and had eyes that said they could take or leave you, but they would probably leave you.

They rehearsed for several weeks before Veronica booked their first gig as part of a cabaret festival. Applying her makeup in the dressing room beforehand, Florence knew she was overdoing it. But becoming more Miss Suki and less Florence Saint Claire in front of her own eyes calmed her, and she applied thick makeup like lacquer, watching herself disappear beneath it.

'Jesus, Florence,' Orla said the first time Florence lifted her head from the mirror's image to meet Orla's eyes. 'We're trying to entertain the punters, not scare them 'alf to death.'

Veronica glided in and said, 'Oh I didn't know it was the Day of the Dead,' and Florence resolved to be a little less heavy-handed in future – less Black Dahlia, more Water Lily.

That first night, when Florence stood with Orla and Veronica on either side of her like bookends, their bodies held in silhouette behind a backlit screen – 'We look like statues,' Orla had complained in rehearsal; 'We look like Greek goddesses,' Veronica had corrected her – Florence wondered wildly, in the few seconds before the screen opened, if she might choke.

What would it feel like if her limbs took hold of themselves again? If her cheeks flared, or her throat folded in on itself?

Puck flashed into her mind, her little brother sitting at the wheel of a homemade go-cart Amanda – was it really Amanda, surely it was Lucas? – had made with them, Puck's hands on the rope, his eyes on Florence. 'Here goes nothing!' he'd said as the cart edged towards the lip of the hill.

'Here goes nothing!' Florence echoed as she lifted her head to sing.

After that it was easy, Florence's fingers automatically closing around the microphone, her voice opening up like a flower's throat.

Richard had been right all those years ago, it was like falling off a bike, but only, Florence thought as the Nightshades shimmied off the stage, if you were dressed like a woman who meant business and not a woodland elf.

The three women met once or twice a week to rehearse, and although Veronica and Orla were close friends outside the Nightshades, going to dance classes together and causing havoc every now and again in nightclubs, Florence did not join them. She liked both of them, particularly Orla, who she knew her mother would deem 'plucky', but she didn't want to blur the edges of her two lives. They were so entwined but so far removed from each other, even Florence sometimes didn't know how she pulled it off.

I am like a superhero, she smiled to herself the second night she performed as Miss Suki, pulling on her midnight-blue, full-length gloves.

I am like one of those characters in a cartoon strip – by day a mild-mannered gardener, occasional children's storyteller and lover of flowers, by night an exotic lounge singer peeping out from behind lamé curtains.

It was, she reflected, quite the leap.

It was also quite the secret, and Florence had always enjoyed secrets.

The backyard of the family home was probably still riddled with the small earthy spaces she had made herself as a child, furiously digging at the dirt with her spade. If her parents thought there was something peculiar about Florence spending much of her time digging out hidey-holes made of curved earth, they didn't say.

As an adult, Florence could never quite work out if Lucas and Amanda's complete refusal to put a name to any of their children's behaviours, much less address some of the quirkier ones – Florence's dug-outs, Puck's vanishing acts, Isolde's *Isoldeness* – was wilfully neglectful or the greatest act of parental brilliance she'd heard of.

Lucas would wave cheerfully at her from the music room window as she emerged from yet another clumpy bush, arms streaked with dirt; Amanda would sometimes say over dinner, 'Did you build any nice holes today, darling?' and Florence continued behaving, from the ages of about seven to ten, as a very small, very industrious human mole.

It was obvious, she thought, what she had been trying to do – find a small space away from the bigness of her family, although it was more than that.

Florence loved the feeling, when she had squeezed into one of her tiny curved caves, of being of the earth.

She would crouch against the damp wall of it at her back, breathe in the petrichor smell of the rocks and clay, and feel the thrill of concealment.

As an adult, she would also wonder how safe her hand-hewn holes were and what her parents would have done in the event of a cave-in.

'Don't be so dramatic, darling,' Amanda said. 'They were only about a foot deep, we would have got you out quick smart.'

She was probably right, but as a child it had seemed to Florence that she was deep beneath the earth's surface – at least past the bedrock and the topsoil – and into the belly of its silence. That this turned out not to be the case didn't bother Florence at all. She could still smell the sharp scents of her hidey holes every time she stepped into the East Elm section of the Mount Bell forest, or feel the thrill of concealment when Miss Suki shimmered into the spotlight, the tiny sequined discs of her dress sending shots of luminous colour into the light.

She loved the anonymity of Miss Suki, the way that, while the Nightshades flirted their way around the stage, she kept a cool distance, and if anyone in the audience ever raised their fingers to form a letter L on their forehead, Florence wouldn't know because Miss Suki never deigned to look at them.

Miss Suki never caught and held their eyes. Miss Suki never gave her audience 'maximum wattage'. Miss Suki didn't give a stuff.

Florence thought she was wonderful.

But despite her best efforts to keep that same sort of cool distance between herself and the Nightshades off the stage, Veronica and Orla were not, as Orla said ''aving it'.

Every now and again they insisted the three of them go out, and tonight it was dinner at an Italian restaurant Orla had heard about and then drinks at East Elm's rowdiest pub, the Gate House.

Getting ready that night, Florence was just putting on her silver hoop earrings when Isolde surprised her by walking into her room – Florence thought she had a Mercy Jones rehearsal.

'Going out?' Isolde asked, stretching her leg against the architrave of the door.

'Mmm-mmm,' Florence answered.

'Who with?'

'Just some friends . . .'

'You don't have any friends,' Isolde pointed out, not, Florence thought, unfairly.

'Yes I do, Issy . . . you've just never met them.'

'Well I might come and meet them tonight then.'

Florence knew by Issy's tone, by the slight lift of her chin and the way she was now leaning into the doorframe, that her sister was in a scrappy mood.

Florence headed her off at the pass. 'Well you can't. They're friends from my course, and we're meeting up to talk about the next module.'

Issy opened her mouth in an exaggerated yawn.

It had become necessary a few months after their first gig for Florence to invent a reason for her increasingly frequent outings. Mostly Puck and Isolde were out at night gigging with Mercy Jones, but sometimes if they didn't have a gig and Florence did, it became tricky. So she had invented a part-time hydroponics course at the local TAFE, knowing that her family would accept this readily and certainly not follow it up.

Florence's interest in growing things was a source of both general indifference and occasional hilarity to her family.

'What do you do, darling, in that forest all day long?' Amanda had once asked over dinner.

'Smokes pot probably,' Isolde had answered.

Florence had rolled her eyes. 'Actually,' she'd said, 'what we usually do is pick a few magic mushrooms and cook them up for lunch, and then we all run around naked together howling at the trees.'

'Your father and I had magic mushrooms once,' Amanda had said, and launched into a tale involving hiking and sea caves and rolling around with Lucas wrapped in seaweed, Florence's forays into the forest immediately forgotten.

Now Isolde appeared to have lost interest too. 'Think I'll give it a miss then, not that I don't think it would be extremely interesting to have a night out with the plant people – where are you going?'

Florence sometimes saw her life as a Venn diagram. On one side was her family and her work with the Green Team, on the other Miss Suki and the Nightshades, and in between lay a neutral, empty space where no one ventured, which was exactly how she liked it.

She looked at Isolde and laughed. 'None of your business, Inspector Poirot,' she answered lightly, walking out the door.

At La Pinisa, the Italian restaurant Orla had booked, there were a few people waiting at the front entrance to get in, and one middle-aged man was becoming agitated at a waiter, his breath coming out in indignant white puffs in the night air.

When they were smaller, she and Isolde would pretend to smoke on cold days, putting two fingers to their mouths and pursing their lips, sucking in imaginary smoke and then blowing it out in one long stream, pretending to be Amanda.

'Darling,' Florence would say, dropping her voice to a throaty thrum, 'try not to glower so at the audience when you sing, Florence.'

'And you, Isolde,' Issy would echo, 'do try to keep still on stage. I said to your father it's like having an electric eel up there.'

They would collapse in laughter, the two sisters wrapped up in each other's skin, sharing a joke only they, and not even Puck, would understand.

Daughter jokes. About mothers. Particularly their mother.

Florence heard her name being called and saw Orla waving her over from inside the restaurant. Florence walked over to a corner table where Veronica sat, a waiter hovering near her like a march fly at the beach.

'Hi girls!' Florence said in what she thought was the right tone, the right level of enthusiasm. Ridiculous, she knew, to worry about such things, but she hadn't had much practice at girls' nights out.

Here was the other thing about being a child performer: that's exactly what you were. Timing. Hitting your mark. Maximum wattage. Stage right. Stage left. Do you like singing with your family, Florence? Does your dad ever give you any advice?

All that, Florence knew how to negotiate. She knew where to stand and where to turn, and how to breathe so the microphone didn't pick it up. She knew how to answer talk show hosts in a way that would make the parents in the audience laugh and wish it was their little girl sitting on the couch in the studio in a pair of adorable denim overalls.

For Florence – and Isolde and Puck – the tricky part was real life.

They had all grown up with adults, and outside of school hours. None of them had – save for Florence's Year of Living Not Very Dangerously with Amy Burton in her long, white socks – many interactions with people their age. Puck didn't care, Isolde didn't notice, but Florence did, she heard it all and saw it all from beneath her sidelong glances. Snatches of conversations about slumber parties and bike rides to the local pool, and later about lipstick shades and boys who pretended they hated you because they liked you, and later still, women would speak of girls' nights out and weekends away, and to Florence it sounded like they were visiting foreign lands even if they were just going down the coast for a night.

You needed practice at these things, Florence thought, to be any good at them. You needed to be able to say, 'Hi girls' with ease, to roll your eyes in exactly the right way at exactly the right moment, to reach over and lightly touch an elbow and say, 'I know,' in exactly the right tone to show that you really did.

Issy was right when she said Florence didn't have any friends, but it wasn't because she was prickly. She was just rusty. She needed to get out more and oil her voice for conversations. She needed to listen to their rhythms with a keener ear so she knew the right moment to come in.

'You look beautiful, Flo' – Orla, the only person in the world she allowed to call her Flo – 'you don't scrub up 'alf bad, does she, Ronnie?'

Veronica nodded then began another tale of another poor bloke she'd accidentally ensnared in her Veronicaness by allowing him to take her out to dinner.

'What is it with these men?' she was saying. 'All I hear about is how reluctant they are to commit, and the ones I meet are talking about holidays together and meeting the parents within two minutes.'

Orla and Florence exchanged glances – Florence secure that this was exactly the right response to Veronica's complaint.

'Well that's because you look like Jessica Fucking Rabbit,' Orla said.

'What about you?' Veronica asked Florence. 'You got a fella hidden away somewhere, is that why you never usually come anywhere with us?'

'Nope,' Florence shook her head, then added, in the spirit of things, 'but there's someone at work I might be interested in.'

'Oooh,' said Orla, 'tell us everyfing,' and both girls leant forward in exactly the way Florence had seen women on the verge of important new information do.

Florence leant forward a little too.

'He's just a colleague, but he's really nice, and he's really kind of solid, you know?'

The girls nodded.

'He smells good.'

Orla nodded vigorously and offered that Gav had smelt like a Sunday fry-up.

'And he's really interested in reintroducing some of the native fungi we've lost in the Mount Bell forest. We've been working together on a species count of them.'

Florence knew from the women's faces that this was not the sort of information they were after, but it was exactly the sort of information that mattered to her.

She liked that Albert was nice, she liked that he smelt a little bit earthwormy, and she liked that he knew about fungi.

'So has anything happened between you and this mushroom man?' Veronica asked.

'No,' Florence answered. 'I think he's not interested.'

'Gay,' said Orla authoritatively.

Florence shook her head. 'I don't think that's it.'

'Has to be,' Orla answered. 'I mean look at you, you're not

the sort of woman a man would frow out of bed on a cold night, Florence.'

Later, much later, when Florence half tumbled out of a cab after continuing on at the Gate House, she let herself in the door and crept up the stairs, not wanting to wake Isolde. It had been a fun night, better than she had thought it would be, Florence relaxing into Orla and Veronica's company, blurring herself at their vivid edges. Climbing into bed and feeling the not unpleasant sensation of the room moving beneath her body – not the full spin, more like a gentle cycle in the washing machine – Florence closed her eyes and smiled.

'I am not the sort of woman a man would frow out of bed on a cold night,' she repeated to herself just before the room stayed still long enough for her to fall asleep.

*

From her armchair, Amanda Saint Claire looked in on her sleeping daughter.

Unusual for Florence to go to bed fully clothed, she thought, good for her, I hope she had fun.

Amanda had let herself in to her daughters' home, as she always did – 'there are no locked doors between the Saint Claires!' she heard her own voice trill.

Amanda wondered what Florence would do if she just crept into bed beside her, as she knew Issy still did.

How would it feel to hold Florence again, to feel the hook of her arm around her waist, and her head resting in the crook of her shoulder, the slow, animal pants of her breath?

When Florence was small, she would leave her own bed to pad down the hall to her parents', climbing up to lie between them, wriggling into position, always turning – and this gave Amanda a ripple of a thrill each time – slightly towards her, instead of Lucas.

Amanda would lie very still and listen to her daughter's grunts and murmurs, and she kept still until Florence's breaths told her she had gone to sleep.

Amanda's own parents, Philip and Nancy Catchpool, had distributed their affection sparingly, they were stiff with her, given to patting their daughter on her head.

To have her own child, this girl, this brown-haired and brown-eyed sprite curved into her body filled Amanda with a quiet, buzzing joy, like she had caught a lady beetle in her hands.

It was easier when Florence was small, Amanda thought, before the other children came, and everyone wanted a piece of Lucas, then a piece of her family.

Before the Saint Claires became the Saint Claire Swingers, and Amanda, suddenly up front in plunging emerald gowns and chandelier earrings, got lost in it all.

Florence had once shouted at her, midway in some fight about a festival she did not want to go to, and some hideous pair of overalls Richard was trying to force them all to wear, that she had 'forgotten how to be a mother'.

Amanda looked at her sleeping daughter, one leg now flung outside of the sheets, dangling like discarded washing over the bed.

It wasn't true, Amanda thought, looking at Florence, I never forgot I was your mother, but I did get distracted.

That was one way of putting those years when she was so busy singing and smiling and making sure that Richard hadn't booked them into time slots that were too late for those members of the Swingers who still had to get up for school the next day.

She approved the costumes, and argued with the venue owners and brought food in Tupperware containers for the kids to eat in the back of the van, and none of it, absolutely none of it, was as exhausting as being Lucas Saint Claire's wife.

Being married to Lucas wasn't easy – actually that was not strictly true.

Being married to Lucas Saint Claire was everything Amanda Saint Claire, nee Catchpool, wanted.

Meeting Lucas at the Conservatorium all those years ago, she in a tartan mini skirt and white leather boots with buttons at the side – God how she had loved those boots, she'd spent winters with them welded to her feet – Lucas in a three-quarter-length sheepskin coat, and every bit the wolf, had tilted everything.

It had raised her up, and taken her away from her parents and their keeping her at arm's length and into Lucas's arms and bed where nothing was off limits, and the more touching the better, and she was nineteen and could not believe her luck.

'Lucky you,' she remembers her friends from the Conservatorium saying, 'Lucas Saint Claire could have any girl he wanted.'

That he wanted her was something Amanda always felt obliged in some way to pay back, to thank him for lifting her from the pack and sweeping his arms out to include her in his embrace every time they walked on stage.

'My wife, everybody,' he'd say, drawing her into him, 'the Gorgeous Amanda,' and she would stand beside him and feel like she had been pulled into the orbit of the sun.

But being the Gorgeous Amanda was a full-time job in itself, it meant eye masks and expensive crèmes and frosted highlights and keeping slim, and never ever being dull.

Somewhere along the way, she became Lamanda, that awful name the children had christened her.

She hated it, and they knew she hated it, but she also knew she wore it well.

Amanda had long ago been displaced by Lamanda, and it was only in moments like these, looking at her sleeping adult daughter, that she knew she was still there, hidden like so many layers of a chiffon dress.

Amanda stood up and quietly left the room, turning to blow a kiss to her daughter on the way out.

5

'Morning Flo,' Victor called as she walked past his house on Monday morning, 'beautiful day.'

Florence smiled at him. 'It is, although I'm a bit dusty.'

Victor smiled at her, 'Oooh, big night?'

'Yep,' Florence answered, 'my head is thumping.'

'Leon used to say he had a head like a fur shoe when he was hungover,' Victor said, then added, 'Want a cup of tea?'

Florence did.

She did want a cup of tea, badly, and some toast and maybe some of Victor's honey, from the hive he and Leon had kept at East Elm's community garden.

'Sure,' she said. 'I don't need to be at work for another half-hour or so.'

Victor opened his gate and Florence followed him into the

house, realising that she hadn't been all the way inside it since Leon's death.

She had gone to the wake. People, mostly men, had crammed inside the tiny cottage, while Victor served up platters of sandwiches and sausage rolls he had made himself, and Leon's immediate family, a sad-looking father and a too-loud mother, served them.

Since then she had mostly spoken to Victor from across the fence, where he stood poised like a Venus flytrap with a watering can, ready to catch someone in conversation as they passed by.

'Sorry about the mess,' Victor called out from the kitchen, 'we haven't had a clean-up in ages. Sit down in the lounge, love, I'll bring you your tea in a jiffy.'

Florence noted the 'we' and the fact that all of Leon's belongings were still in the lounge room, as if he was too. His boots were on the rug; his flat cap was on the hook, and his *Times* crossword was open on the table, a pencil lying diagonally across it.

'I know,' Victor said cheerfully, entering with a tray, 'should get rid of them, but it makes me happy to have his things here.'

Victor shrugged, and Florence nodded.

'Makes sense to me,' she said, thinking of Lucas's music room.

Victor served the tea, asking Florence for advice about propagating begonias, and Florence realised that while she had not been inside Victor's house for several months, she had also not seen him outside of it. Not counting, that was, his front yard.

Usually she could count on at least one Victor sighting a week – at the shops, or the library, or at the community gardens where she sometimes went to get clippings and he tended his hives.

'Victor, have you got any of your honey for this toast?'

'No, love,' he answered. 'I'm sweet enough.'

'Victor,' she asked, 'have you left this house lately?'

'No, love,' he answered. 'I have not.'

'Ah,' she said, 'can I ask you why?'

'Because I'm afraid . . . stupid really.' Victor held up a piece of toast, mid-butter. 'Well, what if Leon comes back?'

He looked at Florence's slightly alarmed face. 'Not the actual Leon, don't worry. I'm not like some queer Miss Havisham tottering around in my wedding frock waiting for him to come home. No, it's more that . . . well, what if his spirit comes back to visit and I'm not here to greet him?'

Florence looked at Victor, holding a teapot with strawberry vines on it, and laughed out loud. 'Victor,' she said, 'that is the most ridiculous thing I've ever heard.'

Victor stared at her. 'Florence, if you are going to make fun of me, you can please leave.'

Florence laughed harder – God, what was wrong with her, was it the hangover? Why could she never say the right thing at the right time? Why must she always wrong-foot it? She looked at Victor's face, and stopped laughing.

'I'm not laughing at you, Victor,' she said. 'I am laughing because if Leon did come back to visit you and you weren't here, if he saw that you were getting on with your life, he would be happy.'

'Well then clearly you didn't know Leon,' Victor smiled and then began to laugh himself, a deep, throaty bellow.

'So you've been sitting here, all this time, keeping the tea on for him?' Florence prodded.

'Yes, you know, just in case he popped by,' Victor was really laughing now, 'to check if he left the iron on.'

Florence laughed with him, and Victor became almost hysterical by listing other absurd things Leon might be popping in to cast an eye over: 'He just wants to see whether there's any library books due', 'He's reading the water meter', until he ran out of puff.

Florence finished her tea and glanced at her watch.

'I really have to get going, Victor,' she said, 'but I'll come and see you soon,' and kissed him on the cheek, which surprised both of them.

She would visit more often – Victor needed looking in on, not walking past as she admired his peonies. She should have popped in earlier, and she should have seen what was standing right in front of her as she walked by Victor's beautifully kept garden every day. It was lush and bountiful, the sweet peas cascading over the fence, the magnolias dotted between the native gardenias, and the raked vegetable garden at the side of the house, its lettuces in neat rows and the curling vines of the butternut pumpkins kept in check.

No, Victor's garden didn't need tending, but its owner did.

Looking around Victor's shrine-like home to his partner of almost thirty years, Florence could see Victor and Leon pottering around inside it. Leon in his Hawaiian shirts and board shorts, Victor in his gardening clothes, the two of them hunched over the crossword or shouting at each other from across a backgammon board. Occasionally she and Issy would watch movies with them, Leon serving popcorn and tall glasses of gin and holding Victor's hand on the sofa.

How could she have missed it?

How could she not have seen the aching gap that Leon's 'Pipeline 68' shirts had left behind?

Somehow she had thought that waving casually to Victor as she sailed past his gate every morning was enough, that as long as he was upright and in his garden, all was as it should be. But it wasn't and if she was truthful with herself, she had known it, Victor's loneliness tugging at her like a distress signal from deep within a mineshaft, not seen but heard.

'Victor,' she said, 'how about we leave Leon a note?'

'What?'

'Let's leave him a note, so that if he does come back to turn on the washing machine or check the mail, and you are not here, he will know that this is still his house, and you are still his husband.'

Victor looked at her, both eyebrows raised, his chin tucked into his hand.

'I would like to get out more . . . where would we leave it?'

Florence smiled. 'On the fridge, of course.'

Florence knew she would be late for work as she sat down to help Victor pen his note, but it didn't matter. What was more important was that once Victor had written his note, which they decided should be, like all good notes, short and sweet – *Dear Leon, I am just out for a bit but will be back soon. Love Victor* – she might be able to propel him out the door.

They had two false starts, Victor getting as far as the hallway then turning back, and the second time making it to the front porch before saying, 'No, I don't think so, Florence.'

She said gently in his ear, 'Oh but you must, Miss Havisham,' and took his elbow to lead him down the front stairs, leaving Leon's note held firmly by four magnets on the fridge door.

They said goodbye at the crossroads, Florence turning around to watch Victor's disappearing back, just to make sure.

Arriving at work, Florence checked her roster on the Green Team's noticeboard and saw she was down for five days in the park, none of them in the library and all of them with Albert as her co-worker.

Florence smiled, thinking of a week-long foray into the forest without Pedro Perkins, and latterly his new sidekick Shawna Carter asking her questions they knew she didn't have the answer to, and also of Victor hopefully checking the beehive frames.

Monty Rollins appeared beside her, peering at the list. '"*And into the forest I go, to lose my mind and find my soul,*"' he said quietly, then added, 'John Muir.'

'Yes,' Florence answered, surprised, 'I like him too, have you read much of him?'

'Oh yes,' Monty smiled. 'I think I've probably read all of his works – *Travels in Alaska*, *Steep Trails*, *Cruise of the Corwin* et al – I've walked a lot of the trails he wrote of too, with Sharon, of course, and some of our friends.'

'Sharon?' Florence asked, and just stopped herself from adding, 'Friends?'

'My wife,' Monty said, his hands adjusting his bow tie. 'Wonderful hiker, puts me to shame, it's her thighs of course, marvellous.'

'Her thighs?'

'Oh yes, dear, she charges up those hills on them like twin pistons going at it when she attacks a trail, it's all I can do to gaze on in admiration.'

'I didn't know you were a hiker.'

'Thought I spent my weekends with my nose buried in a book, did you?' he smiled at her.

'Yes, I suppose I did,' she answered truthfully.

Monty nodded. 'Well I do actually, but it's usually under a tree somewhere.'

'I like to read outside too,' Florence said, 'or inside, or anywhere really.'

Monty laughed, and for the second time that day Florence realised she had missed something. First Victor and his loneliness, and now Monty, who loved the Scottish conservationist, John Muir, and had a wife called Sharon with Teutonic thighs.

What else had she missed?

Who else had she missed?

For someone with not too many friends, Florence thought, she really should make an effort to get to know people better – maybe then she'd make some.

'We don't mind a dollop of cabaret either.'

'What?' Florence asked, her voice a few notes higher than usual.

'Cabaret – Sharon and I go often,' Monty smiled, then turned to push a trolley pregnant with books towards the shelves and vanished into Historical Fiction.

Was Monty letting her know that he knew about Miss Suki?

What had he said? 'Sharon and I go often.' It had sounded, Florence thought, vaguely threatening, but then she remembered

Monty's smile as he said it, which was leaning far more towards the mischievous.

Florence made a coffee in the staffroom, said good morning to Erica Little, the junior librarian, who was wearing a sleeveless dress and, Florence noticed for the first time, had the cover of *Slouching Towards Bethlehem* tattooed on her upper arm.

Now that took some missing. She'd never taken a good look at Erica's tattoo before, and Florence wondered how on earth she hadn't noticed it. Florence felt like she supposed Isolde had the first time she wore glasses. Isolde wore contact lenses now, but when she was about eight a teacher had written to the Saint Claires to suggest that Isolde's habit of bumping into things might be due to poor eyesight rather than 'general clumsiness'. Florence had gone to the optometrist to pick up Isolde's new glasses with her – bright green with studded red arms – and when Issy had put them on outside, she had looked around her, turned to Florence and said, 'Leaves have edges.' Isolde had looked around in astonishment for about two weeks, then left the glasses on her bedside table and gone back to bumping into things.

Now Florence felt, if not quite the same wide-eyed wonder as Isolde had for those two weeks, at least a strange sense of things being pulled into focus. She wasn't sure why, but it had been a steady sharpening since she had begun spending her days tramping through the forest with the Green Team and her nights singing with Orla and Veronica.

That was enough to awaken anyone's senses, every single one of them.

Erica noticed her taking in the image of Joan Didion on her arm, the author's elfin face half wrapped in black, rectangular sunglasses.

'You like it?' Erica asked her.

'I love it,' Florence answered. 'I love Joan Didion.'

Erica smiled. 'You work in a library, Florence, you inhale gardens, you read like a madwoman, of course you love Joan Didion, she's the patron saint of girls like us.'

Florence supposed she was, but she had slotted Erica elsewhere. If she had been made to guess which book cover the junior librarian would have inked on her skin, she would have definitely chosen one of the Brontë sisters – probably Emily.

'It's a beautiful tattoo, Erica,' she said as she left the staffroom for the Green Team office, a little thrill inside at Erica's 'girls like us'.

Florence sipped her coffee. *I am a girl like us*, she thought. *I am in a girl club, I have a crew.*

She giggled as Albert walked in carrying two long-handled shovels.

'I brought these from home, I thought we could use them at the southern entrance today,' he said.

'And good morning to you too, Albert,' Florence answered, then checking the junior librarian was not around added, 'did you know Erica has the cover of *Slouching Towards Bethlehem* on her arm?'

Albert nodded. 'It's good, isn't it? All the librarians do it. Monty's got *Lady Chatterley's Lover* inked on his bum.'

For a moment, Florence believed him, then she laughed. 'His wife Sharon's got thighs like pistons, I bet you didn't know that.'

'I did actually,' Albert said. 'Anyway, how was your weekend?'

'Great,' Florence answered. 'How was yours?'

'Oh, I went for a couple of drinks with Jeremy and Lydia, and I went to a thingy at the Greek Club. Have you been there? Lots of columns and vines?'

'No, I've never been,' she replied. She had, actually: Miss Suki and the Nightshades had performed there during a Paniyiri Festival wearing one-shouldered dresses that had made them look like university students at a toga party.

Florence felt her lips stretching across her face in what she hoped looked like a smile. Just once, she thought, she would like Albert to tell her that he had spent his weekend pottering around. He looked like a potterer to her. But he was always out. With sodding Jeremy and sodding Lydia.

'Are they a couple?' she found herself asking, digging, more precisely.

'Who?'

'Jeremy and Lydia.'

Albert laughed. 'Christ no. Although I don't think old Jeremy would say no.'

Every now and again Albert's speech slipped into the cadence of his other world filled with guffaws and back-slapping and young men who were called old. 'Old Jeremy', and 'Old Liam' and 'Old Freddy'. It didn't, Florence thought, suit him.

She kept her mouth stretched, regardless. 'I went out with my friends Orla and Veronica to an Italian restaurant,' pleased she had an actual, non-paying event to tell him about.

'Orla and Veronica,' Albert echoed. 'I don't think you've mentioned them before.'

'Oh really?' Florence said. 'Well, they're kind of my girl crew.'

The moment she said it, she wished she hadn't.

Bloody, bloody, bloody hell. She blamed Erica for making her feel like she was in some secret sisterhood. Yes, it was Erica's fault. Erica and Joan Didion.

'So, this girl crew of yours, do you have a tag you use when you're spray-painting the outside of buildings?' Albert asked, his mouth twisting in its efforts to stay straight.

'Yes, we do, as a matter of fact,' Florence said. 'It says "Piss Off Albert".'

Albert laughed and handed her the shovel. 'Come on then, Florence, let's go, and if I really piss you off you can always hit me over the head with this.'

They drove to the south entrance of the park, the sun already hitting the windscreen and warming it.

Florence felt her eyes closing, and her head dropping towards her chest, and she jerked it back several times before she let go to the warmth of the car, and the motor's hum beneath her feet and the feeling that it was rather nice to look at Albert Flowers's profile before she went to sleep.

Albert woke her when they got to the car park, reluctant, he said, to leave her asleep in the van in the isolated south-west section of the forest.

'I would have been absolutely fine, you just didn't want to do all that digging yourself,' Florence told him as they got out of the car and slipped behind the green curtain.

At lunchtime they sat on some granite boulders, the surfaces smoothed by time, and when they finished their sandwiches, and she was just about to tease him about his having the crusts cut off, Albert told her about Charlotte Markson and there was absolutely no teasing to be done.

This was not the usual tale of late-night carousing in late-night bars with the sort of people who sometimes reminded her of the crowd who hung off Lucas Saint Claire like flashy baubles on a Christmas tree. Florence hadn't liked those people when she was young, and hadn't entirely liked her father when he was around them either. When he was with them, raising a distracted wave to her from across a room, Florence felt like all his volume was turned up and hers was turned down. It felt like Lucas didn't belong to her family, as if he was on loan. Florence preferred the quieter moments with her father, they all did, times when he would play his clarinet in the lounge room, so it was like a private concert, or sit quietly with Isolde, helping her decipher a score.

Florence was better at quieter moments, like this one with Albert who was rushing his words out, hurrying the telling in a voice so soft that she had to lean in across the granite to catch all the ways that Charlotte could have been a contender.

For the State water polo team, for the position of Ollie's future first girlfriend, for the best friend her girlfriends would ever have in high school, for one of those people life throws forward every now and again, landing like sparking firecrackers.

Florence listened to Albert in the forest and said nothing at all, while Albert Flowers surprised her by crying, his head towards the faint white moon still suspended in the day's sky.

It felt shockingly intimate to Florence, like walking into a room and discovering lovers wrapped in each other's layers.

Albert wasn't crying in any way she had seen or heard anyone cry before. Not like Lucas, who sometimes when he heard a piece of music would bow his head and raise one hand to his eyes as if he needed shielding from so much beauty; or Amanda, who ran the gamut of tears from gazing-into-the-distance sniffs to full-throated sobs. Isolde was a pretty crier, small drifts of tears on her cheeks, while Puck's tears were rare and sprang from his eyes in watery spurts. But Albert Flowers was not so much crying as howling. It was not easy to watch or hear, but Florence held her gaze steady as she slipped her hand into his and began to sing. Florence recognised it as the same sort of song her mother had sung to her as they'd sat outside the Prentices' house, Kinsey awash in red and blue. What had Amanda called it? A song of lament. That was what it was. There were no words or discernible melody, not a hint of a chorus.

She had never sung in front of Albert before, and if he was surprised, he did not show it. Instead Florence sang and Albert got the howl out. It was a strange duet, heard by all the unearthly creatures in the forest.

'I'm sorry Albert,' Florence said when the song stilled.

'Thank you Florence,' he answered. 'I don't exactly know where that came from.'

'My singing or your crying?' she smiled at him.

'Both, I suppose,' he said as they stood up to strike the earth once more, Albert's shovel splitting its skin hard and fast.

*

'Once you have seen a man cry,' Amanda told her that night when she dropped over to see Florence and Isolde, 'all bets are off.'

'What do you mean?' she asked her mother.

'I mean, that's it, darling, it's all over, either way.'

'Either way?'

Amanda smiled her cat smile, the one that said, 'I know things you don't know and will never know,' and drove her children to distraction.

'If a man cries in front of you, Florence, it's a surrender to either a great love or a deep friendship,' she said.

'Or,' Florence said, tired of her mother's romanticising, 'it's because a child died and it's really sad.'

'Well of course it's sad, Florence,' Amanda replied. 'It's the saddest thing in the world. I'm simply saying that this landscape gardener of yours obviously feels very,' Amanda twirled one hand in the air, searching for the right word, 'safe with you, and the person you should feel safest with is either your lover or your best friend. So which do you think you are, darling?'

Florence didn't know. Albert was not like other men she had fallen for, other relationships where she had tumbled into bed with men she couldn't keep her hands off. At university she had gone on a few dates, if attending university balls and trivia nights on the loose understanding that if you had arrived together, you would be leaving together, constituted dating.

There had also been, for a few months in her final year, Adam.

Florence still felt twinges of regret over Adam Best, who never seemed to mind her particular brand of oddness.

He was in his final year of Vet, and his family had a cattle property called Constantine about two and a half hours north-west of the city. The nearest town was Raleigh or, as it was known among its locals and on the billboard on the way into it, 'The Best Little Town in the West'.

Florence had hated it.

She had liked Adam, though.

She had liked the way he spoke to her, always keeping his eyes on hers, and the way he had none of the swagger of the boys in their group but held his own among them. She liked the way he called her mother 'Mrs Saint Claire', even though her entire family, even Puck, had mocked him as he'd said it.

Most of all, she liked the way he used his hands.

Other boys at university – useless boys, Florence thought – behaved like their hands were strange shapes they had unexpectedly found at the end of their arms, uncertain what to do with them.

Adam Best did not have that same trouble.

He did however have five hundred head of cattle, several nippy farm dogs and a mother who wore pale olive jodhpurs and took one look at Florence and knew, just as Florence did, that she would not do at all.

For the rest of the stay, and for several return visits afterwards, Florence had tried. She had tried to imagine herself living at Constantine, creating a garden in the bush, coaxing beds into life and growing wisteria. She would close her eyes to see herself planting a cottage garden in front of the house, lavender at the stairs and bellflowers at the door, but she couldn't. She was like Isolde, she supposed: too much wildness in her.

When she had told Adam it was over, he had cried wet tears into the back of his hands, and she had known straight away that she was losing not a lover but a best friend.

After Adam, there had been other men, but Florence had grown attached to none of them, and she had certainly not seen any of them cry.

'What about Dad?' she asked Amanda, now sitting beside her on the couch, her feet on Florence's lap. 'Did you ever see him cry?'

Amanda shook her head. 'Only over music,' she answered. 'But I did enough crying for the both of us.'

It was true, Florence thought. When Amanda wasn't singing, she was laughing, and when she wasn't laughing, she was crying, or calling out to people from across the room, making sure everyone knew she was in it. Amanda wore her emotions on her sleeve like Erica's tattoo.

'Anyway,' Amanda said, 'I think it's probably time for you and this woodsman to work out if you are to be friends or more than friends, darling.'

'Albert,' Florence said. 'His name is Albert.'

*

In name, plumage and song, the Albert's lyrebird lacked the startling beauty and range of its cousin, the superb lyrebird, with its preening outer feathers curled in the shape of a lyre. Albert's lyrebirds did not have the same instrumental motif; they were,

Florence thought, the avian world's Aunt Margo to its Amanda Saint Claire. But both birds could mimic the sounds they heard around them, the staccato *aaks* of kookaburras, the unsettling mews of green catbirds and, increasingly, the sharp wails of car alarms and chainsaws.

The Albert's lyrebird was the rarer of the two, and its human namesake thought he had seen and heard one in an isolated northern section of the Mount Bell State Forest.

Unlikely, thought Florence. There were fewer and fewer Albert's lyrebirds to be found, thanks mostly to those car alarms and chainsaws they mimicked so gloriously. They were also notoriously timid and did their full-throated courting in winter.

It was summer now, and sitting with Albert Flowers in an already heavy cloak of heat, Florence began to prickle. It was the morning after what she had come to think of as 'The Howling', and they had pre-arranged to meet in this section of Mount Bell.

Florence had thought what had transpired yesterday would lessen the distance between them. She had lain in bed that night drawing Venn diagrams in her mind, and the intersection where she and Albert met had widened considerably, its shape a plump almond.

Now, sitting with Albert behind the clearing where he thought he had seen a chestnut blur and heard a mimicked bowerbird call, Florence felt the intersection instead narrowing.

This was not a coming together at all, but a pulling apart. Albert, she saw, could barely look at her. 'It's not my fault, mate,' she wanted to shout at him. 'You're the one who started spouting like a geyser.' It was uncharitable, but Florence felt uncharitable and scratchy in the heat, as the space and silence between them grew.

It was Albert who broke it, his voice, Florence noticed, a semitone higher than usual. 'Do you know the author Cat Morrison?' he asked, and Florence nodded – so there was to be no new rhythm between them.

'I've read a couple of her books . . . I think one was called *Flourish*.'

'*Nourish*,' Albert said, then added, 'It was pretty good.'

Florence raised an eyebrow at him. 'You've read it?'

'Sure,' Albert answered. 'Or I may have flicked through Addie's copy.'

'And I think I read the second one too. I can't remember what it was called though . . .'

'*The Burnt Chop and Other Syndromes*,' Albert said. 'The one about how women, particularly mothers, will always keep the one chop that's burnt for themselves and give the good ones to their family.'

'Will they?' Florence asked, amused, and mentally added another thing about the people around her she had missed: Victor's fence pacing, Monty's love of Scottish naturists, Erica's homage to Joan Didion, and now Albert's reading habits.

'They will,' Albert answered, 'or at least that's what Cat says.'

'Oh, you know Ms Morrison, eminent American feminist, voice of a generation, woman who wears colourful hats, do you?' she asked.

'Well I'm going to the launch of her new book, *Candy*,' Albert said, snapping a chocolate bar in half and handing a few squares to Florence.

'Who are you going with?' she found herself asking, her voice high-pitched and not her own.

'Oh, the usual suspects,' Albert answered, and Florence nodded.

Of course you are, thought Florence, of course you are going with Jeremy and Lydia who probably hasn't even read Cat Morrison, while she, Florence, had not only read two of her books but had hated them both. Far too self-indulgent. Lots of bath-taking.

'When is it?'

'Friday night.'

'Albert.'

'Yes Florence?' he smiled.

'I've just remembered what Cat Morrison's last book was called,' she said.

'What was it?'

'It was called,' Florence said, slowly getting to her feet and brushing off some small pieces of curling ironbark from her lap, '*Stupid Men, Stupid Women*.' If he really wanted to see an Albert's lyrebird, there was one right in front of him.

Albert frowned. 'I haven't heard of that one,' he said.

'I'm heading back,' she said, and stamped her way out of the clearing.

*

Entering the Savage Reader bookstore, Albert ducked his head beneath a trail of looping ivy above its door, one errant tendril hanging down.

Copies of *Nourish* and *The Burnt Chop and Other Syndromes*, but not, he noted, *Stupid Men, Stupid Women*, were stacked on a table alongside small hills of Cat Morrison's new book, *Candy*.

A young guy sitting behind the books looked up at Albert through a heavy fringe parted like curtains above his eyes.

'You here for the event?' he asked.

Albert nodded. 'I'm a little early.'

'Me too,' the young man shrugged. 'No customers at all yet. I don't mind, it's nice here.'

Albert looked around. It was nice, he thought, particularly as the store had closed trading for the day and the lights from the cafés outside flickered through its windows.

It was like being caught in a Christmas carol.

Albert had always felt at home in bookstores, and libraries, and gardens. Adelaide said he was really a middle-aged woman called Enid.

Albert headed for the drinks table as a tiny bird of a woman with wire-brush hair and a complicated coat gathered around her waist by several buckles walked in, carrying a fedora in one hand.

Cat Morrison, Albert thought, *and her hat*, as the bookstore's owner Fiona Wilson appeared through a doorway behind the cash register.

Albert had met Fiona several times at Savage and liked her. Sometimes she put gardening books aside for him, and once he had been to her house to sort out some invading onion weed.

Fiona nodded at Albert as she walked past him and held out her hand to the author. 'Hello Cat, I'm Fiona Wilson. Welcome to Savage Reader. It's an absolute delight to host your evening.'

The author held Fiona's hand, Albert thought, as if it had one of those electric buzzers in it and did not return Fiona's smile.

Cat Morrison, he thought, was going to be hard work – she reminded him a little bit of Florence.

Albert flinched, thinking of Florence in the forest yesterday morning. It sounded like the title of one of those girls own adventure stories from the forties. *Milly of the Mountains. Primmie in the Pyrenees. Florence in the Forest.* She had been rattled by his silence, stomping off along a wallaby track in her work boots, and he didn't blame her. He had wanted to call after her and explain that sometimes his words travelled all the way to behind his teeth and stayed there.

'Can I get you a drink?' he heard Fiona ask Cat Morrison, and then she nodded again to Albert, which he understood to mean that he should be the one to get it.

He brought both women a wine, Fiona taking hers and then excusing herself to speak to a woman who was hovering around like a dragonfly above water, holding a copy of *Candy*. 'We're doing the signings after the event,' Fiona told her firmly.

As Fiona spoke with the customer, who was telling her a long story about catching a train here and other reasons why she should be allowed to jump the queue, Cat Morison leant towards Albert and said very quietly but very clearly, as if instructing a small child: 'I need to get out of here.'

She jerked her head towards the glass front doors and the people sorting themselves into some sort of line through it.

'Not that way,' she said. 'That's where they are.'

'Who?' Albert said, peering at the gathering crowd, who looked completely harmless, hardly a band of angry villagers brandishing pitchforks.

'The readers.'

Albert looked again.

'Isn't that rather the point?' he said, deciding that he, too, would like to get out, away from Cat Morrison's darting eyes.

But Fiona, having directed the hovering woman to the back of the line, asked Albert to take Cat Morrison into her office, and when he looked surprised by the request, Fiona pretended she didn't notice, instead saying, 'Albert will look after you, Cat, just for a few minutes, I have to go and sort out the seating.'

The three of them walked behind the register, and Fiona said quickly to Albert, 'Just watch her, we thought this might happen. She does this all the time, her nickname's The Bolter.'

'Why?' he asked.

Fiona shrugged her shoulders. 'She's a writer – who knows why any of them do anything.'

Then she turned back into the bookshop before Albert had the chance to explain to Fiona that he wasn't asking why Cat Morrison was called The Bolter, he was asking why he was the one charged with stopping her from doing it.

Inside the office, Cat Morrison was inhaling her breath noisily through her nose, then exhaling it in a rush out of her mouth.

'Are you okay?' he asked. 'Are you having some sort of . . . medical episode?'

Cat Morrison said no, she wasn't, but she wasn't budging from the couch either. 'I'll just stay right here until everybody leaves,' she said calmly, as if this was a perfectly reasonable course of action.

But Albert saw, in the spaces between her breath, in the way her feet were jiggling against the floorboards, that Cat Morrison, author of *Nourish*, *The Burnt Chop and Other Syndromes*, and now *Candy*, but not, as it turned out, *Stupid Men, Stupid Women* (Fiona had looked at him strangely when he'd mentioned it earlier, then said, 'I think someone's been having you on, Albert'), was frightened.

And then, because Albert Flowers knew what that was like, he sat down beside her and said, 'All right, well I'll stay with you for a bit, shall I?'

They sat on Fiona's couch, Fiona's very old and very sleepy cocker spaniel between them, both stroking his deep, silky hair, Albert scratching the dog lightly behind his ears. It felt, Albert thought, strangely companionable, the three of them tucked behind the door. He had never minded silences. In his experience, it was talking that generally got people into trouble.

But Cat Morrison was talking, mostly about hats.

In the beginning, she said, she could write her books and essays and people were happy just to read them. But now people wanted to get beneath the words, they wanted to meet the person who wrote them, they wanted to know how she wrote them, when she wrote them, and it was not, she said, her natural inclination to tell them. She understood that her sort of books invited discussion, it was just that she wanted people to talk about them amongst themselves.

Albert laughed.

The thing was, Cat said, she understood what they wanted – 'I'm not ungrateful' – but with every book, every tour and every signing, each person who waited in line clutching their book with the little yellow post-it note stuck to it with the correct spelling of their name, each person wanted to take a picture with her. In the hat.

Sometimes, she shuddered, they even wore their own hats.

Albert looked at the fedora on the author's lap.

'What's the big deal?' he said. 'It's just a hat.'

But apparently it wasn't.

Because people expected it.

Cat Morrison had never planned the hat thing. She had never sat down and thought, *I shall make my mark by what I wear on my head*, and yet somehow that was what had happened. When interviews were published, when reviews were written, when speeches were given, mention was always made of the hat. 'Wearing her signature hat'; 'Arriving in the restaurant beneath one of her well-known hats'; 'The Cat in the Hat'. It had happened, she said, by accident, and now, Cat told him, 'It's gotten out of hand.'

Albert thought of Florence describing Cat as a 'wearer of colourful hats' and believed her.

He stood up, picked up the fedora and put it on his head.

'I'll wear it for you then,' he said, and held out his hand. 'Shall we?'

Cat laughed. 'You look ridiculous.'

Albert shrugged. 'No one will be looking at me,' he told her. 'They've come to see you, with or without a hat.'

Cat nodded. 'I appreciate you sitting with me,' she said, then stood up and took the fedora off his head.

'I've never needed a man to rescue me, Albert,' she said, 'and I'm not going to start now. So thank you, but I decide who wears the hat.'

Then she put on the fedora and walked past the office supplies, into the rows of her waiting readers wearing a cavalcade of headwear.

6

Florence had spent the evening with Isolde and Puck, the three of them drinking tea, gossiping about other musicians and talking about their father.

It was easier to do this when their mother wasn't around, Amanda taking over each recollection with one of her own, lassoing each memory with hers, always more vivid, never allowing them, Isolde said, to have Lucas Saint Claire to themselves.

'She hated sharing him, even with us,' she said.

'The problem with Dad,' Puck said, 'was there was never enough of him to go around.'

Florence looked at Puck and wondered what it had been like for him, being Lucas's son. With Puck, Lucas had been more physical than he had been with his daughters.

Florence could still see the two of them play-fighting on the lawn, their bodies meshed, fists and hands and legs and elbows rolling down the grass, until Amanda called, 'That's enough, Lucas,' and Puck called back that no, he was all right, and that he loved it, because for Puck, and Isolde and Florence, it was never enough.

When Puck drummed and Lucas played the clarinet or saxophone, that had been physical too, Puck's wrists flying, Lucas's fingers dancing, matching each other, their eyes locked. Florence thought that perhaps the longest shadow cast by their father's death was the one attached to Puck.

'No,' she agreed with her brother, 'there wasn't ever quite enough.'

Looking at Puck and Isolde, Florence wondered, as she had many times, what they would say if she told them what had really happened on the day of their father's death.

She had never told anyone about it.

There had never been, in its aftermath, in the confusion of the days that followed, when the house was awash with tears and lasagnas, space for her to do it.

Kinsey had been in disarray, her family passing one another in the hallway like ghosts in the bardo. Amanda was vague and dreamy from whatever tablets someone was giving her; Isolde was more kinetic than ever, and Puck's hands were shockingly still.

Florence spent most of her time in the music room sitting on the window seat, knees drawn to her chest and arms clasped around them, looking out the window and waiting for the sharp intake of Lucas's breath just before he put his lips to his clarinet.

She would watch from the window as he twirled around on the piano stool and pretended to fall off from giddiness to make her laugh, or scribbled notes on sheets of music and sipped coffee with his headphones on, looking up at Florence and giving her a thumbs-up. Sometimes she spent the night there, lengthening her body along the window seat, breathing in and out slowly, willing sleep to come and, in a house awash with tears, not crying. Florence found she couldn't; she squeezed her eyes together and willed them to fill, but they remained stubbornly dry and empty.

How long had they lived like that? A month? Two? Florence couldn't recall, but she remembered the pushing down of her memory, the act of erasing the day of her father's death, reversing her steps from her street with its spill of red and blue lights, to the café, and the bus, and the school, and the morning and the one sock up, one sock down, until there was nothing there to tell at all.

It was, she knew, an act of self-preservation, one that they had all pulled off, one way or another, as the weeks and months and years rolled on and they had all returned to the business of living.

Amanda, her words no longer blurred at the edges, had summoned her children into the kitchen one morning and announced that it was time to start flying the Saint Claire flag again. She had stridden around Kinsey, raising blinds and parting curtains, lifting up sash windows and opening doors until the whole house was too bright.

Then she had called them up to the music room, where she had opened all the windows, and said, 'I have released your father,' which was so ridiculously dramatic that they had all laughed hysterically, but that night when Florence entered the music room, Lucas Saint Claire was no longer in it.

He was everywhere else, though.

Florence could never tell when he was going to shimmy up beside her. Sometimes she could feel the bounce of his shoulders against hers as she walked to work, or hear his low chuckle at something Isolde said, and once she was certain she saw his grey felt hat bobbing up and down ahead of her at a market.

She remembered sitting beside Albert in Mount Bell forest, the silver triangle of saltbushes brushing against their skin, and hearing her father's voice somewhere beneath the hum of the cicadas. 'Go on, Florence,' Lucas Saint Claire had said, 'ask him. What's the worst that could happen?'

Florence had closed her eyes to feel the heat of the sun behind them.

'You Dad,' she silently answered him, 'you could happen.'

She could lose Albert in a crowd as easily and frequently as she had lost Lucas. There one minute, off with his usual suspects the next, Albert raising his hand towards Florence from a room she couldn't cross. Or worse, stepping off a footpath into oblivion.

Florence returned her attention to Puck, who was asking Isolde if she had felt robbed of their father's attention too.

Isolde shook her head. 'Not really, but I was his favourite, of course – What? I was, it's no big deal. Mum likes the two of you way better than me,' and Florence wondered again what the world must look like through Issy's lens.

'So I do miss him, but I guess I'll always have that.'

Issy leant back on the sofa and smiled, satisfied.

'I really don't think Dad had favourites,' Florence said. 'Unless you count mum.'

Lucas and Amanda. Amanda and Lucas. The Saint Claires, 'like two sexy twins,' Isolde said, then added, 'but not in an incestuous way.'

Florence laughed.

It was true, Florence thought, her parents' marriage seemed unusually close compared to the few others she had seen. She remembered going to Amy's house as a child and thinking it was funny how Amy's parents never seemed to touch each other, the way they spoke to each other from different parts of the same room and sat on different chairs watching television. Lucas and Amanda never stopped touching, one part of one's body seemingly always in contact with one part of the other's. Arms around waists, ankles entwined, hands in hair, shoulders brushing, as if they couldn't bear to let each other go.

And yet, Florence thought, her mother had.

For all her wailing about Lucas, all her long sighs and monologues of memories, the looping of the words 'When your father was here', 'Your father would say', 'How I wish your father could see', there was something she couldn't quite put her finger on, Florence thought, something *amiss* in Amanda Saint Claire's mourning.

She had never voiced it out loud, but there were times, in all the days and weeks and years that had passed since Lucas Saint Claire was run down by a milk truck, that Florence felt there was a small but discernible spring in her mother's step.

'How do you think Mum is going?' she asked her siblings.

'Good, she's all pumped up about that television appearance she's got on *Good Mornings*,' Isolde answered.

'Do you think she's okay in the house still?'

'I think she's fine. Besides, she's never alone there.'

It was true, the Saint Claire house hummed as it always had. Music still filled its corners, musicians still came and went, taking the stairs to the music room, laying down tracks and flirting with Amanda, her throaty voice filled with promise.

Florence sometimes wondered if her mother took a lover from the assorted players who played beneath her roof, but she had never asked her. Amanda's love life was none of her business, and if she needed someone else's arms around her to fill the space left by her father's, then so be it.

Florence noticed both Isolde and Puck looking at her, something a little off-key in their gaze, and she knew, just as she'd known when they were smaller and they had put pepper in her food or sticks in her bed, that something was up.

'What?' she said, and Isolde, being Isolde, jumped right in.

'So we've had an offer, a really good offer, Florence, to perform at Hello 2000!' Isolde said. 'They've asked the Saint Claire Swingers to close the show with Jazz Cat . . .'

Isolde looked at Puck who said quietly, 'It's a really big deal, Florence.'

Florence knew it was.

Everyone in the industry knew. The Hello 2000! concert at the Domain was going to feature an embarrassment of talent to sing in the new millennium.

Florence also knew exactly how it would play out.

Families on rugs waving neon bracelets, the kids overexcited to be in the night air, a male and a female host, both with snow-white teeth, a big name to kick things off, then a smattering of the old and the new, and at least one cool band for the teenagers who had been dragged along by their parents. Then just before the fireworks all the artists would be invited on stage to welcome tonight's very special guests, the Saint Claire Swingers, together again for the first time in many years ('Lucas Saint Claire would be so proud' one of the hosts would say and the other one would say they wouldn't be surprised at all if he was looking down on them all *right now*) performing – what else? – 'Santa Was A Jazz Cat'.

Florence saw Puck tap his sticks together three times and Amanda step forward.

'*On Christmas Eve when the lights are low, all the alley cats know where to go. To where Santa makes his pit stop, puts down his sack, to a little dark club way out the back . . .*'

The crowd would join in, parents holding their kids in their arms, boys hoisting girlfriends on their shoulders, and everyone's arms in the air, a waving, neon sea.

'*He starts to swing and he starts to scat, because the man in red is a fat jazz cat . . . Santa was a jazz cat, Santa was a jazz cat, Santa was a jazz cat . . . purr, baby, purr.*'

Florence felt her throat constrict and wondered if she had an actual hairball caught in it.

Looking at Isolde, hopping from foot to foot, Florence was irritated at herself that she hadn't seen this coming.

She had known that Jazz Cat would top the charts once more, and she had known that her family would once again be in demand to sing it, the song rising Phoenix-like each year from her father's ashes.

But she had underestimated the fact that the one song that would link the old and the new, the song that people would feel they could depend on amidst all the rumours about computers crashing and alien raptures, was the one her family sang.

'We're the closing act, Florence, in the biggest show of the year. They're cross-broadcasting all the millennium concerts around the world. Do you have any idea how many people will be watching us?' Isolde asked.

Florence knew, and wondered how Isolde could have no idea how it made her feel.

'Now this is special – joining her family on stage is Lucas Saint Claire's eldest daughter Florence, who has not appeared in public with her family for quite some time, not since the Jonathan Hammond Christmas Show, *if I'm correct . . .'*

'Sorry Issy, sorry Puck,' she said, 'I'm really happy for you, I think it's great, but I don't want to be a part of it.'

Isolde's arms stopped swinging. 'You need to get over yourself, Florence,' she said, 'you really, really do.'

With that Isolde stomped up the stairs to bed, and Puck stretched out on the sofa for the night, so Florence went to her room too, lay on her bed and closed her eyes.

She had attended a one-day meditation course at one of those health retreats where they think breathing is the answer to everything. She had hated it, especially the teacher who wore his hair in a high bun on his head, like the knot on top of a balloon that Florence wanted to pop with a long, sharp needle.

The teacher told them to take themselves to the one place that soothed them, and Florence had immediately travelled on bare feet to the forest.

She went there again now. Feeling the canopy arc over her, Florence closed her eyes and slept.

*

Wednesdays at the library were the busiest days of the week, with the mother and bub morning, the East Elm Quilt-makers' weekly meeting, Seniors Tech tutorials, the Historical Society meeting and, on some evenings, the Meet the Author events.

Arriving at work, Florence wondered how Albert's own Meet the Author event had gone last night.

She also hoped that Lydia had raised her hand and asked about *Stupid Women, Stupid Men* during the question and answer session.

'How are you today, Florence?' Monty Rollins asked as she walked past his desk.

'Good, thank you, Monty,' she said, then added to show she remembered their previous conversation, and also because she had decided somewhere behind Victor's front fence, Erika's upper arm, and Sharon's magnificent thighs, to be more involved in the lives that ticked on around her, 'How are you? Been on any good hikes lately?'

'Unfortunately Sharon slipped a disc when we were coming back from Barclay Falls, so we're not strapping the old boots on for a while.'

Florence nodded. 'I'm sorry to hear that.'

'It's all right, we have been going to more live music though,' he said, then added, 'Actually, we saw your mother's one-woman show the other night, she was very good.'

Florence nodded – most people at work, she assumed, would know her family background, but most people didn't mention it. Isolde said it was because they knew not to poke the bear.

'I'm glad. I'll tell her you enjoyed it.'

'Do you sing, Florence?' Monty asked, and Florence wondered again whether he was letting her know that, as Amanda would say, he had her number.

She shook her head. 'Not any more,' she answered. 'I haven't performed for a very long time,' which was, in a fashion, the truth.

Miss Suki had, but she, Florence, bare-faced and de-glittered, had not.

She heard Isolde's voice, 'You need to get over yourself, Florence,' and wondered if perhaps Isolde was right.

Did she need to get over herself? Because if she did, she had no idea where to begin, and for the first time in a very long time, she thought perhaps she should ask her mother.

There was something unsettling going on, Florence felt; all sorts of people waiting in the wings to be let in and life edging its way towards her and whispering its approach in her ear.

She sometimes felt that being in the Saint Claire Swingers had been like being caught inside a huge wave that had spat them out again after Lucas's death. The rest of the family had eventually staggered away from the beach, but she, Florence, was still lying on the damp sand, its cold creeping into her bones.

And she thought that maybe Amanda might be able to help her get up.

'That's a shame, dear,' Monty was saying. 'I wouldn't be at all surprised if there's a glorious nightingale resting in your breast.'

God, no wonder she had stopped talking to people.

The Green Team office was quiet. Albert was on a rostered day off, and the other members were in the field, so it was just Florence, catching up on paperwork and deciding that she would pay Amanda a visit. If anyone could teach her about picking yourself up and dusting yourself off, it was her mother.

'Darling, what a lovely surprise,' her mother would say.

*

Later that evening, Amanda looked up from the magazine she was reading as Florence entered her bedroom.

Bedroom, not *boudoir* as Amanda sometimes called it, always irritating Florence when she did. It was one of her mother's affectations, to sprinkle her conversations with French terms like *ami*, even though she was not remotely French – 'not even *un petit peu*,' Isolde said.

Amanda was wearing her silk kimono, its cream background splashed with red and green flowers, the sash tied loosely around her waist, its deep pockets filled, Florence knew, with the caramels Amanda tried very hard not to love. Florence adored that kimono; her mother had worn it for years, handwashing it in hotel rooms and draping it over chairs to dry, and once over a bar heater, giving off a strange, steamy scent until Lucas had asked her if she wanted to burn the place down.

Its colours remained vibrant and it smelt, always, like her mother, years of Shalimar trapped within its fibres. When she was smaller, Florence had loved to breathe the fabric in, tucked beneath Amanda's arm as she sang to her or let her tunnel into her body, Florence always finding, one way or another, a quiet place for herself.

Seeing Amanda in the kimono, Florence felt a strong and strange compulsion to dive right back into its smoky vanilla folds.

'Darling, what a lovely surprise,' Amanda said. 'I didn't hear you come in.'

Florence smiled. 'There are no locked doors between the Saint Claires, remember.'

Amanda nodded, then patted beside her on the bed. 'Come,' she said.

Florence put her bag down on the floor and settled in beside her mother.

'Are you lonely?' she asked, surprising both of them with her lack of preamble.

Amanda took a caramel from her pocket, unwrapped it, then popped it in her mouth.

'Yes,' she said, '*un petit peu*, are you?'

Florence considered. 'Yes,' she answered, realising it was true.

Amanda nodded. 'Thought so,' she said.

It was bloody Victor, Florence thought. Ever since she had written that note for Leon with him, she had flirted with how it might be to love someone like that.

To care for someone so deeply that even when they died, when there was absolutely no chance at all of them coming home again, you left a key under the mat, just in case.

What would it be like, Florence wondered, to be like Leon and Victor? Or Monty and the magnificently thighed Sharon? Or Amanda and Lucas Saint Claire, Amanda's long legs striding in white, knee-high boots on the cover of Lucas's album, *Love Walked In*.

'I'm not lonely all the time, Mum,' she said, and she felt Amanda's small ripple of pleasure beside her.

Amanda loved it when she called her Mum instead of Amanda, and especially instead of Lamanda, and Florence wondered why she didn't do it more often. Such a little thing to give, and yet she, Florence, rarely gave it, some part of her enjoying the tiny thrill it gave her to withhold it; the small, guilty jolt of power.

Florence looked around the room and felt as she always did when visiting Kinsey that she could just tumble straight back into her childhood and teenage years.

In her mother's room, Amanda reading on her bed with the caramels stuffed into her pockets, she could see her father entering it, a page of music in one hand, a pencil wedged behind his ear, saying, 'Two of my favourite girls together!'

She could see Isolde in her leotard, demanding they watch her spin, her long body turning, arms raised above her head. She could see Puck, wandering in with his clothes never quite tucked in or zipped up properly, a little boy who looked, Lucas would laugh, 'like a travelling hobo'. She saw Richard unfurling his glittering costumes from bags, shaking them out and saying, 'Yes, yes, my pretties.' She heard other voices too: Amy's sing-song tones from across the back fence, 'Florence, can you come over?'; their cleaning lady Mrs Winters humming while she vacuumed, and Leticia and Nancy's snatches of long-ago conversations from the lounge room.

'The problem with Florence is that she's too prickly.'

'Like a prickly pear.'

'It kills me that she won't sing.'

Then Nancy's voice faded out, until Florence could hear only Leticia's American drawl. 'Come on, honey, you've been wearing that uniform all day.'

Florence shifted a little on her mother's bed. An extra scene was unfolding in her memory, not one she had replayed before.

She was in her own room the night of her father's death, Leticia's back was to her, the older woman's hands in Florence's chest of drawers, plucking out Florence's flamingo pyjamas. 'We need to put these on, sugar,' Leticia was saying, and Florence remembered thinking, We *don't need to do anything*, but Leticia was leaning over her, her mouth so close that Florence could see the red wine stain outlining her lips.

And then Leticia said: 'Here, Lucas would have wanted you to have this.'

A bright blue feather floated from Leticia's hand.

'Mum,' Florence sat up, her whole body suddenly compelled to sit forward, 'Mum . . .'

'What is it, Florence?' Amanda said. 'Are you choking on a caramel?' and when Florence didn't answer, she began hitting her on the back, in decisive, short, sharp chops.

Florence began to cry the tears she had not shed for Lucas Saint Claire and the knowledge that she had found the source of her prickle.

Amanda put the back of her hand against Florence's forehead, as if Florence was very small again and her mother was checking to see if she had a fever.

'I'm going to make you a cup of tea,' Amanda said. 'Very strong and very sweet tea.'

Florence sat on the bed while her mother went downstairs to make it, thinking of all the other times Amanda had done so, very strong and very sweet tea being Amanda's solution to any kind of trouble.

'You've had a shock,' she'd say when Florence had fallen out of the tree in the front yard; when Florence had cut her hand badly on a knife, blood caught between her fingers; when Florence had been dumped by her first and only high school boyfriend, Bradley Wagner, via a note passed under a desk.

Florence smiled a little. Bradley Wagner was an idiot, but she had cried hot tears when he dumped her in grade nine, and there was her mother, spooning ladles of sugar into a mug, saying, 'You've had a shock, darling.' Amanda had read somewhere that sugar was the solution for those who found themselves cut loose from their bearings, and it had been the elixir delivered in spoonfuls through all of their childhoods.

Amanda came in bearing a tray with two cups, then set it down on the dresser, her back to her daughter.

Florence thought Amanda seemed to be moving very slowly, taking her time to pour the milk and spoon in the sugar. Florence didn't take sugar, she wanted to remind her mother, she hadn't for years. Instead she found herself saying, 'I've had a shock, Mum,' and then added, 'I think I've had a very big shock,' as Amanda turned around, cup outstretched.

Amanda sat on the bed very still and very quietly, looking, Florence thought, like someone else entirely. It was not so much that her face appeared different but that it had stopped moving, stopped smiling and winking and arching its eyebrows. Her mother's face seemed to be like Isolde's limbs, always moving in some way. But now it was flat and calm, as if it had settled into itself at last, as Amanda said, 'Tell me, darling . . .' and so Florence began.

She started with the boy in the yellow jacket, then the stiffening of her body on stage, and the growing chorus of – literally – catcalling, the meows that followed her in the schoolyard. She told Amanda how Lucas had sat with her on the window seat, their feet touching, Lucas rubbing his chin as he apologised for there not being enough of him to go around, and his plans for the two of them to meet. 'Four pm. Java Lounge. Blue Feather. Odd Socks.' She repeated her father's words to Amanda, who smiled and said that sounded like him.

She told her about the waiter asking her to move seats, and how she had looked out the window, then at her watch, then out the window again as people stopped shopping, and started heading home, and knew he was not coming.

She told her about the man asking her for money and how she wished she had given him some. Because she'd wondered ever since whether, if she had, if she had smiled and nodded, yes, of course, and opened up her blue purse with the horseshoe stitched on it, it might have changed things.

It wasn't so much, she told her mother, that she thought the man had somehow cursed her – 'I know it's ridiculous' – but that if she had done the right thing, like Lucas would have, she might have bought them both some time.

The thought, illogical as it was, had tugged at her; the belief that if she could have altered one tiny moment of that afternoon, she might have somehow shifted things and might not have come around the corner to their street, its surface washed in blue and red.

Florence wriggled under the quilt and moved her body to feel Amanda's limbs beside her.

Then she told her mother the new memory, the one with Leticia coming into her room that night and passing her the flamingo pyjamas – 'I remember those,' Amanda said. Florence paused, then told the part about the blue feather, not in her father's hat but nestled in Leticia Pepsi's hand. A cuckoo in the nest.

Amanda nodded throughout Florence's retelling and kept giving her far-too-sweet tea, but when Florence finished, she looked not at all how Florence had expected her to.

Florence thought her mother would look upset or stricken – her mother was very good, generally, at stricken – or perhaps she would be wearing her 'it's all been a big misunderstanding' look and suggest to Florence that perhaps she had been dreaming.

Instead, Amanda Saint Claire looked bloody furious.

'So, Florence, you thought that day, and every day since for all these years, that your father's death was your fault?'

Florence nodded, and Amanda shook her head.

'Florence,' she said, 'I have quite a lot I want to say to you, but first, enough of this ridiculously sugary tea, I'm getting us a wine.'

Amanda went downstairs once more, and Florence waited, hearing her mother making far too much noise for someone who was just getting a bottle of wine from the fridge. There were thumps, then a slamming sound, and then one loud thud and a shattering of glass that made Florence jump.

'Are you okay?' she called from the bed.

'Fine, darling,' Amanda answered. 'I just dropped something. Up in a minute.'

If Florence had gone downstairs, she would have seen Amanda sweeping up the glass she had hurled at the floor.

She would have heard her mother ask, 'What now, Lucas?' as she opened the bin lid to empty the shards into it.

She would have watched her mother put the dust pan and brush back beneath the kitchen sink, take a bottle from the fridge, two glasses from the cupboard, and refasten the sash around her waist, pulling it in crisply.

'Maximum wattage, Amanda,' she would have heard her mother say.

Amanda returned to the room, carrying a bottle of wine and two glasses.

'Let me tell you about Lucas,' she said, as if he was not Florence's father at all, but someone in a fairy tale.

Amanda Saint Claire took a sip of her wine and began, starting with meeting Lucas at the Conservatorium, watching him walk towards her and her friends outside the main rehearsal rooms, their collective intake of breaths as they realised he was heading in their direction.

'Oh my fucking God, Amanda,' her friend Lilian had said quietly, 'I think he's going to talk to us.'

And Lucas Saint Claire, wearing a three-quarter-length sheepskin coat, blue jeans and black boots, had talked to them, his eyes only on Amanda.

'Amanda, right?' he'd said, holding out his hand. 'I heard you sing last night at the concert – I'm Lucas.' And one of her friends, probably Lilian, had snorted, 'Oh we know who you are.'

Two hours later Amanda was in his bed in his small room at Saint Patrick College, and she had thought, she had actually thought, she told her daughter, smiling, 'If I died now, I would be happy.' She had fully expected, Amanda continued, to be sent on her way, like so many other girls she had heard about leaving Lucas Saint Claire's college bed to walk dazed back to their own rooms and think about what had just happened for a very long time.

She had heard lots of stories second-hand, a couple of first-hand accounts from girls he had bedded, and she had giggled out loud, thinking that she would be one of them now.

It didn't bother her one bit.

Lucas had asked what she was thinking about and she had told him, emboldened by everything she had just done – and so quickly. Her parents, so careful in their countenances, so sparing in their gestures, would be shocked at her behaviour.

Philip and Nancy Catchpool, who walked through life like they were picking their way through a minefield, had raised their only child to be wary. Of crossing the road, of making new friends, of putting her hand up in class, of climbing trees or getting caught in the rain and, if they had known what was coming, Amanda smiled at Florence, most certainly of Lucas Saint Claire.

Florence smiled back and tried to remember her maternal grandparents, who had both died within months of each other when she was in her early teens, but she could only conjure a vague vision of Nancy leaning down to give her a stiff, powdery kiss on the cheek. Her only memory of Philip was of him pretending he had stolen her nose and caught it in his thumb, a tedious game he had kept up long after she had stopped laughing, managing only a tight, forced smile.

But Philip and Nancy Catchpool had gifted their daughter their voices, both excellent choral singers who performed at chamber recitals and church concerts, Amanda inheriting the talent that led her out of their home, onto the train to the Conservatorium and into the arms of Lucas Saint Claire.

Lying in his dorm room that afternoon, the two of them curved into each other like question marks, Amanda had looked at his posters of musicians on the wall, his clothes bundled into a ball in the corner, an open suitcase on the floor, with a glittery pale blue scarf at its mouth (a girl's scarf, she thought), and felt completely at home.

'When girls leave your room,' she told him that afternoon as the sun dipped to a sliver of pink neon in the sky, 'they don't call it the Walk of Shame, they call it the Walk of Fame.'

Then she had started to laugh, really laugh, both at the idea that she was now one of them, and also because she felt slightly hysterical at everything that had happened between them in that room, the delicious abandonment, the letting go.

But Lucas was not laughing, he was looking at her with his green, dancing eyes as he said, 'Well, the gorgeous Amanda, I do intend to make you really, really famous.'

What Amanda had not realised then, lying naked in Lucas Saint Claire's college bed, one leg draped over it, her toe touching the floor, was that he had meant it.

She had also not realised, until many years later, that he had sought her out, that he was looking for someone exactly like Amanda Catchpool to orbit his sun.

That she adored him was incidental, as was her beauty – beautiful girls peppered the lawns of the university like flowers. If Lucas was only looking for a pretty girl who worshipped him, he need only stroll across one of its green expanses, reach down and pluck one out. What set Amanda apart, what propelled her to the front of the line and all the way in his pale green Volkswagen to meet his parents, was her voice. That she could sing meant that Lucas would always have someone to accompany him, on the stage and on the road. It meant he would always have someone in the audience.

And so, one Saturday morning after they had been together for about six months, he had taken her to visit what he called

'The Fam', and that too, she supposed, had been an audition of sorts.

The Saint Claires lived in exactly the sort of house Amanda had imagined they would, nothing at all like her parents' brick bungalow on a corner block with its lawns punctuated by dreary rows of her father's rosebushes. Even when they bloomed they looked disappointed to be there, alongside the bird's house letter-box with its *No Junk Mail* sign in her mother's firm hand. The Saint Claires' home was an art deco pearl, hidden from the street by a long driveway, and set on a hill, its white walls curved and seductive, its garden studded with date palms and cacti, with two sleek black cats patrolling among them.

Lucas's family were nothing like hers either. When she and Lucas had walked in to the Saint Claire home, Juliet and Guy Saint Claire had been shouting at each other in the kitchen and they had not stopped shouting just because she and Lucas were there.

Lucas had shrugged and led her up to his bedroom, a girl running down the stairs carrying a guitar case and pausing mid-flight as she passed them. 'Hello, brother,' she had said to Lucas. 'Hello you,' she'd said to Amanda, not unkindly. 'Don't go near the parents, Guy's in the doghouse.'

Lucas had one sister, a slightly unhinged mother and a musician father who was relentlessly, chronically unfaithful.

Amanda sat down on the bed next to Florence and put an arm around her.

'Poor Juliet,' she said, 'and poor all of them, really. Guy Saint Claire was a handful.'

Amanda paused, then added, 'And so was your father.'

The girls had never really stopped going in and out of Lucas's room once he and Amanda had become an 'official' couple, she told Florence; they had just made the commute more discreetly. And Amanda, although she knew that they couldn't all be music students, or girlfriends of friends, or once, she said laughingly, a cousin visiting from interstate, chose to believe him.

'I wasn't the last to know, darling. I *always* knew.

'I always knew but I chose not to see it, not to make a fuss, your father hated fuss.'

'What about later?' Florence asked. 'When you got married, when you had us?'

'Then too,' Amanda answered. 'Especially then.'

'Oh Mum,' Florence said, then again, 'Oh Mum.'

Amanda smiled at her. 'Your father tried, Florence, he really did, but, well, he was a musician, darling,' as if that explained everything.

Florence wriggled deeper under the quilt. 'I didn't know,' she said. 'How could I have not known all of this?'

Amanda looked at her daughter.

'Because I made sure you didn't,' she answered, and everything Florence had thought about her mother tilted.

She saw Amanda hurrying them out of dressing rooms, or shepherding them into Richard's van; she saw her crossing rooms to stand in front of Lucas and adjust his tie; she saw how hard she worked to keep them all in his eye line.

She saw her father and Caroline Prentice in their backyard at a barbecue, Caroline throwing her head back in laughter, and

Professor Prentice hurrying over, spilling his own drink in his haste to get there.

She saw their father lying on the window seat, his head in Amanda's lap as she stroked his forehead, pulling his hairline back slightly each time she did, Lucas relaxing under her touch, his forehead unfurling as his eyes closed.

Lucas Saint Claire wasn't the sun they all orbited around, her mother was.

Once her father had taken the family to Luna Park; they had passed through its lurid, grinning mouth and gone on all the rides, and then to Coney Island with its pathways and distorted mirrors. Amanda, she remembered, had hated it, she had kept insisting they not touch anything, and when a woman approached the family and asked to take a photo, her mother had snapped at her, 'Haven't you got your own family to photograph?' and pulled the children away, leaving Lucas and the woman behind. At the time, Florence thought Amanda was being rude; now she wondered who the woman was.

She and Isolde went on one of Coney Island's wonky attractions together, walking through two large spinning cylinders which constantly moved beneath their feet, making the journey, for Florence at least, an unsteady one. Isolde, of course, had made it through unscathed, even though she had looked like a flapping scarecrow in there, while Florence had stumbled, her palms against the smooth concrete walls, her feet slipping beneath her.

When she got to the other side, Florence had felt disorientated and shaky, and it had taken her body a few moments to settle back into itself.

That was how she felt now listening to Amanda, like everything was slowly coming into focus.

More memories and images were clicking into place: Amanda talking in a low voice to a woman outside their door, her mother pressing her body against its frame; Puck's face when Lucas tucked him under the chin and said, 'Sorry, buddy, you'll have to practise on your own, I'm late'; Richard driving the family home from shows, glancing at Amanda in the passenger seat, her face to the window.

She saw Amy Burton's mother – no, that couldn't be right, but yes, there she was at the back door, talking to Amanda. Caroline Burton seemed agitated, and Florence, walking into the kitchen, heard Amy's mother saying, 'It won't continue,' and at the time Florence had thought she was speaking about her and Amy's friendship.

Now she wondered if it was another Saint Claire they were talking about.

Her mother's hand found Florence's fingers beneath the quilt and laced them with her own.

'It doesn't matter, Florence,' she said. 'It didn't matter then and it doesn't matter now.

'It doesn't change the fact that your father loved you all very much, and he loved me very much, and that we were very happy together for a very long time.

'What does matter is that you know that your father's death had nothing, absolutely nothing to do with you.'

Amanda's voice rose several bars above its normal low thrum, and the fury returned to her face, appearing as two bright red circles on her cheeks.

'It actually makes me feel incredibly angry and very, very sad that you have felt this way, because the reason why your father was run over by a milk truck,' and Florence knew then that her mother really was angry, the 'traffic accident' euphemism dropped at last – in fact her mother looked like she wished she was behind the wheel of that truck, 'is not because he was hurrying to meet you, but in all likelihood because he was late from meeting someone else.

'There was always someone, darling,' Amanda said softly, 'to give a blue feather to.'

There were, Amanda told Florence, quite a few recipients of Lucas's blue feathers. Or signed albums. Or, for some, sets of silver cufflinks shaped like clarinets. Or whatever Lucas gave to whichever one of the many women he saw throughout their marriage right up until the moment a milk truck put an end to it.

'Don't ask me why,' she said, 'feathers, especially, were a little folly of his – I got one too, early on.

'Half of the symphony orchestra had one pinned to their evening gowns in the seventies,' she laughed. 'Can you imagine?'

Amanda's voice was bright, gay – her performance voice, her children called it.

But Florence couldn't imagine it at all.

Amanda's voice wavered.

'But Leticia, I didn't expect Leticia,' and this time it was Florence's hand that found her mother's.

Florence had never been particularly fond of Leticia or Nancy, her mother's oldest friends from school. As a child, she found them both, particularly Leticia, too much, always filling up the spaces around Amanda with swathes of colour Florence couldn't find her way through; bracelets and scarves and layers of gossip. Amanda was always waving her away when they were at Kinsey, and Florence had spent a lot of time during their visits in one of her underground dugouts. But her mother, Florence knew, loved them both, particularly Leticia. After Lucas died, Leticia was at Kinsey for days on end, tussling with Richard for Amanda's attention and taking up too much room in the house. Florence flinched – the gall of the woman, sharing their grieving as if she belonged in it.

But Leticia had moved interstate and her visits had dropped off over the years. Now, Florence knew, Leticia would never come to Kinsey again. Lamanda would smile, turn her back and let her go, as lightly as a feather.

*

Florence stayed the night, calling Isolde to explain she was sleeping at Kinsey.

'What? You're at Lamanda's? What's happened? Is she all right? She's not dying, is she? What could she be dying of? Overexposure?'

Florence did not laugh as she would normally have laughed, and she resolved to tell both Isolde and Puck they all needed to drop the Lamanda thing.

Florence had no doubt her mother would continue to be as infuriating as ever, that the two of them would clash as they always had. But as her mother's eyes closed and her breathing slowed to soft, throaty snores, it was not Amanda Saint Claire Florence saw sleeping beside her, exhausted by the wine and the tears and the telling, but Amanda Catchpool, all cried out.

She saw her mother, standing in a knot with her friends, Lucas Saint Claire walking towards her, about to change everything. She saw her beetling up the driveway to Guy and Juliet Saint Claire's shimmering, curved walls. She could not remember much of her paternal grandparents. Juliet had died before Florence was born – of alcohol; of longing, her mother said – and Guy had blazed along for a few years after that, before falling from a golf cart and hitting his head, never to recover. Both Saint Claire men, Florence thought, destined to die inglorious, transport-related deaths. Lucas's sister Coraline lived in London, and every now and again a postcard with Big Ben or a Beefeater on it would appear in Kinsey's letterbox, with a message scratched across it. Coraline Saint Claire couldn't wait, Lucas once told Florence, to get away from his family, and Australia, and had sworn she would never return. So far she had kept her word, sending flowers and another scrawled note to Lucas's funeral that said, 'Bad luck, brother'. Amanda, Florence remembered, had smiled and said, 'Very Coraline.' Her mother's patience, it seemed, extended to all members of the Saint Claire family.

Florence took the wine bottle and the glasses downstairs to clean up, then returned to her mother's room. She changed into one of Amanda's nightgowns – deep green silk with something scratchy at its neck, the rest of the material slippery against her skin – and crossed the hallway to the music room.

There was no ghost there to greet her. No Lucas looking up from his chair to smile at her or shoo her out or open his arms for her to climb into. It was just a room, Florence saw, and one that was long overdue for a clearing out. It was ludicrous the way they all kept it, her father's books and newspapers still in place, his music scores on the piano, his clarinet against the wall.

This wasn't a room, it was a shrine.

Florence sat at the window seat and looked through the glass to the tree, its spindly arms reaching out into the night.

Why had it taken her so long to remember? How could she have erased the memory of Leticia giving her the feather, or Leticia stumbling out of her room afterwards, smiling as if she had done Florence a favour.

Well, she remembered now. She remembered that she had stood up after Leticia had gone, opened her window and raised the feather to her lips.

Then she had exhaled her breath in a rush, watching it dance from her hand to the street below.

Then she had shut the window.

In the music room, all these years later, Florence remembered and understood it all.

The feather had drifted from memory because she had willed it so.

On the night she had lost her father, she had been sixteen years old and she had known exactly what she was doing.

She had raised the blue feather to her lips and watched it float away to somewhere it couldn't hurt any of them.

7

'So, what was the sleepover about?' Isolde asked when Florence returned to their cottage the next morning. 'Did you have pillow fights? Did you give each other makeovers?'

Florence ignored her. 'Is Puck here?' she asked instead.

'No. He must be at Lance's place.'

Florence nodded. 'So Issy,' she began, putting the kettle on.

The thing that Florence would always remember about that morning, more than Issy's shocked face when she told her about the afternoon of their father's death, or the way she had shocked Florence when she'd shouted: 'I knew it, I bloody knew it!' when Florence spoke about their father's infidelities, was the way Isolde sat opposite her during the telling.

No stretching or swinging limbs, Isolde contained all of her body into one form and kept it there.

'You're so still, Isolde,' Florence said. 'Are you all right?'

Issy nodded, a barely perceptible movement of her chin.

'It's the gravity of the situation,' she said. 'I'm taking it all in, and I can't do that if I'm flapping about.'

'Fair enough,' said Florence.

Isolde continued to sit quietly and Florence, who spent much of her life wishing Isolde would just keep still and stop talking for one moment, found herself wishing that her sister would return to her normal state of a person caught inside the spin cycle of a washing machine, shouting to get out.

'I'm sorry, Florence,' Isolde said finally. 'I'm sorry you thought you had killed Dad for all those years, that can't have been easy.'

'No, it wasn't,' Florence agreed, and then their eyes met across the table and Isolde giggled, her hand going to her mouth too late to catch it.

Florence began to laugh too, at the understatement of Isolde's sentence, and all that lay behind it.

Isolde's shoulders were shaking as she wrapped her arms around her waist and clutched her stomach, and Florence stopped even trying not to laugh, letting it come from deep within her belly.

When their laughter had softened to a few giggles, Isolde tried again. 'No, Florence, I really am sorry that you thought it was your fault Dad was run over by a milk truck . . .'

Florence and Isolde's eyes met as they started laughing again, mildly hysterical now at the absurdity of it, and all the letting go.

Lucas Saint Claire may have been one of the finest clarinet players of his generation, he may have been as spellbinding to his family as he was to his audiences, and there may even have been magic in him, but he was no more and no less than anyone else.

He was just a man, as capable of being hit by a Packers Dairy milk truck as the next.

They could all stop – mostly Amanda, she hoped – saying his name in hushed voices.

There was something else, too, in Florence's laughter.

She had carried the guilt of Lucas's death like river stones deep in her pockets.

She had felt the weight of them in her steps, their heaviness engraved with what ifs. What if she had ignored the boy in the yellow jacket and just kept right on singing? What if she had said to her father that day on the window seat, 'I'm fine, Dad, I just need a break from the Swingers, but I'll be back – you go to your recording session.' What if she had reached down to put some money in the man's guitar case?

What if she took the stones from her pocket, and sent them clattering to the ground?

Florence laughed with Isolde, the hard nub of the prickle inside her dissolving a little more.

'We'll have to tell Puck,' Isolde said. 'If we can find him.'

*

Florence knocked on Victor's door the next morning on her way to work. It was early but Florence knew Victor would be up – gardeners were always up early.

It was, in Florence's opinion, the best time of day to witness a garden, when all the plants and tiny creatures that dwelt within them got busy. They unfurled their leaves and drew in their energy, or dropped down from webs to swing in the morning light, or scurried from beneath the damp leaf matter where they had made their bed.

Birds scattered seeds, and the seeds rolled into perfect divots, and all this activity, all of this life-making work was carried out while the earth spun to face the sun.

Florence could never understand people who slept through it.

Victor opened the door and smiled widely when he saw Florence, a sprig of parsley in one hand and some rosemary in the other.

'Got too much?' he grinned.

'Yep,' Florence answered. 'Acres of both – I was hoping to swap these for some of your honey.'

'Which is a nice way of you asking if I've been out to the hives, and yes I have, twice this week.'

'Good,' Florence answered, 'then you can make some toast with my tea.'

Victor had been to the hives and, he said, also to a book launch for the author Cat Morrison. Did Florence know her? American feminist. Always wore hats.

Leon had been a huge fan of her first book, and Victor had taken it along to be signed for him.

'Bit crazy, I know,' he said, 'but she was in town, and I remembered Leon going on and on about her, so I just took myself there and handed her the book.'

'Did she sign it?'

'Yes, I told her to write, *Dear Leon, better late than never!*'

Florence chuckled and wondered what Cat Morrison made of that.

'I spied your friend Albert there, seemed very chummy with the author.'

'Did he?' Florence asked. 'Did he now?'

'Yes, she was having a drink afterwards and he was chatting to her with a couple of other people like they were old friends.'

Albert Flowers was a dark horse, Florence thought. Probably a Clydesdale.

After she finished her tea and two pieces of toast spread with Victor's amber honey – 'Very nice,' she said, 'buttery, with some notes of acacia if I am not mistaken' – she thanked her neighbour and left for work.

As she left, she noticed a new note on the fridge door.

It said, *Hi Leon, would it kill you to wash some dishes while you're here?*

*

'How was the book launch?' Florence asked Albert at lunchtime in the Green Team's office. Florence usually liked to take her lunch outside, but it was raining, sending spears of water down the library's windows and beating on its roof in a steady, comforting thrum.

'It was very, very strange,' he answered, and then he told Florence about Cat Morrison's strong aversion to her signature hats.

'Well, that's stupid,' Florence said. 'She should just stop wearing them.'

Albert raised his eyebrows a little – and in their arch she saw she had missed the mark again.

She was being flippant, but he hadn't caught her tone. Momentum. Florence realised that was the problem. They didn't have it. They could start out together, but whatever force was needed to help push things along a bit was missing. One of them would be in very grave danger if they were trapeze artists.

'It's not stupid,' Albert was saying. 'I think you'll find it's called being human.'

Florence prickled. 'I think you'll find you sound like a tosser,' she said, as any momentum they had gathered ground to a dull halt.

Albert was about to say something else – and what Albert Flowers wanted to say was, 'Sorry, Florence, that did sound a bit wankery' – when Monty Rollins walked into the office with the air of a man tasked with something very important to say.

'Sorry to intrude,' he said, 'but your mother is here, Florence,' adding with an underline, 'Amanda Saint Claire is in the library.'

*

Amanda's presence in the East Elm's borrowing section had not gone unnoticed by its patrons, drawn to her, Florence saw, like moths to a flame – Mrs Trenton in particular in full flutter.

Except that moths weren't really drawn to a flame, Florence thought, or even to a light. It was more confusion, less compulsion.

Moths had used the moon as a compass for thousands of years. When they wanted to fly in a straight line, they kept its light at a set angle, to their right or left. Then Thomas Edison had come along with his electric light bulb and thrown them all hopelessly off course. With the moon as a lunar guide, it was easy for moths to keep to their flight plan, but a light bulb? A light bulb they would zoom straight past, sense the light was now behind them, and try to correct themselves again and again, flying in ever decreasing circles until they just flew straight into it. Moths thought light bulbs were the moon, and the patrons of East Elm Library thought Amanda's light was equally celestial. They were equally confused as well, circling around her as dazed as any poor moth.

Florence watched her mother nod and smile, her hand lightly resting for a moment on Mrs Trenton's shoulder, and thought that the size of the audience didn't matter, Amanda Saint Claire knew how to work a room, even if that room was the East Elm Public Library.

'Darling,' Amanda said, when she saw her, gently shaking Monty off her arm, 'I'm sorry to bother you at work, but I can't seem to contact your brother. I seem to have lost Puck.'

Discombobulated was Florence's favourite word, and one she was always trying to get the upper primary students from East Elm to use in a sentence. It was also exactly how she felt now, discombobulated by her mother's presence in the library and the words she was saying.

Neither really belonged in the world she knew.

Florence felt detached from both, like she was looking at her mother from one of those terrifying peepholes they have in hotel rooms which make everyone on the other side look like cast members from *The Shining.*

What was Amanda saying? That she'd lost Puck. That wasn't how it worked. None of them ever lost Puck, he just took himself off and came back when he was ready. There was no looking to be done when someone had no desire to be found.

Monty, who had somehow fastened himself to her mother's elbow, took Amanda into the staffroom where she told Florence why she was 'just the tiniest bit concerned'.

'I know he's disappeared before, darling, but Isolde took it upon herself to tell him about our little chat the other evening and he took it rather badly . . .'

Monty Rollins was nodding his head and patting her mother's hand.

'Mmm Amanda,' he said. 'Go on.'

Florence had always hated this, the way people just attached themselves to her parents.

'Monty,' she said, 'would you mind leaving us alone for a few minutes?'

Monty exited the staffroom with a tug on his bowtie that said he did mind, very much.

'What's going on, Mum?' Florence asked.

Amanda had come home from a solo gig to find Puck sitting on the front stairs of the house.

'Is it true?' he'd asked. 'All that stuff about Dad?'

Amanda had played for time. 'Why don't we go and sit inside, darling?' she had said, but Puck had said no, why didn't she just tell him now whether the things Isolde had said were fact or one of Isolde's fictions.

So Amanda had told him that yes, there had been some fidelity issues with Lucas, but that it hadn't impacted on the family, and Puck had shouted that of course it had, stood up and started walking. Where to, Amanda wasn't sure, but he had not come home that night or the next. He wasn't at Lance's either, and normally she wouldn't worry, only it was so unlike him to shout, wasn't it?

Yes, Florence thought, it was unlike Puck to shout, or to make any sort of noise really, apart from that which crashed from his drumsticks.

'What about Isolde?' she asked. 'Has she seen Puck?'

'No,' Amanda answered. 'I went to your house first to check if he was there, and Isolde said she hadn't seen him since she told him about your father's . . . peccadilloes.'

Florence raised her eyebrows at her mother's delicate choice of words.

Amanda sighed. 'She was very rude when I suggested that perhaps it wasn't her place to tell him.'

'Did she tell him the rest?' Florence asked. 'Did she tell him about me?'

Amanda shook her head.

'I'm not sure, he stomped off before I had a chance to find out exactly what your sister said.'

Florence had trained herself not to panic over Puck; she had spent a lifetime being told by Lucas and Amanda and Isolde that he was perfectly fine, that he would come back when he was ready, and that she, Florence, was overreacting. But this time Amanda was worried enough to enter a public library voluntarily, and that in itself was a cause for concern.

The only thing that could have made her more concerned would have been if Amanda had announced she'd caught the bus there.

'Right,' she said to her mother, 'let's go look for him.'

Florence went back into the Green Team's office to get her bag, explaining to Albert that she had to leave to deal with a 'family matter'.

'Of course. Can I help?'

Florence said no but thank you for offering, and Albert seemed to stammer a little as he replied, 'I know I sounded a bit pompous before, Florence. I didn't mean to, sometimes my mouth runs away with me . . .'

'It's all right,' she answered, 'it really doesn't matter,' because it really didn't.

What mattered was finding her twenty-three-year-old little drummer boy and finding out exactly what Isolde had said to him.

She passed Albert's sister Adelaide Flowers as she left, Adelaide half raising her hand as if she was going to ask Florence to look for another book for her. 'I'm not a librarian,' Florence said, and kept walking.

*

'What?' Isolde said, chin lifted, looking at her mother and sister from her bed where she sat cross-legged, a mess of knitting in her lap.

'What is the big deal? Mum, you told Florence, Florence told me, and then I told Puck. It's the natural order of things, when you think about it.'

Florence thought Isolde was being maddeningly unhelpful, even for her.

Florence also thought that Isolde had probably just blurted out to Puck what she had learnt, not choosing her words carefully; not really choosing her words at all.

But whatever she said was enough to set Puck wandering, something he hadn't done in months, maybe a year – long enough, anyway, for Florence to stop noticing he had gone.

'Isolde,' she said, 'what did you say to Puck about Dad?'

Isolde stood up and put her hands on her hips.

'Nothing bad, nothing terrible, I just said that Lucas was a root rat,' then, seeing the expressions on Amanda's and Florence's faces added, 'which he was.'

'A root rat?' Amanda repeated. 'A root rat?' and Florence heard echoes of her mother shrieking, 'A milk truck!'

Florence shook her head at her sister. 'Isolde,' she said, 'you need to choose your words more carefully, you need to choose everything more carefully, you need to pay attention, do you hear me? You need to pay more attention.'

Florence was shouting now, repeating the words every teacher had written on Isolde's report cards since grade one, as Isolde moved her hands from her hips to her face and began to cry. Amanda started crying too, and then Florence, annoyed with herself for doing so, began to cry as well, all three Saint Claire women weeping in the kitchen over two missing Saint Claire men.

Florence looked around the kitchen table and thought she was glad no one could see this display of Saint Claire drama.

Why must her family be so theatrical? Why must her family be such a mess? Why could they not be normal? Why must Isolde cry so noisily, so uncontrollably? Why did Amanda cry as if she was being filmed, looking off into the distance between delicate sniffs? Why was she, Florence, joining in? Must they do everything together? And where the fuck was Puck?

Florence stood up. 'I'm going to look for him,' she said, grabbing her keys, but she did not add that she thought she knew where Puck was.

He didn't need a deputation from the three wailing witches of East Elm.

'What should I do, darling?' Amanda asked, and usually Florence would have prickled at her mother's fluttering hands and blinking lashes, but now she looked at Amanda and saw that she really was floundering.

Lucas Saint Claire may have had his little – what had her mother called them? – peccadilloes, but he had been excellent in a crisis. He had a way of stepping in and saying exactly the right thing in exactly the right tone so that everyone's shoulders relaxed a fraction. When things went awry, he was the guide with the umbrella held steadily aloft in the air, his grey felt hat bobbing beneath it, and its owner completely confident they would all follow.

Since Lucas had died, Richard had taken over the day to day running of her mother's life, so she could concentrate on the full-time job of being Amanda. If Puck wasn't where she thought he was, Florence might call Richard, get him on the case.

Florence shook her head. She was not immune to the odd spot of theatricality either. Why didn't she just pop on a trench coat and a trilby hat?

'I think you should stay here with Isolde,' she told her mother, 'in case Puck comes back.'

Amanda nodded. 'All right, darling,' she said, putting her arm around her still-wailing youngest daughter.

Florence did not feel so kindly towards her sister.

'Enough histrionics, Isolde,' she said, and then, surprising all three of them, added, 'and look after Mum.'

Then she got in her car and drove to Langdon's quarry.

*

The quarry had been closed for so long, nobody seemed sure any more of what had been mined there.

When they were kids, Keep Out signs were posted on droopy orange barriers, not sufficiently alarming to keep anyone out, least of all the kids on bikes and teenagers in cars who turned up on weekends. They smoked cigarettes in the folds of its granite rocks, swam in its rock pools, mostly the deepest one known as 'Gerry's Hole', named after a fat, lazy catfish generations of East Elmers had spied there.

Kids would dare each other to dive beneath the waterhole's milky greenness, to where Gerry purportedly lurked, then shoot again through the blister of its surface.

Gerry was probably long gone, Florence thought, and smiled remembering the time Isolde had shot out of the water when they were teenagers shrieking, 'Gerry's got me! Gerry's got me!' and pulling at her bikini bottom to find only a stick wedged in there.

The signs didn't keep Puck out either. Langdon's was close enough to walk to from their house, if you knew the short cuts, and Puck knew all of them. He'd spend hours at the quarry, going for a quick dip at Gerry's Hole, then he would continue on past a stack of boulders tossed there by giants.

At least, Florence smiled, that's what Lucas had told them when they were children.

The giants' boulders ringed a smaller rock pool, hugged by a half-moon of granite, where sounds grew deeper and richer, and where Puck would sometimes get out his set of bongos and play.

If he picked the right sort of day, with the right wind direction, the sound barely carried at all, so he was largely left alone, which was largely how he liked things.

Florence got out of her car and walked to the quarry's entrance, then along its main path to Gerry's Hole, calling Puck's name and feeling the same familiar bird wings beat in her chest that she'd felt frequently when she was much younger. She wondered if anyone in her family knew about how, while they were all saying not to worry, he'd be back soon, she would do nothing but silently worry, putting her hand on her heart trying to slow its pace.

Isolde never seemed to notice when Puck was missing, and if Florence pointed it out, she would say, 'Oh, well I expect he'll turn up sooner or later,' and he always did, Florence's entire body filling with rushing relief the moment she saw him.

When Puck was a child, she felt responsible for him, and Florence wondered whether this was because she was the eldest or because sometimes her mother and father didn't behave like adults at all and Florence felt that someone in the family ought to. But now Puck was an adult and Florence wondered if they weren't all being a little overdramatic. She was sure other families didn't send out search parties when a grown man was not contactable. But her family, she knew, was not like other families, and Puck was not like other grown men.

There was his name to start with. What had her parents been thinking? She and Isolde had got off lightly, but Puck? Florence's brow furrowed, trying to remember her high school English lessons and the one term when they had been assigned *A Midsummer Night's Dream*. All she could really remember was Lucy Venables snorting, 'Isn't that the one about your brother?' and one line about Puck being a 'merry wanderer of the night'.

Maybe her parents had known what they were doing after all.

Puck certainly did like to wander. Florence wasn't sure how merry he was, though, and she wasn't sure if she was angry at him for disappearing again or not.

When Florence was small, she wasn't sure how small but small enough for it to be a problem, she had slipped her hand from Amanda's in a department store and had had a lovely time with a woman behind a counter who called her 'ducks' and smelled like toffee. An announcement had been made over the public address system and soon Amanda Saint Claire had come click, click, clicking across the floor to glare at the woman behind the counter as if this was somehow all her fault. She had held Florence tightly to her chest, all the while shouting at her for being a 'silly girl for running off'. Amanda Saint Claire was both tender and angry, leaving Florence confused as to whether she was in trouble or not.

This was exactly how Florence was feeling about Puck as she rounded the last bend on the path to the smaller rock pool where he sat, his back against a boulder, his legs crossed in front of him, his eyes closed to the sun.

'Hi Florence,' he said lazily, not opening them.

'I thought this might be where you were. You should know that I've been up all night, worrying myself sick,' she said, reprising an old joke between them, any residue of anger erased with the relief at seeing his slight form against the granite.

Puck smiled. 'Sorry Florence – I'm sorry you felt like you had to come all this way.'

'Oh, it's no problem. I used this thing called a motor car. It really is the most marvellous invention. You might like to try it sometime,' she answered.

Puck was still smiling, so Florence dived in.

'I hear you and Isolde had an interesting chat,' she said, and left it at that. Experience had taught her that the only way to get her brother talking was to stop doing it yourself.

Florence took her shoes off and sat down beside Puck, the sharp heat of the rock settling down after a minute or so to a comfortable spreading warmth across her back.

Two whipbirds sang their duet nearby, calling back and forth to each other, their notes cracking across the bush.

'I went with him, sometimes – actually I went with him quite a bit,' Puck said.

Florence's eyes tracked a mother possum with a baby on its back – they were out early, she thought – making its way along a red cedar branch, then leaping from it to another. Such trust we all put in our parents, she thought, such blind belief that they will not let us go.

'When he took me to lessons or rehearsals, he'd get me to wait in the car,' Puck continued. 'I didn't mind. I'd sit in the front seat and listen to the radio, changing all the channels I wanted – remember how it drove Lamanda crazy when we did that?'

Florence nodded, hearing her mother say, 'Choose one! For God's sake choose one station and stay on it!'

'We'd run into some woman at the studio and Dad would say, "Just go and sit in the car for a few minutes, mate," or he'd give me some money to go the shop and get some hot chips or whatever.

'Mostly I didn't buy anything, I just kept the money to save up for my first Tama kit – remember that, Florence? It was electric blue and I thought I was Jeff Porcaro.'

Florence laughed. 'Of course I remember, Puck – we had to put extra insulation in the music room so we didn't all go deaf.'

She curled her toes around her brother's, wriggling them a little to encourage him to go on.

Puck wriggled his back in answer and continued. 'I kind of knew what was going on, Florence, and I think Dad knew that I did. It was sort of our little understanding that you girls didn't know about.

'And the thing that gets to me, Florence, the thing that feels so messed up, is that I kind of liked it. I kind of liked it that we had this thing he trusted me with, because it was the one thing we had that was just us.

'I'd sit there waiting in the car and I'd get this feeling of almost, you know, pride that he'd trusted me with this information, that he'd enlisted me. And then we'd get home and I'd see Dad kissing Mum and making a big fuss of her, and I'd think how stupid she was, Florence. I'd look at her and think how dumb do you have to be to not know what he's been doing? I was so angry with her, Florence, do you see? I was so angry, not with him, but with her.'

Florence nodded, remembering her own full-throated teenage tantrums directed mostly at Amanda.

'I was angry because I wanted her to catch him out,' Puck said. 'I wanted her to not let him get away with it, I wanted her to say, "I do not believe you, Lucas. I do not believe you and Puck have been caught in traffic all this time," because if she had said that and stopped things, then I could have stopped being his fucking little accomplice.'

Florence looked at Puck's face – all Amanda from his nose down, all Lucas from his nose up.

'And then Dad bought me the Tama,' Puck shrugged, 'so I guess that made everything okay.'

Florence remembered the gift, sudden and unexplained, making her and Isolde writhe with jealousy.

Extravagant, Amanda had said.

'Why would you buy him something so extravagant, Lucas?' she heard her mother asking when she saw the kit in the music room, electric blue and gleaming in the corner.

'I'm sorry Puck,' Florence said, 'you shouldn't have been put in that position. Lucas shouldn't have put you in that position. It was utterly wrong of him to involve you.'

She shook her head. 'And don't worry about being angry with Amanda. You were a child, Puck, and kids put their anger in all sorts of weird places.' Florence remembered that after Monty had told her that Pedro Perkins's parents had split up, she had found a scrap of paper with Pedro's father's name balled up and hidden inside one of the library's pot plants. 'The point is, none of this should have fallen on you to work out, Puck, you were hardly a willing accomplice, you were just . . . there.'

Florence saw Puck at eight, sitting on the white and red leather seats of their father's Fiat, fingers drumming on the dashboard, and thought it was lucky that Lucas Saint Claire was no longer around.

Otherwise she might just throttle him.

'Do you think Amanda knew I was there all those times?' Puck asked her. 'Because that's not really gold standard parenting either, is it?'

Florence shook her head. 'No, Puck, I don't think she knew at all. She knew Dad wasn't faithful, but she thought there were lines he wouldn't cross. I'm pretty sure an eight-year-old boy being deployed as a decoy was one of them.'

Puck nodded.

'Thanks Florence,' he said. 'I'm okay. I just wanted to come here and clear my head a bit.'

Florence smiled. 'How is it in there?'

'Cloudy.'

'Mine too,' said Florence, standing up. 'We can talk more about this any time, Puck, but it's getting late now and we should go home – Isolde and Amanda were worried about you.'

'Really?' Puck asked.

'Well, maybe not Isolde,' she grinned.

She put her hand out to Puck, who took it and stood beside her.

Something niggled at Florence. 'If you knew about Dad,' she asked, 'why did you get so upset when Isolde said he was' – Florence could not bring herself to say 'a root rat' – 'so unfaithful?'

'Because I wanted to be wrong,' he answered. 'I wanted to believe that he really was just helping those women with their musical arrangements, or giving me money to buy chips because he thought I was a good kid, not because he thought it might buy him some more time.'

'You were a good kid,' she told Puck, putting her arm around his neck and drawing his head to hers. 'Still are.'

Puck smiled. 'And you're not a murderer, Florence.'

Florence nodded – so Isolde had told him the whole story.

8

The library's air conditioning had broken down, making everyone in it, not just Florence, prickly.

Monty went around opening windows and turning on fans, but all it did was move the hot air around listlessly.

Florence had not slept well the night before. She had lain on her bed, thinking about Puck. He was, she supposed, the sort of person other people might find strange, the sort of person they might raise their eyebrows at when his name was mentioned. At school he had kept his head down, his fingers drumming, hurting no one, and still he had been singled out for omission. She couldn't remember him having any friends over to Kinsey, or going to any friend's house himself, not even someone from the school orchestra. Music kids tended to stick together, especially in high school. They were herd animals, bound together by their beating, creative hearts. Music kids didn't generally run with the main pack – and the main pack generally didn't want them. But the music kids hadn't wanted Puck either. Outside of rehearsal, he didn't seem to spend any time with any of them. Puck was a solo artist, then and now.

He did have Lance Bueller as a friend – Florence liked Lance, she wished Isolde did too, but not as much as she wished someone would like Puck. Someone who would wander with him.

Florence rubbed her eyes. Through the open windows, she could hear the grade three East Elm Primary class lining up outside the library's doors, laughter and shouts, one big bang – Pedro Perkins, probably – and then Monty's voice. 'Welcome, welcome. Good morning everybody. Now it's very hot in the library today so I want you all to be on your best behaviour for Miss Saint Claire.'

Then Florence heard a collective groan and one child complaining, 'But we wanted Mr Flowers.'

Tough, thought Florence. She had flirted with the possibility she wanted Mr Flowers too, but she, like 3G, had been disappointed.

What was that nonsense he had spouted at her, suggesting she wasn't human just because she'd dared to reason that perhaps Cat Morrison might like to remove her headwear if it was causing her so much bother? Better yet, perhaps the solution to having so much trouble getting a hat off her head was not putting one on in the first place.

God, it was hot in here. She reached to scratch a spot at the back of her neck where the perspiration licked at it, and fanned her face with a pamphlet on hydroponic strawberries.

Albert, she knew, was grappling with a curtain of lantana they'd discovered smothering a thicket of grey myrtle last week. She was glad she wasn't with him, and not only because the air in that particular section of the forest was usually thick with small clouds of gnats that suddenly loomed in your face. Florence was growing tired of Albert opening his mouth to offer sage but maddeningly obscure advice, dropping half-hints about his own life but never following through with details. She had told him about Puck, but what did she know of his family? He had met Isolde and Puck several times, and Amanda? Everyone knew Amanda. It was impossible not to know her – currently there was a giant billboard on the main road leading into East Elm with her picture on it: *Amanda Saint Claire – Stories I Could Tell You.*

Well, Florence, thought, Albert could start telling her his own stories, and not the ones that involved Jeremy and Lydia.

He hadn't asked her to the wedding, even though she was fairly sure his invite would have come with a plus one. He hadn't invited her to the book launch with that stupid woman with the hats welded to her head, and when she had invited him to see the corpse flower, which would have been putrid but interesting, he had declined. Florence knew she was being churlish – part of it was the bloody heat, making her swat and scratch at her skin – but it was clear their friendship was not going to gain the momentum needed to propel them beyond the library's door.

Albert had a full life outside the library's opening and closing hours, and Florence thought it was time for her to expand her own.

She remembered a woman who had written one of those self-help books Florence despised. The woman had turned her entire life around by saying yes to everything, invitations she would normally turn down, food she would normally not eat, activities she would normally not dream of doing. The book was called, unimaginatively, *Say Yes to Everything!* and Florence thought she might try it. Not everything – the idiotic woman had eaten a sheep's bladder – but most things, including the gala evening Miss Suki and the Nightshades had been asked to play.

It was at the big 'ouse, as Orla called Avalon, East Elm's historic estate, once a Catholic convent, now a parcel on the hill for people to point at as they drove past.

She had never been inside, but Florence remembered a long-ago summer when her parents always seemed to be tripping off to Avalon for dinner with its owners, the Elliots, Amanda swathed in off-the-shoulder clouds of fabric and Shalimar. She also remembered when they stopped going, her mother shouting at Lucas in the hallway loudly enough for Florence, upstairs in her room, to hear. 'I will not be trotted out like a performing seal, Lucas. If Rosalind Elliot wants me to sing for my supper, she can bloody well pay for it like everyone else.' The Elliots had left East Elm years ago, and Florence remembered some kind of trouble had been attached to their leaving. Had Lucas been that some kind of trouble? Florence frowned. Was it always going to be this way for her now, raking over memories for signs of her father's straying?

The Bishops, she supposed, had bought Avalon from the Elliots, and she had never met them either and had never particularly wanted to.

Florence wasn't the least bit interested in the house itself, but she was interested in its garden. Avalon's garden had an interesting wildness about it, its hedges not tamed into animal shapes or stiff geometrical forms like military haircuts. Its flowers burst forth with colour all year around, shouty oranges and reds, deep purples and spiky yellows among the standard rows of waxy magnolias and gardenias. Once, walking past the fence that wrapped its iron curls around the property, she had not been able to resist reaching through a gap to brush her hand against the frill of a camellia, and two huge dogs had appeared from the drive, barking ferociously, their lips pulled back from their snapping teeth. Florence had pulled her hand back instantly, shaking and embarrassed but noting that the camellias were sasanquas, too messy for people who liked to keep their lawns pristine, due to their habit of dropping their petals coquettishly almost every day.

She would do the Avalon gig, she decided, although she usually preferred smaller, more intimate shows, and she would touch all the sasanquas she felt like on her way in. She might even steal some.

Florence smiled and looked at her watch. She had five more minutes until she had to disappoint the children of 3G by not being Albert Flowers who told them appalling knock-knock jokes and put on voices for different characters when he was reading to them.

She decided to make a list of all the things she was going to say yes to. Florence picked up her pen and wrote: *Avalon gig. Mum's show. Victor's board game night. Out with Orla and Veronica.* It was a pretty pallid list, but it was better than 'Order water crystals', or 'Remind Isolde to hang out uniform'.

Florence slid open the drawer of her desk and put the list in it, then reached down to pick up a shoebox. Inside it were six fat white silkworms determinedly munching their way through a layer of green leaves from the mulberry tree in Rushton Park. The silkworm, she would tell the children, is not actually a worm at all, but a larva from the domestic silkmoth, the Bombyx mori, from the Latin 'silkworm of the mulberry tree'.

Generally the children were not impressed by Latin – she still remembered the creeping horror on their faces when Monty had leapt up on the table in one of his lessons shouting, 'Carpe diem!' after becoming overly excited by *Dead Poets Society* – but they were interested in eating. So she would tell them how the worms only consume mulberry leaves, and that they ate them constantly between twenty to thirty-three days straight without a break. Their eyes would grow wide and Pedro Perkins would probably say that he could easily do that with pizza, and then she would let them hold the pudgy little creatures in their pudgy little hands and they would forget all about wanting Mr Flowers instead of her.

Albert appeared at her shoulder – that stupid woman who wrote *Say Yes to Everything!* would probably say she had manifested him. 'Thought is intent is manifestation,' she'd trilled on the radio, and Florence had rolled her eyes.

She hadn't manifested him; it was just time for him to start work.

'Silkworms!' Albert said. 'I loved them so much when I was a kid, didn't you?'

Florence stood up and smiled as she made her way to the library door.

'Not particularly,' she said, remembering that Albert Flowers was no longer on her list of things to say yes to.

*

When Florence arrived home that night, she surprised Isolde by asking her if she'd like to go out for a drink.

'Maybe we could ask Puck and all go,' she said, and then Florence really surprised her by adding, 'and I'm going to go and see Mum's show too, if you want to come along.'

Isolde said, 'Really?' and when Florence nodded, she said, 'Really' again, and Florence snapped and said, 'Isolde, it doesn't matter how many times you say "really", I'm going to go and see Mum's show.'

'When?' asked Isolde.

'I don't know, maybe tonight.'

'Tonight?' Isolde echoed.

'If I can get tickets.'

Isolde laughed. 'I'm fairly sure if you asked Amanda Saint Claire she could get you tickets.'

'I know,' Florence answered, 'but I think I'd like to surprise her.'

Isolde shrugged. 'Sure, I'll come, and I'll ask Puck.'

'Great,' Florence nodded and went to look up the number of the Prince Street theatre where her mother was playing. She was not entirely sure why she wanted to hear Amanda's stories she could tell you; none of them had bothered to see Amanda sing professionally in months.

Puck and Isolde, of course, still performed with her as the Swingers, but those gigs seemed less frequent as the years since Lucas's death grew. They just didn't have the same swing without him, she supposed. But Amanda had continued to put out an album every two to three years and then tour it, still swinging for all of them. Sometimes it was an album of standards, sometimes it was themed – Florence shuddered as she remembered last year's hideous *A Very Saint Claire Holiday* with an even more hideous remix of Jazz Cat which Amanda had actually rapped. Florence laughed, remembering her mother rhyming 'purr' with 'myrrh'.

'This is ridiculous,' Amanda had shouted down the phone to Richard. 'It's not even singing, it's just very fast talking.' But Richard, sniffing out a dollar like a bloodhound with its nose to the ground, had pointed out it was also very fast money.

Richard. Florence realised she didn't have to call the theatre, she could just call Richard. She hadn't spoken to him in weeks. Florence's forehead crinkled. Actually, she hadn't spoken to Richard for months. The last time she'd seen him was at Amanda's fiftieth birthday party, at which her mother had not allowed anyone to mention the number fifty, had insisted on no candles on the cake and had quite rightfully refused to wear a badge that said, *It's all downhill from here.* Richard had fussed around Kinsey doing the flowers and rearranging chairs and getting in the way of everyone even more than Isolde, who had arrived late and either pretended (who knew with Isolde, there was every chance she did these things for effect) or truly had not realised Amanda's party was on. All Florence could remember was her sister walking through the doors of Kinsey just before the first guests were due to arrive and saying: 'Oh, is Mum's thingy tonight?' and everyone, mostly Richard, being furious with her.

Florence realised Richard was another person she had let fall from her gaze, another person she had stopped noticing; it wasn't just Issy who was guilty of not paying attention.

Richard had been a huge part of her childhood. He was in so many family photos that people who didn't know the Saint Claires might have assumed he was Lucas. She could see Richard now, pressing their costumes in the hallway of Kinsey where they inexplicably kept their ironing board, people forever tripping over the cord, Isolde once burning her arm on the iron's tip as she paced around it.

Occasionally Richard would pick them all up from school, Florence insisting he park his van far from its back gates, where the students who gathered there couldn't hear 'You Can't Get a Man With a Gun' playing from its speakers.

Richard would dutifully park a couple of streets away, staring straight ahead while waiting for Florence to dash to the van, and not speaking until they had rounded the corner.

'How was your day, sweetheart?'

'Good.'

'Anything wonderful happen?'

'No,' Florence would scowl at him and think if he knew anything he would know that nothing wonderful happened at her school ever, and that life was nothing like bloody *My Fair Lady*.

He and Amanda were always breaking into song around Kinsey – Richard tying a tea towel around his head like a scarf, knotting it around his chin and singing 'I Feel Pretty', making Amanda giggle and Florence stick her finger in her mouth and pretend to gag.

And when Lucas died, the one person who never seemed to leave the house, who remained there days after everyone else had gone, taking their washed casserole dishes with them, hugging Amanda tightly at the door and murmuring 'anything I can do' was Richard. She had hated him being there. In the kitchen baking. In the library rearranging books. In the hallway tripping everyone up with the iron's cord. In their lives, not being their father, stepping into his frame. She had burned with resentment at him every time he had passed her in the hallway, or had sighed long and loud every time he spoke. She had been hell on rollerblade wheels.

Florence picked up the phone. 'Hi Richard, it's Florence,' she said, or at least she tried to, because Richard interrupted, 'Florence, how lovely to hear your voice, how are you, my darling? Well this is just *wunderbar*! I was just saying to your mother the other day, "How is our little flower?" and here you are. Now don't tell me you're calling to say you've finally seen sense and are ready to get the band back together . . .' and on and on, and Florence remembered something else about Richard Miller.

The man never shut up, but this time she found she didn't mind, she just listened and enjoyed the ride until he took a breath and she jumped in.

'Richard, could I have tickets for Mum's show? Three would be great. Isolde and Puck are keen to come along too. I'd like it to be a surprise.'

There was a pause, one that went on for so long Florence wasn't sure if Richard was still on the line, but then his voice, a little muffled, a little quieter – was he crying? – said, 'She would absolutely love that, Florence,' then businesslike again, 'Would you like to go tonight?'

'Really? It's not too short notice?'

'There'll be three tickets at the box office under my name. You'll have to collect them by seven at the latest, curtain is at eight. But I must away, I've got some critics to boot out of your seats.'

*

The crowd in the Prince Street foyer before Amanda's show were exactly how Florence remembered them from her childhood – only older.

The women were in gowns, not dresses, not skirts and tops or jeans and T-shirts, but gowns that fell from their hips and skimmed their ankles. They wore brooches in their hair, gathered in strands behind their ears, and necklaces with red stones that caught the light and made them beautiful. The men wore suits, with pressed shirts and caramel shoes, and they loosened their ties at the bar, and the air smelt exactly like the sort of perfume her mother wore.

Florence thought that the whole crowd looked like it had been caught beneath a Rodgers and Hammerstein snow dome.

Florence knew these people, she half expected one of them to wander over and tuck her under the chin and say, 'My, haven't you grown!' but they just kept talking and laughing. Florence felt giddy from watching them. This was her mother and father's crowd; she knew them so well, and listening to their chatter in the foyer was like hearing a score of music she had practised over and over as a child.

At the top of the foyer's stairs the three Saint Claire children stood momentarily still – even Isolde, who eventually whispered, 'It's like *Jurassic Park* in here. Does anyone else find all these old people a little bit creepy?' But Florence shook her head. She didn't find it creepy, she found it wonderful. She wished she could find Richard and tell him. Never mind. He had just found them.

'Hello! Hello, what a treat to see you all! Puck, I love that jacket you're wearing. Isolde, lovely as always, and Florence, my little flower, in full bloom!' Richard was striding across the room with a suit that appeared to have sequins sewn into the lapels, and somehow pulling it off.

Florence smiled and forgot to be annoyed that he was making such a fuss.

'Hello Richard,' she said, kissing his cheek, while Isolde leant forward and kissed his other one, and Puck shook his hand.

'Oh my!' Richard said. 'It's like being in the middle of a Saint Claire sandwich – how wonderful to see you all in the same room again! I can't even remember the last time!'

'I can,' Isolde said brightly. 'It was at Dad's funeral.'

Florence twisted the side of her mouth. 'No, it wasn't, Isolde. It was at Mum's fiftieth.'

'Oh,' Issy answered, 'I don't remember being at that.'

Richard led them through the foyer crowd, parting the theatre-goers in his wake by holding his arms out on either side, both hands extended in a stop sign.

'I don't think that's necessary, Richard,' Florence laughed as he led them to their – very good, Florence noted – seats. 'I don't think we're in any danger of getting mobbed here.'

Richard smiled as he sat down next to her. 'Got to look after my chickens,' he said, and Florence was taken back to her childhood, Richard clucking and fussing all over them. 'Come on, chickens, into the car!'; 'I think it's time I got you chickens home to bed'; 'Bravo, chickens, bravo, a virtuoso performance.'

Then the lights dipped and Florence felt the crowd settle into their seats, all brushed with the same sleight of hand taking them from where they were a minute ago – bad traffic, unruly children, poor dinners – to here, where all those things faded with the house lights.

Then the lights darkened altogether and Amanda Saint Claire's profile appeared in silhouette against a cream scrim, her head tilted slightly forward, her hair pulled back in a low bun at the back of her neck. It was so unmistakably her mother – the long, flat forehead, the retroussé nose, the perfect triangle of her slightly open lips, the neat, lifted chin – Florence felt strangely like putting her index finger in the air to trace along the shadow's lines, to travel on her mother's skin.

Amanda Saint Claire's profile was so still for so long, Florence knew the audience would start to wonder if it was real or some sort of cut-out. But they didn't know her mother.

Florence looked across at Isolde and grinned, and Isolde smiled back, then leant forward and whispered, 'She'll hang on all night if she has to.'

What Florence knew, and Isolde and Puck too, was that the thing that was keeping Amanda Saint Claire set in stone for so long was sheer will. She would hold that pose until the exact moment when the audience stopped being enthralled and started shifting in their seats.

Florence watched as Amanda raised her hand and began to click her fingers metronomically, and Florence felt the hairs on her arms stiffen as a double bass began to play behind the scrim.

It was sparse, and it was perfect, as the bass player plucked out the first few famous bars of a jazz standard ('Always open with a crowd pleaser,' she heard her father say. 'Get them on your side and then you can do whatever the hell you like later.') and the scrim dropped.

Amanda Saint Claire, in a black velvet strapless dress turned her head, looked the audience in the eyes and took them all on.

'Take me in your arms . . .' she began, and Florence felt tears immediately sting her eyes, although if someone had asked, she would not have been able to explain why. It was something to do with the way Amanda had slowed down the song until she was almost speaking it, the way she had taken all the heat out of it, replaced its febrile tones with something very close to aching, and the way she was on stage, alone with just the double bass player beside her.

No band. No Lucas. No Isolde or Puck and never Florence.

Just Amanda Saint Claire, letting the show go on.

When the song finished the applause spilled through the rows like a Mexican wave, and a couple of people stood up, cupping their mouths with their hands to holler.

Florence hated the hollerers – but not as much as the people she and Isolde called the 'woo-ers'.

'Woo!' a man directly behind Florence called, and Florence didn't have to look to know the Issy would have swivelled her head to scowl at him.

But Amanda loved them all, even the ones who called out, 'Marry me Amanda!' – especially the ones who called out, 'Marry me Amanda!' Florence thought.

She watched as her mother bowed just slightly from her waist and mouthed the words 'Thank you' as she stepped towards the microphone for her next song, and the rest of the band began filing onto the stage, smiling and nodding as if they had all just run into each other at the most wonderful party.

Florence thought back to all those years ago when she had begged her mother in her childhood room not to break into song and Amanda had answered: 'I can't help it.' It was true then, and it was true now, Florence thought, watching her mother toss a smile out to the balcony, her eyes scanning along its rows, making sure it reached everyone.

'Maximum wattage,' Florence mouthed in the dark.

When Amanda had first turned towards the audience, Florence had seen her mother take them in, her three children sitting in the first row of the balcony, seats that Richard had managed to prise someone else's bottoms off.

The thing that struck Florence most was that her mother had not missed a beat. Her eyes had widened a little as she saw Puck and Isolde and Florence, her eyebrows had lifted a little, but she had not faltered or lost her place. She had just kept singing, kept working the stage for the next two and a half hours, with an interval.

It was a marathon, and only at the end of Amanda Saint Claire's seemingly endless stories she could tell you did she say, 'Thank you, everybody. Tonight has been a special night for me as I've had my three children, Florence, Isolde and Puck in the audience.'

She gestured to where they sat, Puck with his head down, Isolde actually waving from her seat, and Florence locking eyes with her mother.

'They are my most treasured stories of all, and the three greatest loves of my life,' her mother added.

Three, Florence noted, not four.

Later that evening, when they sat in Amanda's dressing room and Richard brought in a bottle of champagne in an ice bucket, Florence smiled at her mother.

'You're really good, Mum,' she said. 'You're really, really good.'

Amanda smiled her cat smile at her daughter.

'I know, darling,' she purred.

*

The week after Amanda's *Stories I Could Tell You* gig, Miss Suki and the Nightshades had an appointment to meet Natalie Bishop at Avalon.

The benefit was called Music Under the Milky Way and it was, Orla told them in Veronica's car on the way there, a fundraiser for the art gallery, which had apparently run out of money for new acquisitions.

'Haven't we all?' Veronica sighed from behind the wheel.

Orla said, 'Speaking of which, I fink we need somefing classier for this gig, you know, somefing that makes us look like we belong there.'

Florence thought that somefing might be for Orla to stop saying 'somefing' and calling Avalon 'the big 'ouse' as if it was a correctional centre.

'We do belong, Orla,' she said, 'because they've invited us there.'

'To work,' Orla reminded her. 'They'll probably make us use the maid's entrance.'

In the back seat Florence was mentally going through the costumes they kept hung in suit bags at Veronica's house. They always reminded her of old men in overcoats lined up at a bus stop.

'What about the green satins?' she asked. 'They have a bit of a "to the manor born" look about them, don't you think?'

'Yes, if "The Manor" is the name of a brothel,' Veronica answered.

'The silver sequins?' Florence tried.

'No,' Orla said. ''Alf the sequins are coming off. I always feel like I'm unravelling when I wear them.'

'The black halter necks?' Florence mused. 'They hide a multitude of sins – mostly yours, Veronica.'

Veronica shook her head. 'I don't believe in sin, honey. Thought you might have picked that up by now.'

Florence was tired of the dresses as well, not so much their style but their impracticality. She was tired of pouring herself into sheaths she had to tug down at the hips and cup her breasts into, like she was wriggling into an hourglass.

'What about we rent some tuxedos for the night?' she said and Veronica clapped her hands.

'I love it,' she said. 'Very *Victor/Victoria*.'

''Oo?' asked Orla as Avalon's gates slowly swung open, with no sign, Florence noted with relief, of the two hounds of the Baskervilles.

Veronica parked the car in a spot marked 'Visitors' and Florence wondered what it must be like to live in a house where the parking was designated.

'Let me do the talking,' Orla said, her vowels suddenly far more rounded, her voice taking on its Kensington clip.

'Just be yourself, Orla,' Florence said, 'we're not on stage now,' but as the door opened and Natalie Bishop stood there smiling, Florence felt absurdly like she was; as if she had stepped into the first scene of a Wodehouse play and Bertie Wooster was about to come gambolling off the tennis courts.

Mrs 'Call me Natalie' Bishop led them to a room off Avalon's wide central hallway that had low stuffed sofas, high arched windows, and in between tapestried footstools and occasional tables set with bowls of freshly cut peonies.

Florence's eyes flicked to a tall, clear vase filled with three exquisite bird of paradise stems. Albert called them the punk rockers of the botanical world, all spiky attitude and bright orange mohawks.

'I love your flowers,' she told Natalie Bishop, 'particularly the bird of paradise.'

'Ah yes, the Strelitzia reginae. I love it too.'

Florence noted the Latin, and thought she had been right. Someone who knew their way around a garden lived at Avalon. She just hadn't expected it to be the owner.

She nodded towards a neat pink cluster of flowers growing outside an arched window.

'Daphne odora,' Florence said. 'They're tricky to grow here.'

Call Me Natalie's eyebrows lifted a little. 'Yes, but I've found that the trick is to not overwater them. People think daphnes have to be kept moist all the time, but they don't.' She gestured towards the window again. 'And what do you think of my Anemone hupehensis japonicas?'

'Lovely,' breathed Florence, as Orla whispered to Veronica, 'What are they talking about? It's all Greek to me.'

'Latin,' Veronica whispered back. 'They're speaking Latin – actually they're showing off in Latin.'

After the meeting, which mostly involved Florence and Natalie Bishop wandering around Avalon's grounds pointing at plants, with Orla and Veronica trailing behind them, Natalie walked them to their car.

'My secretary Marianne will send all the details to you,' she said, 'but as I said, it's quite simple, you do three songs in the marquee after the string quartet has led the guests in, and I'll let you know which three from the list you so kindly gave me, Orla,' she added.

Orla bobbed her head and would have gone for a full curtsy had Florence not shot out an arm to stop her descent.

'Thank you, Natalie,' Florence said. 'It's been a pleasure meeting you.'

Natalie Bishop put out her hand. 'I so enjoyed our garden chat, Florence. I do hope you'll come and see my Rhododendron Capistranos when they bloom, it's quite something.'

'I would love that,' Florence answered and the two women's eyes met in understanding.

People could say what they liked about running, or knitting, or skiing, or doing crosswords; they could quote 'there is nothing – absolutely nothing – half so much worth doing as simply messing about in boats' all they liked, but Natalie Bishop and Florence Saint Claire knew they were all wrong.

Gardens were the absolute ticket, as Bertie Wooster might say.

9

When Florence returned home from Avalon, she found the three remaining members of her family waiting for her.

Amanda, Isolde and Puck were sitting in a tableau at the kitchen table, sipping tea and feigning surprise at Florence's arrival, even though she lived there.

Hanging her handbag on the hook behind the kitchen door, Florence turned to her mother and siblings and said, 'What's going on?' because she knew something was. Isolde began to prattle, telling a long and unnecessarily complicated story about how she and Puck had popped into a café and had been about to order a pot of tea when they'd spied Amanda sitting at a corner table, and they'd all thought why not just go to the cottage? Isolde had always been terrible at lying, Florence thought. Amanda had never sat at a corner table in her life. She smiled and kept listening as her sister continued the tale with a completely superfluous detour of going to the service station on the way home to get milk.

When they were small and had committed some misdemeanour, it was Florence who did the talking, Issy under strict instructions not to say a word because of her predilection for saying too much. Nothing had changed, Florence saw as both Amanda and Puck aimed warning glances at Issy from across the table, but really all three of them were hopeless. The only person in their family who was especially skilled at artifice off the stage was Lucas, Florence thought, but then silently added herself and her undulating alter ego.

'So, what's really going on?' she asked, although she thought she probably knew.

November was nudging its way towards December, the jacaranda flowers had dusted their carpets all over East Elm, and everyone was talking about how hot it was. Christmas was on the shelves at the supermarket: jars of chocolate almonds, rows of boxed baubles with paper-thin shells; and Jazz Cat, of course, which seemed to be playing wherever Florence went. And nipping at the heels of Christmas was New Year's Eve.

There had been no more talk about the Hello 2000! concert, but Florence knew that just because she hadn't been part of the conversation didn't mean it wasn't ongoing. She could think of no other reason why what was left of Lucas Saint Claire's Swingers would be pretending to be nonchalant, except if it was something they cared deeply about.

Amanda spoke. 'As you know, Florence, we have been invited to sing Jazz Cat at Hello 2000!'

Florence nodded.

'Your father,' Florence flinched a little; she had not expected the Lucas Saint Claire lure to be trailed across the water so early, 'would have absolutely loved to have performed at it, Florence. I think we all know how much Lucas would have wanted to play this particular show.'

There was the slightest ripple of difference in the way Amanda said Lucas's name now, Florence thought. Amanda Saint Claire used to say her husband's name as if everyone should quickly perform the sign of the cross afterwards, but while her mother still said her father's name with a lick of reverence, Florence was sure she could detect a far less deferential tone.

Amanda gave Florence a brief smile and continued. 'It would have meant a great deal to Lucas to have the four of us play together on stage once more.

'Your father used to say to me, Florence, that after you left the Swingers, we never sounded the same again, that there was always something missing.' Amanda smiled. 'I remember once asking him what he thought it was, what exactly was absent, and he said that it was "essence of Florence".'

Not fair, Florence thought, *not fair for Amanda to tell me this now.*

'And he was right, darling, we never did sound the same without you. I remember those first few dress rehearsals looking across to see you in one of those ridiculous costumes Richard kept putting us all in, and you were not standing in your spot. Of course, there was no spot because you weren't there any more – I think we might have popped a chair there in your place . . .'

And there, Florence thought, was Lamanda, still lurking beneath the surface like Gerry the Catfish beneath the softer version of her mother.

'We had to rejig everything because we had gone from a six piece to a five when you left and then a four when Lucas died.'

Amanda was waving her hands about, as if moving the remaining Saint Claires into their new positions.

'It was like when Geri Halliwell left the Spice Girls,' Isolde said.

'The point is, Florence,' Amanda continued, 'that in light of recent events, we have all – Isolde, Puck and I – decided that we do not want to play the show.'

Florence blinked.

This was not what she was expecting.

What she was expecting was a three-pronged, coordinated ambush using the entire Saint Claire weaponry – loyalty, legacy, guilt, debt and familial duty to keep the Saint Claire flag flying.

Instead, it appeared her family was voluntarily lowering the flag and folding it away.

Isolde leant forward. 'Because you thought you'd murdered Dad,' she said, explaining as if to a small, not very bright child.

'No, I didn't,' Florence said. 'I never thought I murdered him . . .' God, Isolde and her endless exaggerations.

'Yes, you did,' Isolde said, then leaned forward and whispered hoarsely, 'because of the Blue Feather.'

'Isolde,' Florence repeated firmly, 'and you too, Puck, you need to know I never thought I murdered him, I just thought I was partly to blame for his death – there's a difference.'

'Manslaughter then,' Isolde said, and Amanda shook her head.

'Stop it, Isolde,' she commanded. 'I want all three of you to listen to me, especially you, Florence, and Puck, no drumming.'

Puck's fingers, beating out a rhythm on the table, stilled, and he folded his hands in his lap, his fingers, Florence knew, still tapping mutinously on his thighs.

Amanda straightened her back. 'The person who caused your father's death is the unfortunate driver, whose name, by the way is Greg Calloway, if any of you had bothered to find out, from the Packers Dairy company,' she said.

'The rest,' Amanda clapped her hands together, making Florence blink, 'is life.

'None of us, not you Florence, or you Isolde, or you Puck, or me, has much say in it, not in the big things, not the death things.

'Your father died because he stepped in front of a truck.

'What happened before that is inconsequential, so unless you physically pushed your father into the path of the oncoming truck, Florence, unless you shouted at Mr Calloway, "Here's a live one for you!", then it is time for you all to accept that fact in full.'

Florence looked at her mother, Amanda's nostrils slightly flaring, her gaze steady on her children.

'It is also time for us to accept that Florence does not wish to be in the Swingers, and to stop pushing her to be. But it's not just you, Florence. Puck has also expressed his reluctance to perform Jazz Cat, and Isolde,' she smiled at her youngest daughter, 'says she now doesn't care either way.'

Amanda straightened a little more. 'As for me, I find that I no longer have the stomach for it.'

She nodded, as if dismissing them all from a board meeting. 'So that's it,' she said, clapping her hands together once more. 'I'm going home now to listen to Chopin's "Raindrops" and have some sweet tea.'

'I'll do it,' Florence said.

'What?' shouted Isolde – Isolde always shouted when she felt unsure about anything.

'I said I'll do it,' Florence repeated. 'I'll sing Jazz Cat with you at the concert. I want to do it, I really do.'

Florence was astonished at herself. The words had come before she had formed them in her mind, but the moment they had tumbled from her mouth, she knew she meant it. She did want to sing Jazz Cat with her family. She wanted to very much. She wanted to open her mouth and sing about the stupid damn cat again with her mother and sister and brother and draw them to her like a tide coming in.

Essence of Florence, her father had said, but he was wrong.

It was the essence of all of them that was needed.

Even Lucas.

Especially Lucas.

When the Saint Claire Swingers walked onto the Hello 2000! stage just before midnight – Puck first, she thought, to duck behind the kit; then Isolde smiling and waving like a home-coming queen; then she, Florence, probably scurrying to the microphone; then last of all, Amanda casting her light like shards of glass – a frisson of energy would spark through the crowd.

Women would whisper to each other that they'd once had the most enormous crush on Lucas Saint Claire, and look, there was Amanda, the wife, still so gorgeous, how did she do it? And the children! So grown-up! And so brave, singing without their father.

Some of the younger people in the audience wouldn't know who they were, but it wouldn't matter. They would know at least some of the words to Jazz Cat, because everybody did. They would notice – Florence hoped – that Puck was worth watching, his hair falling over his eyes as he played, and that Isolde was frenetically herself, and that she, Florence, was, well she'd be there, doing something, she supposed, with her hands and feet.

But what none of them would know, would ever know, was that Lucas Saint Claire was a root rat who sometimes used his son as a wingman; Amanda Saint Claire had a narcissistic twin called Lamanda; Isolde was a kinematic stick insect with an alternate view of reality; Puck was every bit as weird as his name; and that she, Florence, had spent most of her adult life walking around like a bag of shattered glass and only felt truly comfortable around shrubbery.

They would not know that the Saint Claires were just a family, as glorious and inglorious as any other.

Looking at the faces at the kitchen table – Amanda's shocked, Puck's still processing the information, and Isolde's face failing at pretending not to be wholly delighted – Florence knew she had made the right decision.

It was time to say yes to her family.

'So, can I have my spot back?' she asked, feeling Lucas Saint Claire's beaming smile upon her.

'That's my girl,' he said.

*

'You are not!' Victor said when Florence told him the Swingers were playing at the Hello 2000! concert.

'I am too,' she said, smiling at Victor's face, his hand splayed across his mouth.

'You are not!' he repeated, removing his hand to say it, then clamping it fast across his mouth again.

'Look, Victor,' Florence said, fastening a small cable tie to some jasmine he was trying to train along his side fence, its star-like flowers in full, bursting bloom like thrown confetti, 'you can say I'm not all day long, but it won't change the fact I am playing at the millennium concert and I am – for one night only – singing "Santa Was A Jazz Cat".'

'Christ, I hate that fucking song!' Victor said, then immediately apologised.

'That's all right, Victor, I hate it too,' Florence said cheerfully, 'but as I said, it really is for one night only.'

Florence felt it was important to clarify this, to Victor and her family, and especially to Richard, who had received the news of Florence's change of heart by falling in a swoon to the floor. 'Get up, Richard,' Amanda had said. 'Florence has only returned to the Swingers, not back from the dead.'

'You also hate cats,' Victor reminded her.

'I don't hate all cats,' she corrected him, 'just that one.'

Victor patted down his hair, damp with sweat. 'Why, Florence?' he said. 'Why now?'

Victor – and Leon when he was alive – knew most of Florence's musical history, and they both adored Amanda, buzzing around their front fence like native bees when they knew she was due to visit Isolde and Florence. Once, when Florence had drunk several glasses of Leon and Victor's homemade beer, she had told them about her choking incident on the *Jonathan Hammond Christmas Show*. They had listened gravely and Leon had said, 'Oh honey, if I got upset by every boy in some hideous jacket who told me I was a loser, I would have spent my entire teenage years locked in the closet.'

Florence smiled, remembering.

Victor and Leon. Leon and Victor. Everything about them, even their names, belonged together. How hard it must have been for Victor to step outside his front door again, without the sound of Leon's step behind him. But he had done it – the last couple of times she had visited, there had been no one home. Victor had returned to trivia night at the Shandon Pub, and he had renewed his State Theatre subscription ticket. 'I always buy two tickets,' he told her. 'I just pop Leon's programme on the seat.'

Good for him, Florence thought, good for Victor, stepping out.

Victor was squinting at her in the sun, waiting for her answer.

'Why am I singing Jazz Cat again?' she said. 'Because like you, Victor, I have decided to rejoin the land of the living.'

Victor nodded.

'Fair enough,' he said. 'Cup of tea?'

*

The East Elm Library was gradually turning into a Christmas-themed art installation.

Outside, the lower branches of the trees that hugged its corners were looped with red and green baubles, and the bike rack outside its front door had been wrapped in silver tinsel. Someone – Monty probably – had put a *Santa Stop Here!* sign in the herb garden, which the graffiti kids hadn't got to work on yet. Florence knew it was only a matter of time before Santa was turned into Satan.

Inside the library, crepe-paper bells hung in low rows across the room – Isolde would have to duck if she visited – and the craft table in the children's section was littered with glue guns and paper-chain snowmen.

Where the Book Marks display usually stood, with its notes handwritten by the librarians about books they had read, which Florence loved reading, especially the grumpy ones ('There's three nights of my life I'll never get back'), was the tree.

An absolute beauty.

It had been Albert's idea to replace the library's tired artificial tree, its green plastic branches looking like they had been gnawed by dogs, with the Araucaria heterophylla or, 'in English please, miss', a Norfolk Island pine.

'Actually,' she had told the children, 'it's not really a pine at all, it's an evergreen conifer,' but they hadn't been impressed, they had just wanted to get their hands on its feathery branches so they could string tiny lantern-shaped lights on them. The tree was now the first thing library patrons saw when they came through its double glass doors, standing tall with its branches extended upwards and outwards – 'like jazz hands,' Albert said.

He tended to the tree all year around, before bringing it in from its spot on the library's back verandah where just the right amount of light bathed it, and Albert made sure just the right amount of water quenched it, and Florence was sure, although she had never actually heard him, just the right words of encouragement were murmured to it.

In the next couple of years, Albert would have to perform the tricky task of removing it from its pot and planting it outside, but for now it stood sentry among the books, simple and majestic at the same time, something Florence thought only trees could really pull off. Trees. And music. And her mother, with the right lighting.

Every year a different class was chosen to decorate the tree, and Florence was admiring 6B's handiwork – red crepe bows and silver paper chains – when she heard Albert's voice behind her.

'They did a great job, don't you think?'

'They did,' she agreed, 'and so did you.'

Albert bowed a little from his waist. 'Thank you, Miss Saint Claire.'

'You're very welcome, Mr Flowers,' she smiled as they walked into the Green Team office together.

'What are you doing for Christmas, Florence?' Albert asked, hanging up his daypack.

'The usual, just going to Kinsey with Isolde and Puck.'

'That's the family home, right? I've read about it,' he said.

Every now and again Albert would say something that let her know he knew all about her family background, but unlike Monty he didn't press. Once, she remembered with a shudder, Monty had brought a Saint Claire Swingers album into the library, her family on the cover standing behind Lucas in descending order, their hands on each other's shoulders, heads turned to face the camera. Florence was wearing a blue and yellow tartan pinafore and a grimace. She remembered the day the photo had been taken. Her parents had been fighting, Puck had complained of a stomach ache, and she'd had her period and had convinced herself everyone knew it.

She smiled at Albert. 'Kinsey is the family pile, but it really is just a pile of old bricks, with lots of rooms no one goes into any more. It's nowhere near as fancy as its name suggests.'

There was a thawing between them, Florence thought. It was something to do with the general festive mood in the library, and her own decision to keep their friendship between the shelves, or in the forest where they shed their outer layers like papery sheets from the melaleuca trees.

Albert certainly seemed relaxed as he asked her casually, 'So everything turn out all right with Puck?'

Florence nodded. 'Yes, thanks, he's fine.'

She didn't want to explain Puck's quarry visit, or the reasons behind it, to Albert. That would be like stripping all the melaleuca's layers, from its shaggy, outer bark to its spongy white core. Florence did not want Albert Flowers seeing her core.

So instead she said, 'What about you, what are you doing for Christmas?'

'Just at Mum and Dad's too,' he answered, 'with my sister Adelaide if she can be bothered turning up.'

'I should introduce her to Isolde,' Florence smiled, 'then they can glide through life not showing up to things together.'

Albert smiled. 'And there's all the usual silly season parties, of course,' he said.

'With the usual suspects?' Florence asked, her smile stretched taut all the way to her earlobes.

Albert nodded. 'It's all a bit exhausting, actually.'

Florence nodded back to Albert Flowers, who had so many parties to go to he was tired just thinking about it.

'I know what you mean,' she said. 'I'm going to about,' Florence plucked the number like a lemon snapping off its branch, 'four or five already.'

Albert, the words tumbling out of his mouth before he had a chance to catch them, said, 'Really?'

Florence met his eyes. 'Really,' she said. 'Might run into you at one of them,' her words a light soufflé.

'Have you got much on this weekend?' Albert asked.

'Oh, a couple of things,' Florence smiled. 'You?'

'A couple of things,' he echoed. 'And of course the non-negotiable dinner with my parents.'

Ah, Florence thought, Georgina Flowers's Sunday roast that waits for no man. Not even the exhausted-between-parties Albert Flowers.

*

Albert Flowers sat across from his sister Adelaide at the dining table, Georgina and Laurence Flowers at either head of it.

Ridiculous for the four of them to be spread out like this, but this seating arrangement was how his mother liked it, probably, Albert thought, because that was how she imagined they might dine at Avalon.

Addie kicked him under the table, harder than necessary, which Albert thought described his sister well. There was an edge to her, no trace left of the tiny girl who had followed him from room to room in the house, trailing a corner of a cut-off sheet behind her. This bit of fading flannelette was Addie's best friend Boo, who was, she said, an elephant.

But there was no trace of Adelaide Flowers and her imaginary elephant friend in the woman sitting across from him, kicking his shins in lazy, repetitive knocks for no other reason than she felt like it.

Instead of making a fuss, Albert shifted his chair back so her swinging foot couldn't reach his legs.

Georgina Flowers hated fuss at her table, most particularly her Sunday roast table, which seemed to come around, Albert thought, more quickly every week.

His phone would ring on Sunday morning and his father would say, 'Dinner tonight, six o'clock,' and sometimes add, 'chicken', or 'lamb' or 'beef' or whichever animal Georgina was going to slather in gravy and surround with her Italian herbed potatoes.

He never wanted to go, and Addie hated it too, his mother fussing and hot in the kitchen, his father talking to him and

Addie about real estate, and Addie sneaking out for a cigarette every half an hour. 'God,' she'd sigh when he joined her, telling his father he was just popping out for some fresh air, although the air gathering around Addie in grey, wispy smoke was anything but. 'Why, why does she insist on keeping this bloody Sunday roast thing going?'

But Adelaide knew exactly why, and so did Albert.

His mother made the roast and his father carved it like clockwork every Sunday so that at least one thing in their lives remained the same when everything else had changed, and they could all pretend not to notice the empty place at the table were Hamish had once sat.

Hamish should be here, home from university, and everything would be all right because Hamish was at the table and there was magic in that.

He could have been a bastard, Hamish. He probably should have been a bastard. He was so fucking good at everything – school, sport, friends, girls – that he, by the laws of nature and school ovals, should have been a prick.

But he wasn't, he was great. Albert's big brother Hamish was so fucking great that Albert never even thought to feel less than around him.

Hamish wouldn't let him. When Albert, so big in his skin but so lost in it, fell over his own feet, Hamish covered each stumble quickly and easily. When his mother grew morose about her lot – she actually called it her lot sometimes – that she wasn't Natalie Bishop snipping away at her roses with a pair of garden shears with a ribbon on them, Hamish would tease her until she laugh-snorted out of her nose. When his father began to bore whole rooms to death about real estate – even people who actually cared about it – Hamish would change the subject or say, 'Give it a rest, Dad,' in a way that made everyone, including Laurence, smile. When Addie was younger, and someone hurt her feelings, Hamish would say, 'What's the girl's name?' and then pretend to report her to the police saying, 'Hello, I'd like you to go around to Melanie Exton's house and arrest her immediately for crimes against fresh breath,' and Addie would stop crying and start laughing and ask for a piggyback. Or he would tease her about which boy she liked, calling out names alphabetically. 'Archie . . . no? Barnaby? Okay, Callum? Derek? Engelbert? No, no, anyone but Engelbert,' and Adelaide would blush and squirm and almost die from laughter.

And when Albert wasn't sure of himself – and Albert was a kid who was never entirely sure of himself – Hamish never pushed him like his mother did ('What about joining the photography club?'); instead he made him feel like it was entirely all right to not be entirely sure of himself. 'You'll be right, mate,' he'd say in their room, blowing cigarette smoke out the window while Albert watched wide-eyed from his lookout position from the door. 'Don't worry about the olds – you just do your own thing, yeah?'

When Albert, awkward and uneasy in social situations, standing just outside the periphery of a group, hesitated to say anything, Hamish would throw in, 'What do you reckon, Albert?' as if it was the most natural thing in the world that Hamish, and therefore everybody, valued his opinion.

Diversion was Hamish's greatest skill, Albert thought.

If Albert stammered out his reply, or didn't have one at all, Hamish would find a way to take the heat off him, suddenly remembering they had to go somewhere, looking at his watch and saying, 'Mate, we better get going, we've got that thing at Mum's,' then tossing to the semicircle of boys around them, 'You know how the olds get.' They would all nod their heads and agree that yes, they knew how the olds got, and Hamish and Albert would head off, Hamish's arm loosely around his little brother's shoulder.

As a child Albert had understood very clearly, from an early age, that Hamish – if he'd been like other big brothers he had seen in action . . . Willy McIntyre's made him shudder – could have made his life hell. He could have pinched him, or kicked him, or taken his things, or mocked him in front of his friends, or frozen him out of every single thing he did, but instead he let him in. At school Hamish walked him to his locker in the mornings, laughing and joking and drawing an invisible line around Albert, so that everyone knew and understood he was not to be touched. He was not to be teased about spending his lunch hours looking up botanical books in the library, or his general crapness at every single sport, or his startled eyes when someone addressed him directly, or his utter uselessness around girls.

'Don't sweat it,' Hamish told him, 'you'll come good, you're just a bit shy, who gives a fuck, mate, you'll get there . . . big, strapping lad like you, the girls will be lining up for you, mate, you just wait and see, I'll have to get a baseball bat to fend them off.'

And Albert had believed him, because Hamish might only have been seventeen, just four years older than Albert, but he knew absolutely everything there was to know in the world. Hamish had access to information other people didn't. Hamish knew some code that other people couldn't decipher, some way of understanding how the world worked and how to gain entry into it. Hamish knew, Albert thought as a thirteen-year-old boy, what was what. If Hamish said it was so, it was so, and if Hamish was around, it meant that everything, absolutely everything, would turn out all right.

So when the lump under Hamish's arm wasn't just a lump and his big brother became lost in a world of specialist rooms and clinical studies and treatments that worked and then didn't; when time slipped past and no one cared any more if there was roast dinner on the table because Hamish couldn't eat it; when Hamish himself slipped past them just after his twenty-first birthday and there would be no party and no Hamish bringing home some wonderful girl he had met at university who they would all fall in love with, after that there would be no more absolutely everything turning out all right again.

Albert raised his fork to his mouth. 'Lovely dinner, Mum,' he said.

Georgina smiled brightly at him. 'Thank you, Albert. I know roast chicken is your favourite.'

It wasn't his favourite, it was Hamish's.

Albert wondered if his mother's mistake was forgetfulness or wishful thinking.

'You look great, Mum,' he said, and Georgina Flowers did look great – pressed linen blouse, floral skirt, her hair pinned back by tortoiseshell combs, a pair of milky pearl earrings at her lobes.

'Thank you,' she answered. 'So how is everything with you, Albert?'

'It's pretty shit, Mum,' he wanted to answer, 'it's pretty shit because I am doing a job that no one except the people who do it really care about, and there's about five of us trying to keep a whole forest alive, for a wage you and Dad would be appalled by; I keep putting my great big fucking feet in my mouth when I speak to this girl at work who I think I might like quite a bit and who thinks I'm a tosser; and I know that if you had a choice, if you really had a choice, it would be Hamish sitting here having dinner with you not me. How's tricks with you?'

Albert swallowed.

'Good thanks,' he answered, and she gave him her bright smile again.

He felt uncomfortable around her, he always had in that way of children who see between the blink-and-you'd-miss-it look of disappointment, or worse, distaste, from parents who'd wanted so much more than you turned out to be. How many of us are there, he wondered to himself, how many of us not-quite-good-enoughs?

'Your father thinks we should go on a cruise,' Georgina said so suddenly it sounded like she was making an admission.

'A cruise . . . where to?' Addie asked, jumping on Georgina's words like a gambolling labrador and thinking, Albert knew, of having the house to herself.

Addie had temporarily moved back home. She was between flatmates, between jobs, between boyfriends, and between here, at the Sunday dinner table, and whatever came next. Albert knew he should ask his sister to move in with him, but he didn't think he could stand being around all that brittleness.

'Oh, some group of islands in the Pacific,' Georgina answered Addie vaguely. 'Tonga, I think, and some other one.'

'Vanuatu,' Laurence threw in from across the table.

'You don't sound terribly interested, Mum,' Adelaide said.

'Don't I? Well, I expect I'll enjoy it.'

Albert expected she wouldn't. Albert expected she would, instead, endure it, as she did everything since Hamish had died.

Albert's mother had perfected the art of going through the motions, just as she was doing now, fussing around the table, clearing the dishes and insisting on doing the washing-up herself.

Laurence started talking to Adelaide about negative gearing, and Albert, seeing an opening said, 'I'm just going to make a quick phone call,' and headed up the stairs to Hamish's old room.

There was nothing left of his brother's belongings in there. Thank God his parents hadn't, as he knew some people did when they lost someone they loved, kept their rooms exactly as he or she (oh Charlie Markson, Albert's heart murmured in his chest) had left it.

The Flowers hadn't done that. Instead they had turned Hamish's room into an office. Where Hamish's bed had been, there was a desk, his Farrah Fawcett posters had been replaced with framed prints of wooden sailboats tied up together somewhere in Greece, and his bedside table, once stacked with books, was now a side table with a telephone on it.

But Hamish? Hamish was still there. Hamish was there right now, lying on the floor, wearing his white tennis shirt and shorts, his hands locked behind his head, caught in time, like a butterfly pinned to a board.

Hamish didn't change; he didn't put on weight or lose it; he didn't grow a beard or start wearing suits. He appeared to Albert just as he always had, and they had the same conversations over and over, in a loop.

Now he was grinning up at Albert, saying, 'Had to get away did you, mate?'

Albert nodded.

'You okay?'

Albert shook his head, as Hamish began singing the same old song.

'Albert, you've just got to get out more, you know, you've just got to get out and see what happens. You can't wait for things, mate, you could spend your whole life waiting.'

Hamish lay back down again, looking up at the ceiling.

'I do go out all the time now, Hamish,' he told his brother, trapped in time in his tennis whites, 'I go out all the bloody time.'

But Hamish was no longer there, the floor smooth and empty, his brother as much of a phantom as the phone call Albert was pretending to make.

He waited a few more minutes and then went back downstairs to Georgina Flowers, who told him she had made apple strudel for dessert, his favourite.

Again, it was Hamish's favourite. Again, Albert ate it anyway and pronounced it Georgina's 'best yet'.

*

If Richard Miller had been allowed, he would have hired a sky-writer to announce the return of the Swingers on New Year's Eve writ large across the skies.

Richard would have taken out full-page press ads, booked radio and television spots and arranged a series of thoughtful, sit-down interviews with Amanda.

But he wasn't allowed, and he wasn't happy about it.

At the first meeting with the Hello 2000! producers, held in what appeared to be an abandoned car dealership on the outer fringes of East Elm, a man called Kip with curated face stubble told Richard the producers wanted to keep the final act of the evening a surprise.

It was what was known in the industry, Kip explained to Richard, whom he called 'Rich', as a 'moment'.

Then he said: 'I expect you've had a few of those in your time, Amanda?' and his team, also dressed in head to toe black, laughed appreciatively, a murder of crows on a telegraph wire.

Florence laughed too, because she knew what was coming.

She had been watching her mother's face throughout the meeting, her eyes flicking between Richard and the Hello 2000! team who were treating Amanda's long-time manager like a drink-spilling uncle at a wedding, smiling politely at his words but not paying any attention to what he was saying and looking over his shoulder for an exit.

When Richard spoke of logistics or the Saint Claire technical requirements, or brought up sound checks or the terms of the contract, Kip waved his hand lazily through the air and said: 'Taken care of, Rich,' or 'We've got this,' and Florence wondered how long it would take her mother to tell them that they didn't have it at all.

Florence met Isolde's eyes, her sister making a quick chopping motion across her neck; then Florence looked at Puck, who was looking at the floor, shaking his head almost imperceptibly. You wouldn't have caught the movement at all, she thought, unless you knew him very well. You wouldn't have caught any of the signals between the Saint Claire family unless you were in it yourself or, like Richard, an honorary member.

You wouldn't, for example, know from Amanda's enraptured expression while listening to Kip's plans for the 'big reveal' – at one stage her mother had even clapped her hands delightedly and said, 'Oh bravo, Kip!' – that Lamanda was about to emerge from that charming smile and smooth, porcelain skin to flick at him with her lovely tongue.

Amanda stood up.

Here it is, thought Florence, wishing she had brought some sort of snack along. Buttered popcorn, for example.

'Thank you, Kip,' Amanda said, lightly touching his arm, 'it's been so interesting listening to you, hasn't it, Richard? If only someone had explained all of this to us when Barbra last came to Australia and we sang "Evergreen" together with the Sydney Symphony Orchestra at the Opera House. Was that what you might call a "moment", Kip?'

As she spoke Richard was picking up his briefcase, Isolde was putting on her cardigan and Puck was already walking towards the door.

Florence dipped her head to loop her handbag across her shoulders. The meeting was over, they all knew, even if the Hello 2000! team hadn't quite grasped the silent ballet that was going on before their eyes.

Amanda lifted her hand from Kip's arm.

'We won't be available to play at your concert, I'm sorry to ruin your surprise – perhaps you could provide one by shaving properly.'

Then she, Richard, Florence, Isolde and Puck walked out the door and into the waiting mini-van, the driver looking up from his paper as Amanda slid into the front seat beside him.

'I'm not scheduled to take you home for another hour,' he said.

'Change of plan,' Amanda smiled at him, then turned to face the passengers in the back. Nestled in her hand was a familiar gold packet. 'Caramel?' she said.

Sometimes, Florence thought, she really loved Lamanda.

In the van on the way home, Amanda engaged the driver in conversation, finding out about his eldest daughter who was nursing in Cambodia, and his son who was doing not much at all, as far as he could tell. When they pulled up at Kinsey, the driver passed Amanda his business card and was gifted with maximum wattage.

It wasn't until they were inside that they spoke about the meeting, everyone scattered like cushions on the lounge room's couches.

'I'm sorry things didn't work out,' Puck said. 'I know how much you wanted to play the show, Mum.'

'Of course we're playing the show, darling,' Amanda said.

'I don't think so,' Isolde said. 'You insulted the man's facial hair.'

'Doesn't matter,' Richard said, 'all your mother really did was put our price up.'

Poor Kip, Florence thought, it really was all a game, and no one had told him who the real players were.

When she saw him backstage at the New Year's concert in a few weeks' time, she would be sure to throw him a smile. As Amanda would say, there was no need to skite.

10

'We look like piano keys,' Veronica said.

'Sexy piano keys,' said Orla.

'What do you think, Florence?' Veronica asked.

Florence considered the three of them in the tuxedos she had rented.

'I think we look like we mean business,' she said.

'Sexy business,' said Orla.

They were in Veronica's flat, getting ready for Music Under the Milky Way.

The three women were smoothing each other's collars, tucking shirts in and gliding their hands through each other's hair to affix high ponytails. Florence supposed this was the same sort of feeling some girls got from slumber parties, the brushing of hair and spritzing of perfume. She didn't know for sure, she'd never been invited to one, but she thought it might feel a little bit like this.

When they were finished dressing, they considered each other in Veronica's full-length mirror.

All traces of Miss Suki and her Nightshades had been erased, and in their place these women, both feminine and masculine – even Veronica. Their hair was pulled tight from their foreheads, eyebrows heavily pencilled like bird wings, and their lips outlined in a deep scarlet crayon. Florence thought the effect was more startling than sexy, but she still preferred it to Miss Suki and her Nightshades' almost cartoonish curves.

She leaned forward and peered closely at her face in the mirror; stripped of some of Miss Suki's layers, she saw the familiar outline of her eyes and lips, the lift of her chin. Becoming Miss Suki rendered her unrecognisable, which was, of course, the point.

Or had been. Florence thought it was nearing time to retire Miss Suki, send her off with a series of farewell concerts, pack up her greens and silvers and blacks and watch her shimmy off stage with, being Miss Suki, no backward glance.

She would miss her, Florence thought, but only as much as you could miss something that was never really there.

'Right, ladies,' said Veronica, 'we'd better get going to the big 'ouse.' The women slung their bags across their shoulders and walked out of Veronica's flat to her car, Florence, her legs freed from the slippery confines of Miss Suki's dresses, striding out in front.

'I still think we look like penguins,' Veronica said.

'Sexy penguins,' said Orla.

On the way to Avalon they passed the East Elm Library and Orla said, 'That's where you work, isn't it, Florence?'

'Yes, we have an office inside.'

'Pretty different from this,' Orla said, turning to face her in the back seat, 'pretty different from us.'

Florence nodded. It was different, but she had grown used to straddling the two worlds, one foot in stilettos, the other in work boots, and Florence somewhere in between.

'Did you ever crack it with that fella you liked?' Orla asked.

'No,' Florence shook her head.

'Why?' Veronica asked, her eyes on Florence's in the rear-view mirror.

'We never met in the middle,' she answered honestly.

'His loss,' Orla tossed over her shoulder, as they drove through East Elm and up the climbing roads to what the real estate agents called 'Upper East Elm', although nobody else did, not even the people who lived there.

The name had never caught on, and Florence was glad of it. She was sure the people who lived behind its sandstone walls and trailing ivy were aware that their gaze fell from loftier heights than the other citizens of East Elm. There was no need to press the point.

The car rounded the last bend to Avalon's perch at the top – Upper, Upper East Elm, she supposed – the house throwing out light from every window, like a restaurant birthday cake held aloft and shimmering through the crowd.

'Bloody 'ell,' said Orla as they entered Avalon's gates and began the climb up its driveway.

They passed staff in black and white uniforms moving through the grounds, carrying trays and vases of fresh flowers and shaking out silver tablecloths.

Orla turned to face Florence. 'We look like the bloody waiters.'

Florence looked at their outfits and began to laugh. 'Sexy waiters,' she corrected her.

They did look quite similar to the wait staff, she thought, but it was too late now; if anyone asked Florence for a canapé, she would just go and fetch it.

At the top of the drive, a man in a hi-vis vest directed them to the rear of the pool house where two small marquees had been set up as dressing rooms. A small woman wearing a headset and carrying a clipboard was darting between the two, tapping at the headset with her fingers. Marianne, the event planner, Florence thought. She usually hated dealing with event planners, snappy and overexcited with the delicious power of being the keeper of the clipboard.

Veronica pulled into a parking bay and switched the engine off.

'Right,' she said, 'here goes,' as everything in the car shifted.

A brief transference occurred, a wrinkle in time, as Veronica, Orla and Florence remained in the car and Miss Suki and her Nightshades exited it.

They were third on the bill, after the string quartet in the courtyard welcomed guests in – Vivaldi's Four Seasons, for sure, Florence thought – and a duo called Sugar and Spice who Florence had seen before and sang far better than their stage name suggested.

The woman with the clipboard came over to where Florence, Orla and Veronica were standing just outside the performers' marquee.

'I'm Marianne, you must be the Nightshades,' she said. 'We've spoken on the phone. Now which one of you is Miss Suki?'

Florence raised her hand a little.

'Natalie is very busy at the moment, but she said to tell you that the moon flowers are out.' Marianne laughed, a startling honk from someone so tiny. 'I thought she was talking about another group at first, but then again I also thought you were waitresses when I first saw you.'

She honked again and then showed them where to put their things.

'So, I'll come and get you about half an hour before you're due on at eight. I understand you've brought your own PA and backing tracks?' Veronica nodded. Marianne smiled. 'Wonderful. I'll be about if you need me.' Then she scurried off again, still tapping at her headset.

'I told you we look like waitresses,' Orla sulked.

Veronica had insisted they dress at home, and looking around the small marquee, Florence was glad. Sugar and Spice were in the corner, wriggling their bodies into matching silver jumpsuits and bumping into its soft white walls.

Orla was reading a paperback, Veronica was doing and redoing her eyeliner, and Florence was feeling restless in the increasingly cramped dressing room as the string quartet and all its instruments entered it.

Florence thought she recognised the viola player, a slight woman with a pixie haircut and a glinting blue nose ring.

She might have been one of Lucas's backing players – or something else – and Florence turned her head slightly away.

'I think I might go for a walk,' she said to Orla and Veronica, 'and see if I can find those moon flowers.'

'But you're in costume,' Orla protested, 'you can't go outside in it.'

'Yes I can,' Florence said. 'I'll just grab a tray and blend right in.'

Outside the marquee, Florence walked slowly towards the back of the big 'ouse, keeping to the darker side of the path and sniffing the air for traces of the moon flower. Breathing in deeply through her nostrils, she caught the bubblegum notes of plum magnolia, the sharp and sweet scents of jasmine, and the heavenly aroma of the angel's trumpet.

You could get drunk on an evening like this just by inhaling, she thought.

Natalie Bishop had timed this benefit perfectly, when Avalon's night garden unfurled its most heady scents.

There was one thing, however, that Natalie Bishop hadn't got quite right.

Florence looked up at the night sky.

Music Under the Milky Way was missing its biggest component.

Wrong time of year, Florence thought, to glimpse that particular part of the galaxy's billions of stars and planets. May or June would have been better, when the Milky Way appeared across the sky like a smear of white paint to anyone who cared to look up. But at this time of year, the Milky Way and the Goddess Hera who ruled it were not inclined to make an appearance.

But it didn't matter, and Florence doubted anyone else would notice its celestial absence – except Albert.

That was just the sort of thing Albert Flowers would notice – the Milky Way missing.

Florence walked the edge of the path, watching as the grounds of Avalon transformed into its own Midsummer Night's Dream. The staff were putting centrepieces of silver candelabras swathed in boughs of ivy on each table, and tying huge creamy bows on the back of each chair, as if they were dressing small children.

A man pushing a wheelbarrow filled with bags of ice wobbled it towards each table, filling the buckets that stood at either end and then wobbling off again.

'Can I help you?'

Florence started. She had not heard the man, who was now standing close behind her, approach at all.

'No, I'm just looking,' she answered, irritated, and taking a step back from him.

'Are you staff?' he asked, and somewhere in the tone of his asking, the way he said 'staff' as if it had quotation makes around it, made her prickle.

'No,' she said, looking at his tuxedo and glancing down at her own. 'I'm your long-lost brother Geoffrey.'

The man laughed, a shouty guffaw.

'I'm sorry, that sounded rude – Mama's got me patrolling the grounds, checking the perimeters, that sort of thing.' He smiled and put out his hand. 'Oscar Bishop,' he said.

Florence took it and answered, 'Miss Suki – and I am staff, I'm one of the performers.'

'Ah, my mother told me about you,' he answered. 'You're the girl who knows all about flowers.'

He was about her age, she thought, but he had one of those boy-man faces that made it hard to tell: slightly fleshy cheeks, full lips, and wavy, coppery hair tucked behind his ears.

'Yes, your mother and I had a pretty long chat about the garden.'

'She's mad about it,' Oscar said. 'So who are you when you're not Miss Suki?'

Florence smiled – it was an excellent question.

'I'm not at liberty to divulge that information, and I'm not allowed to fraternise with guests either. They'll be gossiping like mad below stairs,' she said and turned back towards the pool house.

'Nice to see you after all these years, Geoff,' Oscar called after her.

'About time,' Orla grumbled when Florence walked into the tent, just as the string quartet were walking out, moaning about having to play the Four Seasons again.

'I would like to murder Spring,' said the woman with the blue nose ring.

Florence and Orla and Veronica ran through their vocal exercises and Orla's 'facial calisthenics', a series of grimaces and exaggerated expressions she believed loosened their airways and jaw, and Florence believed made them look like they were collectively having very bad sex.

'Right,' said Veronica when they were finished, 'hands in.'

Veronica insisted they complete this ritual before every performance, and sometimes, particularly in the early days when

Miss Suki and the Nightshades played much smaller gigs, Florence found it unnecessarily theatrical. But she had grown to like it, the brief touch of Orla's and Veronica's hands on her own, the moment their eyes locked, the belonging.

Florence put her hand out on top of Orla's and Veronica's and smiled.

They walked out of their tent towards the back of the stage where Sugar and Spice were shaking it about with more enthusiasm than Florence felt was strictly necessary.

'I still fink we look like zebras,' Orla huffed.

'Sexy zebras,' Florence said.

Peeking through a gap in the draped silk of the stage marquee, Florence felt like she was looking at a giant chessboard, Avalon's guests moving like smooth, gleaming pieces about the grounds. The women wore long evening gowns with flowers tucked behind their ears; the men were in black tie, and all of them, Florence thought, looked utterly at home here, gliding around the board with ease.

What might that be like? she wondered, watching a woman approach a group at one of the tables, the men standing to greet her, the women smiling, heads tilted. To know that you belonged in such a place? That your family knew that family who went to school with that family who were cousins of that family who played football with that family who married into that family? It would either be wonderful, she thought, or suffocating. Probably both. Florence remembered Albert telling her about the wedding of one of the Bishop boys. Who was it? Simon, she thought, older than the one she had just met – Oscar – who had asked if she was staff. There was a sister too, she recalled, trying to remember what else Albert had told her about that night. Something about the groom being annoying and a conga line. There was always a conga line, she thought, although she couldn't imagine Albert being in it. Florence couldn't really imagine him here either, although he was close enough to at least one of the Bishop brothers to be invited to his wedding. But he hadn't mentioned this particular party on his dance card. It had been one of the reasons she had said yes.

Sugar – or Spice – said, 'Thank you very much, you've been a wonderful audience,' as Veronica pressed the tips of her fingers to Florence's shoulders: 'We're on'. Sugar – or Spice – whispered as they passed them at the back of the stage, 'No, they haven't, they've been shit, good luck.'

It was not one of their better shows; they hadn't settled into their new skins properly. Later Veronica would say they should have worn the silvers, and Florence would agree. As much as she had liked the tuxedos, Miss Suki had resisted. Florence found she could not get into character, and neither could Orla or Veronica, the teasing banter between them sounding, to Florence's ears, rehearsed and stiff. But it didn't matter. No one was listening. After a polite smattering of applause when they first walked on, and a thimbleful of silence, everyone went back to talking to the person on their right or left and Florence didn't blame them. It wasn't really the sort of night to pay attention. It was the sort of night to lose yourself in conversation, wine and your own luck at being in such a place, loosening your tie.

After their last number – thank God there had been only three of them to trawl through – Florence said a hurried thank you, and she and Orla and Veronica exited, stage left, Orla not turning around as she usually did to flatten out her palm and throw a kiss.

'Well, that was 'orrible,' Orla said when they got back to the dressing room, pulling at her ponytail.

'Dire,' Veronica nodded.

'Oh, I don't know,' Oscar Bishop said, strolling in, Florence thought, as if he owned the joint, which she supposed he did. 'I thought you were very good.'

He had his hands in his pockets, his bow tie untied to hang slackly on his chest, and his head tipped slightly to one side.

Florence knew she was meant to be charmed but she was not.

It was a sliver too louche.

At her mirror Florence swivelled her head around.

'You're not allowed in here,' she said. 'You should have called out before you just walked in, this area is for performers only.'

Oscar dipped his head. 'My apologies. I am really not getting off on the right foot with you, am I, Geoffrey? Anyway, I'm Oscar Bishop, Natalie's son,' he said to Veronica and Orla, 'and Mum has sent me to ask if you'd all like to stay for a drink?'

Orla and Veronica declined, but Florence hesitated. She felt like she should stay, Natalie Bishop had been so kind to her, and she wanted to ask if she could come and plunder Avalon's gardens for clippings one day.

'I'll stay,' she said. 'I'd like to say hello to your mother.'

Florence said goodbye to Orla and Veronica and walked with Oscar towards the party, now in full, throaty swing.

A seven-piece covers band was playing and most of the guests were now shoeless and dancing.

Florence wished she could join them, take off her own shoes on the wooden dance floor and pretend the Milky Way was above it.

Were these people Albert's sort of usual suspects? She supposed they were. She supposed he and Jeremy and Lydia would feel right at home here, mimicking each other's dance moves and putting their arms up in the air, or whatever it was DJs were always exhorting people to do.

Florence smiled. She couldn't actually imagine Albert putting his arms up in the air at all – unless it was to pick a sticky berry from a mulberry branch.

'What sort of drink would you like?' Oscar asked. 'There's all the usual, and we have a Pimm's bar, and a mobile mixologist – whatever that means,' he laugh-shouted in her ear above the music. Oscar gestured to a bar with 'Cocktails' written in curling, pink neon letters above it, and a chalkboard of drinks beside it.

Florence considered the list – Long Island Iced Teas, Sidecars, Strawberry Daiquiris and Manhattans. She thought she might have a Long Island Iced Tea, because although she had no idea what was in it, it seemed to be exactly that sort of night where you could say to the bartender, 'A Long Island Iced Tea, please,' as if you were in West Egg instead of East Elm.

Oscar and Florence joined the small line at the bar, Oscar's hand on the lower part of Florence's back as if she was a ventriloquist's dummy, needing his touch to propel her forward. Natalie Bishop might be lovely, she thought, but Oscar Bishop wore his entitlement like a smoking jacket. He would not be on her list of things to say yes to. The line moved again, and Florence moved with it, stepping away from Oscar's touch, then she stopped as everything tilted alarmingly off centre.

The bartender was leaning across the bar, passing a tray of drinks to the woman in front of Florence, and smiling.

Florence knew that smile. She knew how it grew to settle into its corners. She knew how it would part to reveal a slightly chipped front tooth.

It was Albert.

Albert Flowers was behind the bar wearing a long black apron tied at his waist, scooping ice into a tray of glasses and laughing at something the woman was saying.

Florence was holding her breath between the familiarity and unfamiliarity of him. What was he doing here? What had he said at the library? He had so many parties to go to, he was exhausted just thinking about it. Was this one of them?

'Oscar, you complete fag,' a voice boomed behind her as a tumble of men descended on the line.

They circled around Oscar, bumping into his shoulders.

'Bishop, get us a drink from your mummy's bar.'

'Where have you been anyway? You left our table ages ago, you bastard.'

There were four of them, all tugging at Oscar, and then one of them let go of his shoulder and said: 'Wait, is that you, Bertie? Is that B-B-B-Bertie F-F-F-Flowers?'

'It is! It is you, B-B-B-Bertie,' the tallest of them spluttered, while the others grasped at each other's coat sleeves in laughter, one burying his head into Oscar's shirt.

'B-B-B-Bertie F-F-F-Flowers,' said one with braces tracking across his teeth, 'could I have a S-S-S-Sidecar, old mate?'

Oscar, she saw, was not laughing but flicking their arms away, a scowl settling on his face.

'Leave it,' he said, stepping away from them towards Albert.

'I'm sorry, mate,' he said, 'they're just really pissed, don't serve them if you don't want to.'

'Ooh I'm s-s-sorry too, B-B-B-Bertie,' said the man in the braces, 'will you f-f-f-forgive me?'

Florence took a step back, then turned and strode away as quickly as she could without breaking into a run – thank God she was wearing trousers.

She was not sure what was happening. She did not know why Albert was behind the bar or why Oscar Bishop's mates were stuttering at him. She had seen an arc of spittle spray from one man's lips as he laughed. She had seen Albert's face. She had seen his head lift as his name was spoken, then dip again as he heard the stammered words. She had watched him fold into himself, somehow getting smaller in his space behind the bar. Whatever was happening, she thought, she was absolutely not meant to see it.

Reaching the driveway, Florence did begin to run down it. She could not wait to get away from the place where she had seen Albert Flowers break.

He hadn't seen her, she was sure of it. Or if he had, he hadn't recognised her. There hadn't been enough time for Albert to find her face beneath her makeup. Florence slowed her pace as she neared the end of the driveway and saw a garden seat tucked beneath a spreading fig. She sat down, her breath sharp and quick from her sprint from Avalon, and put her hands to her face.

'You all right?'

A girl in a dress, long and silver and strappy, stepped out from behind one of the tall green lampposts that guarded Avalon's gates.

Florence started. Another bloody apparition out of the dark. Avalon was teeming with them.

The girl smiled. 'Sorry to scare you. I have to come all the way down here to smoke, otherwise my mother will have a conniption – perhaps two,' she laughed, sitting down beside Florence.

She was, Florence saw, more than a little tipsy, tilting her head back to rest against the top of the seat, closing her eyes and throwing an arm around Florence.

'Sadie Bishop,' she said.

Another one – all the Bishop children apparently bestowed with a genetic gift of materialising from thin air, this one looking like a slightly drunk, slightly demented angel.

'Do you want a smoke?' Sadie Bishop asked, sitting up and retrieving a packet from a small silvery clutch.

'No,' Florence shook her head.

'You're crying,' Sadie said.

Florence nodded, putting the back of her palm to a wet cheek, surprised. 'So I am. Bit of a rough night.'

'Me too,' Sadie sighed. 'All of Oscar's stupid friends groping at me.'

'I met Oscar,' Florence offered, 'and his stupid friends.'

Sadie leaned towards Florence, crinkling her nose. 'Do I know you?' she asked. 'Or are you staff?'

Florence smiled. Orla would expire with laughter.

'I'm a singer,' she answered. 'I just finished performing.'

Sadie nodded, lighting up. 'I'm a singer too,' she said, 'in the shower mostly,' and giggled, adding, 'You sure you don't want a cigarette?'

'No thank you, Sadie,' Florence answered, 'but you might be able to give me something else.'

'What's that?' Sadie's eyes narrowed. 'I don't do drugs, if that's what you're thinking . . . well I do, but only with people I know really, really well.'

'No,' Florence shook her head, 'information.'

Albert clearly had some connection with the Bishops – he had been at Simon Bishop's wedding and he was here again tonight, albeit behind a bar and wearing a ridiculous apron. Sadie Bishop might know why.

'I don't suppose you know Albert Flowers?' Florence asked.

Sadie clapped her hands together, the cigarette falling from one hand as she did. She pitched forward to retrieve it then righted herself next to Florence and said, 'B-B-B-Bertie, 'course I do.'

Florence prickled. No, this wasn't a prickle. It was a steadily rising anger. She had felt it build since Oscar Bishop's friends had pecked at Albert with their words. Now this stupid girl wearing a nightie for a dress was purposely stumbling around inside her sentences as well. Florence breathed through her nose and expelled the air slowly from her mouth, a relaxation exercise she had been taught by Lucas.

'Don't kill her, Florence,' she heard her father say close to her ear. 'Listen.'

Florence looked around. Was Lucas lurking in the bushes as well? Was her mother about to float down the driveway on a sea of gossamer fabric exclaiming, 'There you are, darling, I've been looking all over for you!'

'Just listen,' Lucas Saint Claire repeated in her ear, so Florence breathed some more through her nostrils, and did.

'Albert . . .' Sadie was saying, 'I don't know him too well, but my brothers do, well they did at school, well not him so much but his brother Hamish, you know, the one who died.'

Florence shook her head. No, she did not know. Albert had never mentioned a brother. He had certainly not mentioned a dead one.

'Hamish Flowers,' Sadie was saying dreamily. 'God, he was gorgeous, everyone was in love with him, even me, although I was so small, it was more like a crush . . . everyone had a crush on him, even my brothers.' She giggled and tossed her cigarette to the ground.

'No one had a crush on Albert,' Sadie pronounced solemnly. 'It was hard to believe they were related.'

'Why?' Florence prodded. 'Why was it hard to believe?'

Sadie Bishop laughed. 'You really didn't know them, did you? Because Hamish Flowers was spectacular, and Albert was like a . . . like a big old dugong with a stutter.' Sadie smiled, pleased with her description.

'But they were really close, I think,' Sadie continued. 'Mum said Albert had to leave school after Hamish died, and that his stutter got worse . . . poor old B-B-B-Bertie Flowers,' she finished, a hand through her hair.

Sadie stood up abruptly – she was, Florence saw, now bored with the story and with Florence's company. 'I better get back – nice to meet you, strange woman in a man's suit.'

She began to walk back up the path and Florence stood up hurriedly to catch her.

'Sadie,' she said, 'why is Albert here tonight? Why is he working here behind the bar?'

Sadie paused, her eyes narrowing. 'Why are you so interested? Do you like him? I don't blame you, he's much better looking now, isn't he? I tried to flirt with him at Simon's wedding, but no go,' she sighed.

Florence tried again. 'What was he doing at Simon's wedding?'

'Working,' Sadie answered. 'You know, at his bar business, like he is tonight – Albert Flowers, Mobile Mixologist.'

Sadie continued walking up the path, stumbling a little over her trailing hem.

'He does all the best parties,' she said over her silver shoulder. 'You should hire him sometime.'

Florence began to walk back down the driveway, leaving Avalon's gates just as fireworks sent their hot sparks above its roof lines – Albert Flowers, Mobile Mixologist, somewhere beneath them. Florence kept walking. She would walk all the way home, she thought, if she had to.

She would walk and think about Albert who was not who she thought, who kept this part of his life apart from her, who had a brother who had been spectacular and who had died.

Albert Flowers, who was not a part of East Elm's A-list, or perhaps any list at all. There was no band of usual suspects. There probably wasn't even a Jeremy or a Lydia. Good. She had hated them both, especially Lydia, even if she was fictional. Why would Albert make them up? Why would he make any of it up? The weekend parties, the tennis afternoons, the weddings, the house-warmings? Florence scrolled through all the social occasions Albert had told her about, as if she was flicking through a Rolodex. Lucas had one of those on the desk in his office, its name, he told her, a portmanteau of 'rolling' and 'index'. Probably full of women's names he had given blue feathers to, Florence thought, as the orange shimmer of a cab's lights came towards her.

The cab's light blinked closer; Florence struck out her arm and it slowed down.

'Where to, mate?' the cabbie said as she got in. Orla would spontaneously combust.

She was glad the driver was not a talker, telling her about new roadworks or complaining about the Premier. She didn't want to think about any of those things. She wanted to sit slumped in the back seat and stare at East Elm tucking itself in for the night, house lights switching off as the cab cruised past them, and digest what Sadie Bishop had told her.

Drawing up to the cottage, Florence was relieved to see Isolde's bedroom light out. Usually Florence changed out of her costumes after a gig, so she didn't have to explain to her sister why she was wearing a floor-length silver sequined gown to her horticultural class. But she had left her clothes at Veronica's, so if Isolde had been awake, she would have had to slip past her somehow in her tuxedo. Florence turned off the kitchen and outside lights and went up to her bedroom to change into her pyjamas and think about Albert Flowers's duplicity.

Florence stopped short on the stairs, her own Rolodex of fabrications flipping over its silver rings. Albert wasn't the only one keeping secrets. Florence opened her bedroom door and flung herself on the mattress, eyes on the ceiling. She had lied to Albert many times and in many ways, all of them boring. What did you do on the weekend, Florence? she heard him ask. Oh, you know, she answered, this and that. Pottered around. Spent time with Isolde and Puck. Visited Amanda. Went to the movies. Bought a bag of Valencia oranges. Florence grimaced. She had, she remembered, actually said that once. She, Florence, never said, 'Performed at the Kit Kat Club', 'Sang at a twenty-first', 'Got a bunch of limp flowers tossed to me on stage'; instead she pretended she was possibly the dullest woman to tread the earth, endlessly on her way to the grocery store.

Albert, on the other hand, always told her exactly where he was going and recounted the details to her. She remembered his description of Simon Bishop's wedding. What was the name of the girl? It was unusual, something Amanda and Lucas might name a child. Siobhan, that was it. Albert had called her dress 'decidedly frothy'. He had told her what the music was like, how pretty the small jetty over the lake was, what drinks were served – well, that made sense now, but had he ever specifically said that he had been a guest there?

Or anywhere? Florence stood up to change into her pyjamas, brush her teeth and begin the shedding of Miss Suki from her face. She stared in the bathroom mirror, toothpaste bubbling at the corners of her own lying mouth. Had Albert ever lied to her? Had he said: 'I went to the wedding as a guest of the bride and groom'? Or 'I went to Cat Morrison's book launch as her plus one'? Or 'I attended Charlotte Markson's funeral because I am a very close friend of the family'?

Florence stopped brushing. No, Albert would never lie about that, which meant there was a very good chance he hadn't lied about the other events either.

What exactly had he said about Simon Bishop's wedding? That he liked the bride and had an awkward conversation with the groom, whom he did not like at all, down by the jetty. Something about a conga line, and Simon being thrown into the ornamental lake? He could have done all that, she thought, from behind a bar, or on a break. Charlie Markson's funeral? No. Her wake. Albert hadn't gone to the funeral. What had he told her that day in the park when he had cried and she had sung Amanda's song of lament? Florence squinted in the mirror, trying to remember. Albert had told her all the ways Charlotte Markson could have been a contender. The water polo. The boy she liked. The way she brought joy with her when she entered a room. But those could have been someone else's words, recounted. A mother's words, perhaps, uttered to just about anybody to keep her daughter in the room. Albert had told her about giving Charlotte Markson's parents his van to drive away in from the wake when they could not stand upright a minute longer. Surely that showed how close he was to the Markson family? Who gave their van away to strangers? Albert Flowers would, she thought. Albert Flowers would hand over his keys without giving it a second thought, turning back to the wake to serve drinks to people whose mouths had turned to gravel. He was not at the funeral because drinks were not generally served at funerals. He had told her he had gone outside to get some air when he saw the Marksons holding each other up beneath a tree. He could easily have witnessed that on a break. Florence couldn't imagine they'd be knee deep at a bar shouting for daiquiris at a wake. Did they serve alcohol at wakes for children? Florence thought grimly that if there was one place where people might desperately need a drink, that would be it. Florence shook her head slightly, remembering Albert saying that he wasn't sure whether to hand the keys over to Greg Markson, worried that he may have had a drink. Had Albert served it?

Florence spat in the basin, returned the toothbrush to its holder, and turned off the bathroom light.

Getting into bed she saw Cat Morrison's face looming large on a book cover. She heard her own voice – 'Oh you know Ms Morrison, eminent American feminist, voice of a generation, woman who wears colourful hats?' she'd asked Albert. Florence sat up in her bed. What had Albert said?

'Well I'm going to the launch of her new book, *Candy*,' she heard him reply, so he hadn't answered her at all. Florence had been to a book launch at Savage Reader earlier that year, for Colin Jenkins, the ABC's resident garden expert's new book on succulents. Had there been drinks there? Of course there had. A table set aside with rows of glasses and bottles of red and white wine, a few champagne bottles too which had run out before

Colin had arrived. Florence smiled, she loved Colin Jenkins, he always looked like he had just emerged from some potting mix. *Focus, Florence*, she told herself, *get to the bottom of this particular garden*. Albert had spoken about that night as if he and Cat Morrison were old friends, but they could just as easily have been new ones. Either way, he hadn't lied.

Wriggling under the covers, Florence thought of all the times she, however, had opened her mouth to lie to Albert Flowers, and her family, and anyone else really who strayed onto her path.

Albert had just neglected to mention things; he was guilty only of the sin of omission, while she, Florence, was a walking fabrication.

The question was, why did either of them do it?

She knew, of course, why she did it. She had permanent stage fright. From life. From being a child star under everyone's stares. From freezing on national television. From thinking for years she had caused her father's death. From being Lucas and Amanda Saint Claire's daughter, and Isolde and Puck's sister, and all the negotiating that required. She was a mess, really; no wonder she hid within Miss Suki's satin folds. But Albert? Why did he keep his secrets so close to his great expanse of a chest? Why had he never mentioned his brother Hamish who had died and left Albert stuttering? And where had his stammer gone?

Florence put one forearm across her eyes in the dark, listening intently for Albert's voice.

'F-F-Florence, do you know where I put those acacia seed samples?'

'W-W-Watch out Florence, Monty's on a coffee mug rampage.'

Florence heard snatches of sentences from hundreds of conservations, and the occasional hesitation in his delivery. Albert Flowers had, she realised, every now and then stuttered out a sentence in her presence.

Not that it mattered. Florence couldn't care less if Albert stammered or not. Florence also couldn't care less, she realised, if he had lied to her or not. She was hardly a shining paean to truth. But she did care, very much, for Albert Flowers. She had begun caring from the moment he said, 'They asked me if I wanted Bertie,' that first morning in the Green Team's office.

And anyone who hurt him, like those buffoons in the penguin suits at Natalie Bishop's party, could f-f-f-fuck off.

Florence curled her toes beneath the covers, and settled in beneath them, resolved.

She was going to stop lying. She was going to retire Miss Suki from the footlights. And she was going to help Albert Flowers. But first she was going to sing Jazz Cat with her family. The Saint Claire Swingers had their first rehearsal tomorrow. Florence flicked off her light. Both she and Albert had things to face in the morning.

*

Albert walked through the melaleuca track, listening to his boots stamp on the leaf litter, and the odd set-to between birds, shrieking and pipping above. People had no idea, he thought, how dramatic birds were, always fighting and loving and drawing their battle lines. It was the morning after the Music Under the

Milky Way party, which had been, he grimaced, a mistake. An Albert Flowers–sized mistake. He should not have agreed to take the booking, he'd known it even as Natalie Bishop had said, 'I do hope you'll bring the mobile mixology bar, Albert, it was such a hit at Simon and Siobhan's wedding, and the boys will be happy to see you.'

He doubted very much if the Bishop boys, who were, of course, men with gradually retreating hairlines, would be happy to see him. But he liked Natalie, whom he had first met at the library when he overheard her asking Monty for books on natural pesticides and offered to help. Since then he'd been to Avalon a few times to work as a pair of extra hands in the garden, and it was Natalie who had suggested to her future daughter-in-law that she hire Albert for the wedding. He had also liked Siobhan Peters when he'd met her to discuss it at World's End one night after work, still in his Green Team uniform and his calves streaked with dirt after a short tumble down an embankment. They'd found each other easily – Albert guessing the girl at the bar in the pressed linen shirt and chunky gold fob chain was Simon Bishop's fiancée, and Siobhan recognising him from his description: 'I'll be in khaki, covered in dirt, and wearing a badge with my name on it.' Albert smiled, remembering their easy conversation and Siobhan's polite, feigned interest in his box weed problem.

So when Natalie Bishop had asked him to work at her gala, he'd found himself saying yes, even though he generally avoided gigs that felt too close to home – literally in this case. His parents' back fence met the lower edges of Avalon's grounds, where a small creek occasionally still ran. Georgina Flowers was forever patrolling the boundary with her watering can, in the hope of running into Natalie Bishop and striking up a lifelong friendship.

At the party he'd kept his head down, his hands busy pumping out Sidecars and Long Island Iced Teas, and his conversation limited to bar banter. A few women, including Sadie Bishop, had flirted with him, Sadie asking if he'd like to take a cigarette break with her at the bottom of the garden. Albert had said no but had offered her his coat because she looked freezing in some silvery slip of material, and Sadie had answered, 'No thanks, Dad,' and walked off, throwing a pout over her shoulder. He'd kept the line moving steadily and had been thinking about taking a quick break to see if he could find the moon flowers whose scent teased through the night air, when Oscar Bishop's friends had descended on the line like magpies.

Albert had automatically ducked his head, more out of habit than fear, but one of them had met Albert's eyes and the past had come nipping at his heels. The thing was, Albert thought, kicking a stone along the path, their words hadn't hurt him that deeply at all. Some sort of muscle memory had flinched at hearing them, but he hadn't been B-B-B-Bertie F-F-F-Flowers for a long time now, and school-ground taunts no longer filled him with the dry-mouthed horror they once had. When Oscar Bishop's mates had begun to peck at him, Albert had been filled not with any sense of humiliation but with a sharp and overwhelming urge to see his brother. To see Hamish step out from the line and say: 'Boys, you're embarrassing yourselves. Oscar, take your children back to the kindergarten, I think it's nap time.' But the sudden yearning to see his older brother materialise beside Natalie Bishop's immaculate flowerbeds had not been because he needed Hamish's protection – not now anyway – but because of how it would feel afterwards. What Albert missed was the after part. The walking off together, Hamish flinging his arm around Albert and doing imitations of his tormentors: 'Mark McIntosh has a dick the size of the rubber at the end of a pencil,' and the two of them laughing as they kicked a stone between them all the way home.

Albert looked down at the stone he was now kicking and pushed it off the path with his toe. Missing Hamish felt like someone had dropped a knee to his chest and was holding it there, seeing how much weight his heart could take before he folded into himself.

Hamish had not given a stuff about Albert's stutter, or his size. Hamish hadn't bothered about Albert's shyness, or his way of blurting out the first thing he thought of when he was trying to make friends, which was always the wrong thing. Once, when Georgina had pushed him out the door to 'make friends with those nice Shaw boys', he had wandered over to where they were shooting basketball hoops outside, stood silently on the edge of the game for what seemed like a very long time, then shouted – at least it had sounded like shouting in Albert's ears – 'I'm a vegetarian,' even though he wasn't.

The first doctor his parents took him to for his stutter wondered whether Albert's habit of saying the wrong thing was the source of the problem. Did it, Doctor Feldman mused to a big-eyed Georgina and fidgety Laurence Flowers, make him subconsciously trip over his own tongue in an act of self-sabotage? Albert and Hamish thought Doctor Feldman was full of shit, and thankfully so did the conga line of speech pathologists who came afterwards. Albert was thirteen when he began to stutter, an unusually late onset, everyone agreed. There had been no trigger, no internal warning system that he was going to have to start thinking about every word he said; he had just found himself stumbling over the first letter of butter when he'd asked Hamish to pass it to him over dinner one night. 'Could I have the b-b-b-butter please,' he had said, and he remembered being more interested than alarmed at the way his lips held the sound behind them, stubbornly refusing to let it go. Hamish had just slid the butter dish across the table and the moment had slid away with it, but the next day and the day after that more words began to trip Albert up.

He grew watchful, doling out his words carefully while his parents listened so intently to everything he said that he found it was easier not to say anything around them at all. The speech therapists and pathologists and hypnotherapists – except for Doctor Feldman – all assured his parents that their son's stutter was not psychosomatic. It was not the result of some terrible psychological trauma or an attention-seeking device, it was more likely genetic, they said, causing Georgina and Laurence Flowers to look sideways at each other. Albert didn't know why he started stuttering, but he knew that it was worse at school, better when he sang, and non-existent when it was just him and Hamish building paper planes in Albert's bedroom. They gave the plane designs names like 'The Wasp' and 'The Stinger', but their favourite was 'The Comanche Dragon', which Hamish said was quick and elegant and always landed where it was meant to.

When Albert was with Hamish, making their planes loop and dive in Albert's room, his words flowed like water over river stones. At school he increasingly fell over them, like someone had set out a trip wire, and Hamish began to walk him to his locker. It wasn't the stutter itself that bothered Albert, but that he had spent most of his thirteen years on earth being embarrassed by the utter uselessness of his size, his lumbering body proving no good at any sort of football or basketball or any of the sorts of things it might have come in handy for, and in the end it had not been his body that would betray him, but something as small as his voice. It had pissed him off in the way that only a thirteen-year-old boy can be pissed off, full of anger that rose up through his fists, which he wrapped in towels so his parents wouldn't hear him driving them into walls. That, however, was nothing compared to the molten rage that was to take hold when Albert was seventeen and Hamish got sick.

Albert felt the forest cooling around him, the slight drop in temperature, and he kept walking, remembering when missing Hamish first really began, when it moved from what Albert thought of as a temporary state into a permanent one.

'You cannot talk to the parentals about this because they, my brother, are currently floating down a river in Egypt,' Hamish had said from his bed, a poster of Farrah Fawcett in a red swimsuit taped to the ceiling, Farrah smiling down at his brother in a tumble of hair, teeth and erect nipples.

Albert had screwed his face up at the old joke between them.

'De Nile?' he had asked.

Hamish had grinned.

'That's the one. They are going to tell you and Addie that I'm going to get better, but I'm not. The oncologist has been straight with me, if not with them, though I can't imagine why. Come here, mate.' His brother patted the smooth part of the bed beside him and Albert sat on it, leaning into Hamish's knees.

'I'm dying, Albert,' Hamish said. 'It might be a year, it might be six months, or it might be six weeks, but it won't be any longer than that, so you and I have to sort some stuff out, all right?'

Albert nodded.

'First off, I'm scared as fuck. Don't tell the parentals that either, but I am and the only time I'm not scared as fuck is when I'm with you and we talk about shit like we always have, and we make The Wasp and The Stinger and The Comanche Dragon like we always have, or we play poker or listen to music, and you get all the words wrong . . .'

Hamish laughed, running a hand over his skull, tufts of hair like tumbleweeds sprouting from it.

'Everyone else can barely fucking look at me, Albert. The blokes from school come and they look at the floor, and girls I like come and look everywhere but in my eyes, and Mum and Dad and Addie look away when it's too hard, but you look at me all the time, Albert, in exactly the same way you always have. Do you see what I'm saying?'

Albert shook his head. He had no idea.

'I'm saying thank you, and I'm saying stop thinking that you're shit, Albert. So what if you're a bit bigger than other guys your age? So what if you can't kick a ball, so what if you're a bit shy, so fucking what if you stammer out your words here and there?'

Hamish took Albert's hand and put it on his chest – it was like covering it with an enormous saucer, Hamish's ribs like sparrow's bones.

'You're the only one who still looks at me like I'm bearable, Albert, and the only time I'm not scared shitless is when you are in the room with me, so what does that say about you? What does that say about you, little brother?'

Albert shook his head again, as Hamish covered Albert's hand on his chest with his own and pressed it.

'It says you are the best, Albert. The best of the best. You are The Wasp, you are The Stinger, you are The Comanche Fucking Dragon. You are quick and elegant, and I promise you will land exactly where you are meant to – now fuck off and let me go to sleep.'

When Hamish died a little after his twenty-first birthday – a limp celebration held in his hospital room where the nurses had hung balloons and a banner that said *Happy Birthday, Hot Stuff!* – Albert walked the same bark-strewn path he was walking now.

It was the afternoon after Hamish's funeral, which hundreds of people had attended, spilling out of the church onto the grass and listening to the service through outside speakers. There were past and present students and teachers from Hamish's primary and high schools, members of his football and cricket teams and swimming and rowing squads, university friends and lecturers, people Hamish had worked in part-time jobs with, and girls – so many girls who had caught his eye or shared his bed or wished that they had. There was, it seemed to Albert and Addie, battalions of relatives they had never met before, and people peppered throughout the pews that nobody knew at all. Hamish had collected them all somewhere along the way. Hamish was the Pied Piper of East Elm, no shortage of people wanting to join his merry, doomed dance. At the wake, a horrendous affair in the church hall where the sun streamed in through the windows and everybody clung on to the idea that it was a sign from Hamish, Albert stayed long enough to be seen to have stayed, then he walked out the back door and kept walking. The Our Lady of the Bower church grounds met a little-used southern section of the Mount Bell State Forest that led to a short cut to the melaleuca track. The path dipped, then climbed steeply until it reached an escarpment overlooking the gorilla-shaped mountain locals called King Kong, the ape's sleepy granite eyes half-closed and granite fists curled and tucked by its side.

Albert stepped forward to the edge of a small rocky outcrop and reached into the backpack he had brought with him, his mother asking why he had that disgusting old bag in the church. First The Wasp, which wobbled a little before catching a slight upwind and dancing briefly across the valley on it; then The Stinger, which dived immediately and sharply downwards, hitting a bush not too far from its launching pad: and lastly The Comanche Dragon.

Albert took his time, smoothing the plane's edges and its tail, waiting until the breeze lifted, then he drew back his arm, opened his hand and let its paper wings take flight.

Albert was heading to the same escarpment now, to swing his legs over the outcrop, scan the valley below and wonder where his brother's plane had landed under King Kong's sleepy eyes.

After the funeral and the wailing that went on under the Flowers' roof for weeks, Albert missed days, then weeks of school, the last term slipping by without Albert in it. When Farrow's class of 1987 graduated, his was missing from the shower of hats tossed to the air. Instead he stayed in his room, or scanned the shelves in the library's botany section, or took himself into the woods, his world growing smaller and quieter.

His stutter was more pronounced after Hamish died, but not, Albert thought now, because Hamish had died, but because he had stopped practising the words and sounds designed to unlock his teeth, lips and tongue. He had found it increasingly difficult to speak to people he didn't know well. The worst ones were the people who jumped in to supply the word for him, as if he didn't know it, or they couldn't stand the suspense for a second longer. 'I'll just get my b-b-b-b,' he would say, and inevitably some kindly woman with lipstick on her teeth would say, 'Book? Bag . . . Bike!' Albert wanted to tell them all to b-b-b-b-bugger off.

He began to spend more time in the Mount Bell forest, taking the less popular trails where there was very little chance of having to make small talk, and where, despite all the evidence to the contrary, his brother could still be found. Months later, Hamish Flowers would turn up at home, lazily talking to Albert from his bed, or appearing in the television room, smiling from the couch. But for the first few weeks after Hamish died, the forest was the only place Albert could hear his brother in his ear saying: 'Don't worry about Stinky Bates, a girl I know kissed him and said he had an old wad of chewing gum in his mouth.' Albert remembered Steven 'Stinky' Bates at Hamish's funeral sitting in one of the pews and chewing gum, his jaw constantly moving throughout the service. Albert wondered if it was the same piece.

That Albert did not graduate from Farrow did not bother him at all. He remembered watching his classmates whirl past the windows of Bougainvillea Gardens the night of the school formal; he'd slouched down in his car seat and spun his tyres as he'd driven away. *So much fury inside of me then*, Albert thought. Nothing of it left now, sitting down at the outcrop's ledge, in the shadow of the mighty Kong. He had first begun studying horticulture through a correspondence course, following Georgina Flowers's insistence that he 'do something'. He was driving her mad at home, his broad frame getting in the way of all that wailing. Surprisingly, it had been Laurence who had brought home the brochure, tossing it on Albert's desk and saying, 'Might be worth a look.' It had been worth so much more than that.

Albert's love of plants deepened, and his rambles took him further and further afield from Mount Bell's trails and brought him small, emerald green and muddy brown slices of peace.

Hamish had left him some money, which Albert hadn't touched and had thought he quite possibly never would. But when Marcia Mittford, a girl he knew vaguely through Addie, told him she was leaving East Elm and had to sell her mobile cocktail business, he bought it. He purchased every last piece of it: the van, the bar, the alcohol, the shakers, the stirrers, the plastic blue mermaids and the tiny paper umbrellas. He was nineteen and he had no idea what he was doing, but Marcia's price for her business was the exact amount Hamish had left him. He took this as a sign from Hamish at a time when he still spent his days searching for scraps of his brother.

His journey from Albert Flowers, bedroom hermit and roaming woodsman, to Albert Flowers, Mobile Mixologist, was surprisingly smooth. He spent an afternoon with Marcia taking him through the cocktail list, learning how to make the perfect martini, slicing maraschino cherries and salting tequila glasses, then falling into bed with her afterwards, Marcia bestowing him with the great gift of finally ridding him of his own maraschino cherry.

After that, everything became easier, like someone had expelled a little air from his tyres.

'This gig is made for you, Albert Flowers,' Marcia told him from between the sheets during that long afternoon. 'All you have to say if you don't feel like chatting is "What can I get you?" or "Shaken or stirred?" or "No, I don't want to come home with you," and I can promise you that you'll get a few offers.'

Marcia bartended his first two events with him before she left, and Albert found she was right. Most people were happy just to get their drinks and go back to the party. But at his first solo gig and the next few after that, Albert found his hands busy and his lips loosening. When he ducked behind the bar, when his fingers found their way to his lower back to tie his apron, when he was Albert Flowers, Mobile Mixologist, his mouth, he found, unlocked.

Albert progressed from 'What can I get you?' to 'How do you know the bride and groom?' and 'I'd recommend a Manhattan, if you want something a bit sharper' to finding himself in loops of conversations with the lovelorn, the disenchanted and the really, really pissed. He was two people: Albert Flowers, stutterer, loner, brother of the dead guy; and Albert Flowers, Mobile Mixologist, teller of stories, 'the secret ingredient', a client wrote in a recommendation, 'to every successful party'.

Did it matter that he wasn't invited to any of them? Not really, Albert thought. He wasn't hurting anybody; genuinely having places to go had got his parents off his back, and having constant conversations with people at social events kept his lips well oiled for talking to Florence.

He kept his business even as he became a full-time member of the Green Team. The two jobs never intersected, and Albert found he could shed the uniform for one easily before putting on the other. When Florence joined the Green Team, with her name badge that said *Flo*, Albert sensed a small leap inside of him, some sort of quickening and, although he could not be certain, his brother was in his ear saying, 'Here we go!' The first few times he spoke to Florence and she asked what he'd done over the weekend, he had panicked. He should have said, 'I've got a little bar business I work at most weekends.' He should have said, 'I'm serving pitchers of Pimm's at a woman's fortieth birthday party,' or 'I'm working at a twenty-first on a boat on a river, and I'm afraid I won't be able to get off,' but instead he implied he was front and centre at all those events – often with his made-up friends Jeremy and Lydia.

But while he had conjured up his 'usual suspects' – and what a terrible phrase that was; it had fallen from his lips before he could catch it – they were in fact real people. Jeremy was a friend of Hamish's from his first-year engineering course, and Lydia, an arts student, was the girl Albert was sure Hamish would have one day brought home to meet the family. She would get out of Hamish's car with her long, loose limbs and raise a hand in greeting, a satchel slung across her shoulder, and they would all fall in love with her. Because she was Hamish's girl, which of course made her *the* girl. Lydia Woolcock, Hamish had once told him, had hair the colour of butter.

He could not remember when he introduced Jeremy and Lydia into the stories he spun to Florence, but she seemed to like to hear about them, especially Lydia. By the time Albert realised that Florence would not care less if he had a social life or not – her own appeared to be sparing and largely centred around her family – it was too late. Albert was caught in his own lie. What would Florence think of him, he wondered as the sunset's first colours began to bruise the sky, if he told her the truth? Not much. Florence could be prickly, and this would certainly make her prickle. Everything about Florence was straightforward, from the way she wore her hair pulled back, with her middle part running through it like a train line, to the way she strode through the forest in front of him, her face bare beneath its hat. There was no dissembling with her, no shady areas at all.

Albert stood up, bowed his head slightly to Kong, and turned back on the path. He was fortunate that Florence's own lack of social life meant their paths never crossed. There was very little chance of running into her at any of the parties he worked at. Or anyone else he knew. He did encounter former Farrow boys from time to time, mostly drunk, mostly friendly and mostly having trouble placing him. They would peer at him from across the bar, and Albert would watch their faces pucker in concentration. 'Where do I know you from, mate?' Sometimes Albert told them, other times he let them work it out for themselves, but mostly they did not remember him at all. If they did, they remembered Hamish in the very next breath. 'Oh, you're Hamish Flowers's brother . . .' and their faces would pucker again, this time in memory and sadness. They would mumble something inaudible, and once a Farrow boy from Hamish's year had shoved a crumpled wad of bills into his hand. They rarely mocked though. Oscar Bishop's troop of clowns had been an anomaly.

Albert walked a little faster. He had lingered longer in the forest than he realised, the trees darkening as if, Florence would say, someone had turned down the dimmer switch. He didn't mind the forest at night, but he did mind the insects that flew at him when the switch dimmed, so he made his way back to his car at the park's entrance. The gala hadn't been so bad, apart from missing Hamish. He could handle any rambunctious Farrow boy these days – he was just glad that his parents or Addie or Florence had not been there to witness it. But if Florence had been there, he thought, she certainly would have noticed the Milky Way was missing.

11

'One, two, three, four.'

Amanda was counting in the beat, and Puck hit the snare drum, the session musicians moving into position.

'*On Christmas Eve when the lights are low . . .*' Amanda had her hand curled around the microphone as if it was welded there, Isolde and Florence bookending her on either side.

Florence smiled across Amanda to Isolde, twitching her body about the stage.

Amanda stopped. 'Isolde,' she warned. Isolde stopped. It was like watching jelly settling onto its plate.

'What?'

'Darling, we are performing "Santa Was A Jazz Cat", not "Santa Was Caught In A Sudden Downpour".'

The musicians behind Amanda sniggered, and Florence prickled. People always sniggered at Isolde, they had done so her whole life. On Isolde's first day of school she had worn a messy, homemade crown of flowers on her head, and neither Lucas nor Amanda had stopped her. When Florence had protested, Lucas had said, 'Oh let her be, honey bee,' and Florence had wanted to scream. It was up to her, walking Isolde up the crumbly, concrete path that led to her little sister's new classroom, to duck behind the school library and gently lift the crown of daisies and gold foil milk-bottle tops from Isolde's head. 'But why, Florrie?' Isolde had asked with her big, dark eyes, and Florence had answered that crowns weren't allowed at school. What she wanted to tell her was that people like them weren't allowed at school. People who didn't understand the signals. People who 'brought attention to themselves', as a teacher had once said to Florence, even if they didn't mean to do it. Particularly if they didn't mean to do it.

Florence had a two-year head start on Isolde in the playground, and she didn't want her little sister to stumble at the first fence. So it was off with the crown, stuffed into Florence's backpack. Not that it made a whit of difference. Isolde, like Florence before her, and Puck to follow, had her own strong scent of otherness curling around her that first day, and all the days that followed. Florence had waited outside Isolde's classroom, watching as other little girls streamed out in patterns already knitted together. Florence waited until all the children had been expelled out the classroom doors, except Isolde. The teacher, Miss Harris, who wore long, batik skirts and smelt of sandalwood, had come out and said, 'Florence, how lovely to see you. Isolde is still inside, come in.' Miss Harris, Florence thought now, had a distinct whiff of the other about her too.

Isolde was sitting at her desk, colouring in, and when she saw Florence the first thing she said was, 'Can I have my crown back now?' and Florence knew she had been wrong to take it. Isolde had been completely at home in her body since she first found herself in it, just as she was now, flicking around the stage, limbs pulled by unseen hands.

'Oh let her be, honey bee,' Florence said to her mother, who, she saw, remembered the echo of Lucas's first-day words.

'You're right,' Amanda said. 'I'm sorry, Isolde. Please continue dancing as if nobody is watching.' She smiled at her second daughter, then gestured to the musicians. 'All right, everybody, from the top, one, two, three, four.'

It was the first day of a three-day rehearsal set aside for the Saint Claire Swingers' New Year's Eve appearance on Hello 2000! It had played out exactly as Richard had said it would: a string of apologetic phone calls from a nervy Kip, an extremely good bottle of whiskey for Richard and a huge bunch of flowers for Amanda. Kip had delivered the bouquet personally, standing on Kinsey's front porch, his head and torso half hidden by the sheaf he was carrying. Amanda had opened the door, said, 'Kip, what a lovely surprise, do come in,' and by the time he'd left, the Saint Claire Swingers were back on the bill at a considerably higher fee, and Kip looked like a crumpled suit left in a laundry bag.

Now, Florence saw, Kip was shadowing Richard, listening intently to everything the older man had to say, Kip's hand curled thoughtfully around his chin. She almost felt sorry for him, but he was wearing too-tight leather trousers with a silver chain looping from one pocket to his hip, so really, she thought, he could only blame himself for any misfortune.

Amanda started again. '*On Christmas Eve when the lights are low . . .*' and the Saint Claire Swingers, like old friends meeting in the street, began to swing.

Later, when they would stroll out onto the Domain's stage, first Puck, then Isolde, then Florence, and lastly Amanda throwing her arms out wide and smiling, 'Well, Hello 2000!' the crowd's collective roar would fill Florence's ears, and sweet waves of nostalgia would roll towards her, but it would feel nothing like this.

From the moment she opened her mouth to join Amanda and Isolde in the chorus, Puck's driving beat behind them, she felt herself return to the rhythm of her family. The four remaining members of the Saint Claire Swingers – five if you counted the one Florence spied in the wings – found their way easily to exactly where they belonged in the song.

When they finished, the crew applauded and Richard nodded at Kip.

'There's your moment mate,' he said, grinning.

*

Afterwards, back at Kinsey, they opened a bottle of champagne and sipped some of Kip's excellent whiskey, which Richard poured into tumblers.

'Thank you, my dears,' he said, raising his glass. 'You've made an old man very, very rich.'

Florence lifted her tumbler. 'To the Saint Claire Swingers.'

'And Richard,' Amanda smiled.

'And Kip,' Isolde said.

'And his trousers,' Puck added.

'And Lucas,' Richard said.

'And Lucas,' they all repeated.

Florence took a deep gulp of her whiskey, feeling the burn at her throat. It was time, she thought, for her own moment.

'I really enjoyed today, singing with you all again,' she began. 'You might have thought I'd be a bit rusty vocally because I haven't sung for a while, but that's not entirely true.'

She paused.

'It's not true at all. I've been singing quite a bit in a group with two other girls, Orla and Veronica – Orla is British and Veronica looks like Jessica Rabbit . . .' Florence felt herself teetering off the path and took another deep drink until only the tinkling ice cubes remained. 'We do cabaret shows, mostly old standards and then some contemporary ones with our own arrangements. Anyway, I probably should have told you from the beginning, but I really wasn't sure if I was going to stick at it . . .'

Isolde stood up and put out her hand to Florence. 'Would you like me to refresh your glass, Miss Suki?' she asked.

Florence felt everything tip off centre again.

'What did you say, Isolde?' she asked.

'I said,' Isolde drew out the words slowly, 'would you like another whiskey, Miss Suki?'

Florence looked at her family. They were all laughing, Richard giggling from behind a hand, and Amanda's shoulders shaking. Everybody knew.

'Mum?' Florence tried.

'Yes, Miss Suki?' Amanda spluttered, then let out her laughter in a joyous rush.

'You knew?'

'Of course, I knew, darling, we all did,' Amanda answered. 'And I must say, although Isolde would disagree, that I absolutely love Miss Suki. I find her fascinating, all that deathly makeup and antagonism, she's like an angry corpse.'

Florence was caught between the dawning knowledge that not only did her family know of Miss Suki's existence, but they had also seen her perform.

'Isolde?' she said.

'I'm not in love with Miss Suki,' Isolde answered. 'Too studied. Too much like hard work. Too much slap covering her face. I like the Nightshades though, particularly the one who looks like she could eat you alive.'

Florence smiled. 'That's Veronica.'

'I like the other one,' Puck said, 'the one with the posh accent.'

'Orla,' Florence said automatically, 'and she's not posh, she's got a mouth like a London sewer rat.'

Florence stared at her family. 'How many times,' she asked, 'have you seen me? Mum?'

Florence could understand how she might miss Isolde or Puck in an audience, how they could slip in to a back table between sets and slip back out again, if the bar was dark enough, and the bars the Nightshades played usually were. But Amanda?

Amanda Saint Claire couldn't go to the laundromat without making an entrance. Sometimes people started spontaneously clapping when she walked into a room, and then looked surprised at themselves when they did.

'Oh three or four, darling. Richard usually takes me. You're very good, all of you, but I don't agree with Puck about the posh one, I find her very pitchy.'

'How is it at all possible that I have never seen you in the audience, Mum?' Florence said. 'You're not generally known for blending in.'

Amanda shrugged. 'I just go as myself, darling. I take all my makeup off, pop on a shirt and some jeans, and leave Lamanda, as you children so rudely call her, at home. People don't recognise me without all the . . . fuss.'

Amanda smiled at her daughter. 'Of course, it helps that no one's seen my bare face since 1972.'

Florence laughed. Amanda's method of concealment had been to take all her layers off, whereas hers had been to trowel them on.

'How did you find out?' she asked Isolde, for surely it would have been Isolde.

'Followed you,' Isolde said, stretching, 'didn't believe that hydroponics course guff – not even you would study something that boring.'

'You followed me?' Florence asked, letting the comment about hydroponics – which she did intend to study one day – go, in favour of imagining her sister shadowing her out of the house.

'I had an inkling you were up to something,' Isolde said, 'always scurrying up the stairs carrying bags you wouldn't let me look at and taking the phone into another room and not letting me listen.'

Isolde walked over to Florence and put her hands on her older sister's cheeks.

'I was worried about you, Florence, we'd never had any secrets between us, well, apart from the one about you killing Dad.'

'Isolde!' Amanda flung her daughter's name across the room. 'Would you stop saying that!'

'Sorry,' Isolde said, 'but I was worried, Florence. I was afraid you had taken an unsuitable lover, someone who was married or voted for the National Party, and you didn't want to tell us. So one night when you said you were going to your course, I waited until you were in your car and then Victor and I followed you in his.'

'Victor! Victor knows?'

'Oh, everybody knows, Florence.' Amanda shrugged. 'And although I cannot for the life of me understand why you would want to hide all that talent under a bushel, it is your business, not ours. Personally, I don't understand why anyone in this family does anything, but I have found it is best to let you all just get on with it.'

'When you say everybody,' Florence asked, 'do you think the people at my work know?'

Amanda shrugged and Florence saw Monty Rollins twinkling at her from beside the shelves: 'We don't mind a dollop of cabaret either . . . ' Monty knew, she was sure of it. Had he told anyone in the Green Team? Had he told Albert?

Florence thought of all those walks with Albert where he filled her in on his social life with the now almost certainly fictitious Jeremy and Lydia, and she regaled him with raucous stories of her weekends spent trimming Victor's sweet peas, both she and Albert talking through their lying, rotten teeth. She concentrated on remembering Albert's responses to her tales from behind Victor's picket fence. There had never been, she was sure, a flicker of disbelief across his face. She had never seen a slightly twisted mouth, a lifted eyebrow, or heard an 'Oh, really?' And she was certain that if Albert Flowers had come to a Nightshades gig, she would have noticed him, no matter how quietly he slipped in or what he was wearing. *I would know Albert in a grizzly bear suit*, she thought. No, she was sure Albert had not seen her alter ego, but she had seen his. It had been more shocking than it really should be. Plenty of people liked to keep their work and personal life separate. But plenty of people weren't hiding a dead brother, a one-time stammer, and life so lonely they filled it with make-believe friends.

That Albert Flowers was achingly lonely had come to Florence along Sadie Bishop's words, delivered from across her shoulder.

'He does all the best parties,' Sadie had said. 'You should hire him.'

Bugger Sadie Bishop, Florence thought, *I hope she caught pneumonia in that nightgown*.

Florence pulled herself back from Avalon to her family, and Richard who was holding out the whiskey bottle to her.

'Another wee dram, Miss Suki?' he asked, and Florence wondered how long she would have to endure them all using her stage name. Isolde, she knew, would be relentless.

'No thank you, Richard,' she said. 'I'm going to head home. Do you want a lift, Isolde?'

'Yes please, Miss Suki,' her sister answered.

*

'What ho, Albert!' Florence said when she walked into the library on Monday morning. She was overegging it, she knew. She had never uttered the words 'what ho' to anybody in her entire life. She was not sure anyone ever had. Bertie Wooster notwithstanding. But she was nervous, skittishly nervous that Albert may have glimpsed her at Avalon, and the words that fell from her mouth were a clumsy attempt to mask her concern with enthusiasm. Somewhere on her walk to work she had decided that her best line of defence was jauntiness. She would look like a woman without a care in her world, and not at all like one who had witnessed a car crash in a drinks line. When she saw Albert, she would not wear a question mark on her face, she would, instead, wear an exclamation mark – and she supposed that was where the 'what ho' had sprung from. If Albert had his own question mark, if he was wondering if she had been the woman who had dashed from the line like Cinderella bolting at midnight – stupid girl, ramming her feet into a pair of glass shards for some sappy prince who let his parents tell him who to marry – then Florence would remove all traces of doubt with, among other things, maximum wattage. She opened her mouth and exposed the whole horseshoe.

'Are you all right?' Albert asked. 'You seen unusually . . . happy, Florence,' and she knew in that moment that he had not seen her.

'Fine,' she answered. 'Lovely morning,' and then pushed her luck by adding, 'How was your weekend?'

'All right, I did a bit of gardening and I went to a party at the Bishops' house, Avalon, you know the old Sisters of Mercy convent on the hill? They say the ghost of Sister Patricia still nicks biscuits from the kitchen.'

So this was how he did it, Florence thought. This was how easily he covered his tracks. She was right. Albert never actually lied to her. Instead, he used details – the convent was haunted, the bride's dress was frothy, the lake was ornamental, the author's hat was problematic – as distractions, so that the listener didn't notice what was missing.

He was, she conceded, rather good at it.

Albert was kneeling in front of the Christmas tree, gluing rings of a silver paper chain that had come apart. 'It's a bit fiddly,' he grinned at her. There was something in his kneeling, the paper chain like a dainty silver necklace in his big, flat hands, that Florence found difficult to watch. She felt her eyes blink with the particular sharpness of unexpected tears.

'I know Avalon,' she answered, 'but I've not been there myself. Mum and Dad used to go, when the Elliots had it. Mum said Rosalind Elliot kept a donkey there until the council made her get rid of it.' She could do it too. Cover her tracks. Throw in some decoy details.

'Carry on,' she said brightly, tapping him lightly on the shoulder. Then she walked past Albert towards the Green Team's office and put her hands to her eyes. It was all, she thought, a bit fiddly.

12

'Isolde?'

'Yes, Miss Suki?'

Florence frowned. Isolde's use of her stage name had continued unabated since the first Hello 2000! rehearsal, and Isolde showed no signs of flagging. They were home from the last rehearsal, lying on opposite couches, Isolde's legs flung over the end of hers, one arm trailing the floor.

'I need your advice.'

'Really?' Isolde sprang from her supine position, her eyes on Florence. 'Really?' she repeated. 'No one ever asks me for advice. You've never asked me for advice.'

It was true. Issy lived her life haphazardly, as if she had just wandered into its frame. She seemed wholly unqualified to navigate it for herself, and even less so for others. There was no forward planning with Isolde, but there was a certain crisp decisiveness. Where other people vacillated, Isolde dived in; where Florence saw everything in palettes of colour, Isolde's gaze was monochromatic. 'What's the big deal?' she'd shrug. Black or white. Yes or no. Stay or go. Throw Albert Flowers a party, or not.

Christmas activities had taken over both the library's and the Green Team's offices. Florence and Albert had not spent many hours in the Mount Bell forest at all, and when they had, it was not together. Most of Florence's shifts had been alone, while Albert had been paired with a new recruit, a loose-limbed teenager called Gabriel who had made a fuss about wearing the uniform with his name on it. When Albert and Florence did meet, things were exactly as they always had been between them, which was to say their lies continued to fall so lightly from their lips, they barely felt them when they hit.

Outside of work, Florence had spent hours dissecting conversations she'd had with Albert, parsing sentences for clues into his existence. She would wake from dreamy nights to sit up in bed, slide open the drawer of her bedside table, and jot down the name of someone she remembered Albert telling her about.

Eighteenth birthday party, Megan Stewart. Party on boat at Mariner's Harbour, Joseph and Jenny Jackson. Engagement party, the Coxes – son or daughter? Forty-year wedding anniversary, Mr and Mrs Davenport. Wedding, Simon and Siobhan Bishop, and the most recent entry, *Book Launch, Cat Morrison.*

When she looked at the list, Florence felt like an intruder, scribbling stranger's names down who were oblivious to her scrutiny. She felt like she was somehow spying on them. But Albert had mentioned he held Megan Stewart's hair while she vomited into a pot plant, helped Mrs Davenport keep Mr Davenport relatively sober at their party by pouring him watered-down drinks when he began to wobble – a glaring clue she had missed – and given Cat Morrison her choice in headwear back.

Surely at least some of them would like the chance to show him they had appreciated it?

What she wanted Isolde to tell her was whether she should ask some of these people – not all of them, just those Albert appeared to have established a connection with; the Davenports, for example, had sent him a postcard from their holiday in Greece – to a small party for Albert. It was either a wonderful idea or a terrible one, and she needed Isolde to tell her which.

Isolde's eyes widened and narrowed as she listened, and when Florence had finished, Isolde leaned back on her elbows.

'So, what you are telling me is that Albert has no friends and has created an entire other universe to make up for it, and also has an entirely different persona?'

Florence nodded – it sounded far stranger when Isolde said it.

'So, he's basically you,' Isolde said.

'What?'

'You're the same person. You both have very few friends to speak of, other identities that you actually have costumes for, and you both skulk around between two different lives.' Isolde lay back down again on the couch, stretching her arms behind her. 'And people think I'm the weird one in the family.'

Florence laughed. 'So is holding a party for him a wonderful idea or a terrible one?'

Isolde briefly considered.

'It's wonderful,' she said, 'but you'll have to be really careful about the wording on the invitation. Don't say, *Please come to a party for Albert Flowers because he has no mates, and a dead brother who everyone liked more than him*, you know?'

Florence knew.

'And maybe don't mention the stutter thing.'

Florence nodded. She hadn't planned on mentioning the lack of friends. Or the stutter. Or the dead brother.

'I'm just not sure who to invite, or how to get in contact with some of them,' she said.

'Didn't you say he had a sister?'

'Yes, Adelaide, her book club should be meeting at the library sometime this week.'

'Well there you are,' Isolde said. 'Ask her.'

'Really?' Florence asked.

'Really,' Isolde answered.

'Why do you think she'll know?' Florence asked.

Isolde sat up again.

'Because sisters know everything, Miss Suki,' she smiled.

*

Adelaide Flowers was sitting on one of the benches outside the library, encased in a pall of grey smoke and glowering at library patrons who were glowering at her as they passed.

Smoking wasn't permitted in the library grounds, but Addie Flowers either didn't know or didn't care. She was a study in insouciance, puffing away.

Florence watched her from the window, Monty appearing at her side making audible 'tsk, tsk' noises.

'Do you know who that young lady is?' he asked Florence.

'Albert's sister,' she answered.

'Yes, Adelaide Flowers, and if he was here himself, I'd ask him to do it, but as he is not, I'm going to go out there and tell her to butt out.'

Florence saw that Monty was raring to do so, his nostrils flaring a little at the prospect of enforcing a library rule.

'I'll do it,' Florence jumped in. 'I was just leaving, I'll tell her on the way out.'

Monty nodded, nostrils deflated.

'If you're sure, Florence,' he said, and Florence nodded, not sure at all.

Florence grabbed her bag and headed to the library's door, which slid open automatically, letting in a blanket of heat.

Christmas Day was going to be a scorcher, she thought as she headed towards Adelaide Flowers, who looked up from the book that sat in her lap.

'I know, I know, I'm putting it out,' she said, dropping the cigarette to the ground, and grinding her heel on it.

'Thank you,' Florence said, 'the head librarian was going to come out and give you a talking to, but I said I'd do it, and save you the wagging finger – I'm Florence Saint Claire,' she said, putting out her hand. 'We have met before, briefly, you thought I was a librarian? I'm not, but I work with the Green Team, and I'm a friend of your brother, Albert's.'

Adelaide Flowers gave a small laugh.

'Albert doesn't have any friends,' she said, and Florence prickled. What was it with these girls? First Sadie Bishop and now Albert's own sister, blithely puffing away and dispensing casual personal information like they were handing out peppermints.

'Actually, that's not true,' Florence countered. 'He's got me.'

Adelaide took Florence's outstretched hand.

'Pull up a pew,' she said.

Florence sat down. At first, she trod carefully, sketching out the bare details of what she knew of Albert's life and why she thought it might be fun – *Don't say lark*, she told herself – to ask people to raise a glass to Albert, but Adelaide Flowers surprised her.

She listened to Florence carefully, and then filled in the gaps herself.

Addie Flowers thought of her family in two time periods: when Hamish was there, and when he wasn't. When Hamish was there, she told Florence, the Flowers had been happy in the way most families were happy, which was happy enough. It was not what it became in the retelling, a suburban version of Jackie Kennedy's recreation of Camelot. To hear Georgina Flowers tell it, when Hamish was there, the Flowers home was suffused in its own golden light. When Hamish wasn't there, it was as if someone had gone through the house and turned off all the lights, then left again. It wasn't easy to live with parents who were always looking over their shoulders at the before, while she and Albert were trying to make their way into the after.

'It was harder on Albert,' Adelaide said. 'I loved Hamish so much, we all did, but he and Albert were close in a different way.

The two of them were always squirrelled away in Albert's room. It's weird, but I never felt left out, I knew I could go in there any time I wanted to, but I left them to it. I knew, even when I was really little, that Albert needed Hamish more than I did. Albert had a way of standing out, and Hamish had a way of helping him to fit in.

'Me,' Adelaide Flowers looked down at her floral wrap dress and smoothed it across her lap, 'I can make myself fit in anywhere, it's a particular skill of mine. But Albert never could. Every time he got in some sort of scrap, Hamish just stepped in and fixed it,' she said, snapping her fingers. 'Which was wonderful, but it meant Albert never had any practice at fixing things for himself.'

The last patrons had left the library, nodding or waving at Florence as they passed, Erica Little wobbling by on her bicycle with Joan Didion riding shotgun, and Monty coming out to say good evening and sniff the air for any errant traces of tobacco.

Florence liked this time at the library; the parents walking to the cars with their children, the mother or father holding bags of books, the children cartwheeling ahead. She liked to see the older patrons walk slowly to their cars, Mrs Trenton always one of the last to leave, taking slow, measured steps with her walker. Florence liked to tease Albert that Abigail Trenton stayed late hoping for a glimpse of him, and another 'alley-oop' in his big strong arms.

Adelaide Flowers, seeing the coast was clear, lit up another cigarette.

'It was so easy to be eclipsed by Hamish. He'd walk into a room and it was like the sun had passed over your moon.' Adelaide sighed, blowing out a steady stream of smoke. 'And when Hamish died, it was a total blackout. We were all just stumbling around in the dark, looking for the matches.' Adelaide laughed, a brittle crackle from her throat. 'That's when I first started smoking, Mum started joining any committee that would have her, Dad started going to real estate conferences, and Albert started stammering more and preferring plants to people.'

Florence froze. She and Albert really were the same person.

'The thing is,' Adelaide said, reaching down into her handbag to retrieve a small notebook, then digging around again for a pen, 'I love both my brothers. I loved Hamish but I love Albert too, he might not know that, but I do. God will probably smite me down for saying this, but I might even love him more. Everyone worshipped Hamish because he was perfect, but I probably preferred Albert because he wasn't.'

Florence smiled, as Adelaide continued.

'I love my family, Florence, I do, but I find I work better when I keep them at a distance.'

Adelaide Flowers was full of surprises, Florence thought. Albert had told her that his younger sister 'opts in and out' of his family but hadn't told her why Adelaide was often in absentia. Looking at Adelaide, puffing away, Florence thought that, having lost one brother she had loved fiercely, Adelaide was not taking any chances by getting too close to the other.

Adelaide passed Florence the notebook. 'Write down your number,' she instructed. 'I can help you with Albert's party. He keeps his Mobile Mixologist books at Mum and Dad's because there's an office there, so I can get you all his contact numbers. I can probably help you with the asking as well.'

Florence took the book and pen. 'So you think the party is a good idea?' she asked, writing down her number.

'Who knows?' Adelaide shrugged. 'Could be a disaster. You're keeping it casual, right?'

Florence nodded.

'Just a few Christmas drinks?'

Florence nodded again.

'Well, we'd better get cracking. When are you thinking of holding it?'

'I thought Christmas Eve, early in the evening, just for a couple of hours.'

Adelaide nodded. 'That could work.'

Florence retrieved her list from her own bag.

'I wrote down the names of a few people who might want to come,' she said, passing it to Addie who flicked her eyes over it.

'I know a couple of these,' she said. 'I'm friends with Siobhan Peters, and the Coxes are friends of my parents. I know Meg Stewart as well, and I can check Albert doesn't have an event on that night.' Adelaide stood up. 'I'm glad you're doing this, Florence, I really am. Even if it just ends up being you, me, Albert and a sad bottle of chardonnay.'

'Thank you, Adelaide,' Florence said. 'I really appreciate you giving this your time.'

'Oh, I've got all the time in the world, Florence. I'm between everything at the moment.'

*

Amanda Saint Claire was lying on a chaise longue, her eyes masked by two circles of cucumber and her face covered in a thick peach-coloured crème.

She looked like a magazine advertisement caught between the pages from another era, when women like her still existed. Florence looked to her mother's feet. Was she wearing slippers with tufts of faux fur on them? She was, the fur tickling at Amanda's rosy pink toenails. The sash of her kimono hung loosely around her waist, the red and green flowers sprinkled in its satin folds. Watching her mother, Florence clearly heard her father say, 'The Gorgeous Amanda,' and she turned her head quickly to look for him. Lucas had not been making so many guest appearances in her life lately. She hadn't heard his gravelly chuckle for a while, or seen his felt hat bobbing up and down anywhere. But he was here now, just long enough for Florence to see her father drinking in her mother. But Amanda, eyes closed behind their cucumber patches, was oblivious to his gaze. Just as well, Florence thought; there had been too much yearning in it.

Amanda put her hands to her eyes, plucking the cucumbers from the lids and placing them in a small china dish on the table beside her. 'That feels better,' she said. 'Now, what did you want to talk about, darling?'

Florence had gone to Kinsey directly from the library to ask her mother what she thought about Albert's party. She had let herself in and called out to Amanda, who had answered, 'I'm in here darling, wallowing behind garden vegetables.' Florence smiled, no wonder Lucas yearned.

Isolde and Adelaide both seemed to think the party for Albert was a good idea, but something tugged at Florence, a niggle that made her think that it wasn't. She had never given a party and most of the ones she had gone to had been the 'after' kind for opening nights when she was younger. She and Puck and Isolde usually ended up asleep on a couch somewhere, with coats flung over them. But Amanda and Lucas had given plenty at Kinsey over the years, Florence usually upstairs in her room with her headphones on, reading *Are You There, God? It's Me, Margaret* and trying to ignore the reverberating bass line in the walls.

Now she was throwing what she had always considered the worst kind of party, a surprise one – all that whispering and leaping out from behind couches. But beneath the niggle that told Florence this was a bad idea was a smaller but stronger one that told her something else. It told her to throw Albert Flowers this party. He might feel ambushed, but he might also feel welcome. It was all in the execution, she thought, which was where the woman on the chaise longue came in.

Amanda listened to Florence, occasionally popping a caramel from one of her pockets into her mouth. When Florence had finished – 'Thank God this is a slow-setting mask, darling, it's a very long story, isn't it?' – Amanda stood up and redid the sash around her waist. 'Tea?' she said.

Florence nodded. 'But no sugar.' The last time Amanda had made her tea at Kinsey was when the blue feather had floated back into their lives, its descent taking everything Florence knew with it. But that had not turned out to be an entirely bad thing, she thought, listening to Amanda moving about the kitchen below, as if Amanda Saint Claire making her tea and dispensing advice was the most natural thing in the world. The blue feather had given her family a jolt, and perhaps this party would give Albert one too. Albert Flowers could do with a jolt, Florence thought.

'Here we are, darling,' Amanda said, bringing in the tray and putting it down on a small side table. She sat down on the chaise longue and patted the space beside her. 'Come and sit next to me while I tell you how to throw a party that doesn't make you want to set yourself on fire with the bombe Alaska . . .'

Florence was right, Amanda said, it was all in the invitation and the execution. The invitation, she said, set the tone of the party, so that everyone knew how to behave, and the execution made sure they did.

'You just say that you are holding a small drinks party to celebrate Christmas, and also to raise a glass to Albert for all the festive cheer he's brought to all of you over the years. Then you give the details, mention you'd like to keep it a surprise for Albert, and say you hope to see them there. You don't want to sound desperate, darling, you want to sound as if you've just thought of it in passing. Your Aunt Margo used to sound so desperate when she asked people to her parties, like she was one of those little animals caught in a trap, trying to gnaw off its own leg.'

Amanda poured the tea and looked around the lounge room. 'It's been a long time since we've had a party here, it will be nice to see people filling in the corners again.'

Florence stared at her mother. 'I'm not having it here, I'm having it at the cottage.'

Amanda sighed. 'I don't think so, darling. From what you've told me, the numbers might be a bit low. But if you say you're holding it at Kinsey, at least some people will come just to have a good old look at it. And at me,' she said, sipping her tea. 'I'm not being vain, Florence, I'm being practical.'

It was true, Florence thought, they might not come for Albert, but they would come for her mother. Florence looked around the lounge room and thought it was just the right room for a drinks party. Or for anything else that might happen at it.

'All right, Lamanda,' she said, 'we'll have it at Kinsey.'

*

Monty Rollins smiled at Florence as she knocked on his glass office door.

'Come in,' he said. 'I'm just attending to some last-minute library business before we close our doors for the holidays.'

Florence sat down opposite Monty, who was wearing a bow tie patterned with dancing sugar canes.

Monty glanced down. 'From Sharon,' he smiled. 'The woman can't resist a holiday accessory. Now what can I do for you, Florence?'

Florence plunged in before she had a chance to bottle out.

Monty and Sharon and their Maltese terrier Ruby had lived with Albert for two weeks earlier in the year while their own home was being renovated. 'What's it like to live with them?' Florence had whispered to Albert in the Green Team office the morning after they had moved in. 'It's all right,' Albert had whispered back, 'sort of like being in the first row of a vaudeville act.' Monty, she knew, would want to come to Albert's party, and so would Sharon and her holiday accessories.

'I'm having a small Christmas party for Albert, just a few of his friends to say cheers for all the things he does for people . . .'

'Will he be serving the drinks as well?' Monty asked. 'Because he makes an excellent Tequila Bon Bon.'

Florence didn't falter, of course Monty knew about Albert's second job. His eyes saw everything as he glided his library trolley around, gathering intelligence.

'Sharon and I have attended two events now where Albert has provided the liquid conviviality,' Monty smiled, 'but on both occasions he was unaware of our presence, and we decided it behoved us to remain undetected.'

Florence looked again at Monty, past his bow tie and into the place where he knew how to keep a secret.

'You know who I am, too, don't you, Monty?' she said. 'You know I'm Miss Suki.'

Monty bowed his head briefly. 'Guilty as charged, Florence, and I must say you have inherited every bit of your mother's talent. I said to Sharon, why that girl doesn't let her light shine, I will never know, but then we both agreed that you'd have your reasons. Quite the pair, you and Albert, aren't you?' he smiled.

Florence smiled back. 'The party is at my mother's house – at Kinsey,' she said, 'and she would love to see you there.' Florence wasn't sure, but she thought she saw Monty's bow tie give a shiver of excitement.

'Albert doesn't know the party is for him, Monty, so I'm going to ask him to arrive half an hour or so after everyone else is there.'

Monty clapped his hands. 'And then we'll all leap out at him from beneath the candelabras!'

Florence sincerely hoped not.

'Something like that,' she said, although what the something was, what she'd say to Albert Flowers when he stepped through Kinsey's heavy front door and straight into the overlapping parts of his own Venn diagram, she hadn't thought of yet.

Florence stood up. 'I'll let you know all the details as soon as I have them, Monty.'

'It's going to be some enchanted evening, Miss Suki,' he beamed.

*

Adelaide Flowers was no shirker, Florence discovered. And it seemed she really did have a lot of time on her hands. A couple of days after they had settled on a date and time, and Adelaide had made sure Albert wasn't donning his black apron that night, she rang Florence and said, 'I've had a yes from the Coxes, their daughter Laura, the Davenports, Megan Stewart and her mother – who probably wants to thank him for getting all that vomit out of her daughter's hair – Natalie, Simon and Siobhan Bishop, a maybe from the Jacksons and a no from Eve Blake, the Lanzos and Hannah Luck. Everyone's promised to keep mum. Who have you got?'

'Mum, Isolde and Puck, Monty Rollins and his wife Sharon, and Fiona Wilson from the bookshop. Not Cat Morrison – that was a long shot, anyway, and a yes from my neighbour Victor. How many is that?'

'Including you and me, about twenty, I think, and if my parents come, two more.'

'Have you asked them?' Florence said. 'Have you told them what we're doing?'

She and Adelaide Flowers had become co-conspirators, Florence realised. She hadn't said, 'What I'm doing'; she'd said, 'What we're doing'. *We are in cahoots*, she thought.

'Not yet,' Adelaide answered. 'I can't decide if Albert would want them there or not, or if they'd want to come or not.'

'I don't know about that, but I think Albert would like them to come.'

Florence also thought it would be good for Georgina and Laurence Flowers to see their son outside the shadow of his older brother.

'Mmm,' said Adelaide. 'I'll have a think about it and let you know, but otherwise we're all set.'

Florence felt the niggle's tug but ignored it. It was easier to do when you were knee deep in cahoots with someone, she found.

*

The shoe was still on the post, Florence noticed, cutting through the park to the library the next morning – Cinderella, or her mother or father, failing to claim it. It was far grubbier than when she had put it there weeks ago, sooty patterns of mould on its fabric and its laces gone, undone by clever hooked beaks.

All the tiny marvels, she thought, the micro armies marching all around us, all the unseen work being done.

The park was empty, its swings still, its jacaranda carpet thickly damp and pungent.

Florence sat on the swing, her feet on the ground, her hands curled around the chain, and began to pitch herself slowly back and forth. She lifted her feet a little off the ground, feeling the swing take her weight, and pushed them down again, leaning her body back, then pitching it forward as it gathered its slow, metronome strokes through the air. *I am gathering momentum*, she thought. She closed her eyes and let the swing take her higher, then as it was returning to the ground, she uncurled her hands and let go.

It wasn't the most graceful of landings; her body jerked when her feet hit the ground and she had to run a little to regain her steadiness, but it was, she thought, what you might call a lark.

Florence picked up her handbag from the grass and slung it over her shoulder. Then she walked into the Green Team's office and, carried along by the swing's momentum, asked Albert to the party.

'It's just Christmas Eve drinks at my mother's house, next Friday night, if you're free,' she said, hoping she didn't sound like one of Aunt Margo's poor trapped animals. She waited for Albert to say, 'I've got Christmas drinks with my imaginary friends Jeremy and Lydia,' even though she knew he was free because Adelaide had checked the date.

Instead, he said, 'I'd love to . . . so it's at Kinsey?' and Florence thought that even Albert Flowers was not immune to fame's siren song. Or her mother's.

'Yes, Isolde and I thought our house might be a bit small, even though I'm not sure how many people are coming . . . I've left my run a little late.'

'Well, I'll be there with Christmas bells on,' Albert said, and Florence didn't have to look at his face to know he wished he hadn't.

'Great,' she said. 'Monty's coming too, and you'll know Isolde and Puck, and Victor as well. Don't let him corner you to ask about the whiteflies on his hydrangeas.'

Albert smiled. 'I won't. Thanks for asking me, Florence. What should I bring?'

Courage, she wanted to tell him.

*

'Ooh, a party,' Orla said, 'and 'ere's Veronica finking you didn't 'ave any friends.'

Veronica snapped her head around. 'I didn't say she didn't have *any* friends, Orla, I said she didn't have *many* friends.'

'No, you said *any*,' Orla insisted.

They were sitting on the floor of Veronica's flat, having a glass of wine while sorting through costumes and deciding which ones were, as Orla said, 'done for'.

Florence laughed. She would miss this. She would miss them both when Miss Suki and her Nightshades bowed out, Orla throwing her signature kiss to the audience, Veronica leaving rows of bloodied men in the aisles. The costumes were arranged in piles of colour on the floor, the greens and silvers and hot pinks vibrant against the timber, making Florence feel like she was sitting in one of Natalie Bishop's flowerbeds.

She had not told Orla and Veronica of her decision to retire Miss Suki from the footlights, but she thought perhaps they wouldn't mind. The act, as most did eventually – except, apparently, Amanda Saint Claire's unflagging stories she could tell you – was growing tired. It happened to the best of them, Florence thought – Miss Betty and her Bon Bons, Miss Otis Regrets and the Ragtime Dolls – and it was happening to them. Florence sensed Miss Suki and the Nightshades were calling it a night, and her departure would only hasten things along a little. Orla, she thought, might return to London. She had begun to speak of pints and crisps and London's sodding rain with increasing fondness. Veronica would probably go with her, crossing the ocean to break an entirely new nation's hearts, having depleted the supply at home.

'Remember these?' Orla said, unzipping a suit bag and pulling out three long red sheaths they had worn for their first, early performances.

'I do,' Veronica said. 'We looked like blood clots.'

They began to laugh, Orla putting her hand to her mouth, eyes darting, and Veronica throwing her head back, Florence's chuckle somewhere in between.

Veronica was wrong, Florence thought. She had friends. She had these two.

She would tell them about retiring Miss Suki another time. For now, she just wanted to sit on the floor between them and listen to their bickering. She found it strangely comforting. 'Tell us about this party, Florence,' Orla was saying. 'Any good sorts going?'

Florence didn't know. She didn't know who was going yet, and if she did, she wouldn't know if they were good sorts or not. She was giving a party where she didn't know what most of her guests looked like. Florence straightened. 'Well, you're going, Orla, so that's one,' she said 'and Veronica, so that's at least two good sorts already.'

'No fit fellas then?' Orla sighed. 'There never are – and Veronica's not a good sort, she's hideous.'

Veronica tucked a russet curl behind a perfect creamy ear and smiled.

'I know,' Florence said. 'I can barely stand to look at her.'

Florence found she was delighted at the thought of Veronica and Orla both being at Kinsey, Veronica undulating up the front stairs, Orla taking them two at a time behind her. Of course, neither of them knew Albert, which strayed from the point of the evening, but Florence needed them to bookend her.

Veronica refilled Florence's glass. 'So the party is at Kinsey?' she said. 'At Amanda Saint Claire's house?' and Florence flinched.

She had never discussed her family with Veronica or Orla, just as she knew only the bare bones of their backgrounds. Particularly Veronica. Florence still had no real idea of where she had sprung from. Veronica Allen could have been poured from a tall glass of water for all Florence knew.

'How is your mother, these days?' Veronica asked, and Florence answered calmly, 'Well, thank you,' because it was clear the jig was up.

'We knew your name wasn't Florence Jones from the first day we met you,' Orla rushed in. 'Your 'and got all shaky when you wrote it down at the audition, didn't it, Ronnie?'

Veronica nodded. 'Plus, Jones is a stupid name to pick,' she said. 'So obvious. You may as well have said your name was Florence Smith. Anyway, we figured it out eventually.'

'Why didn't you say something?' Florence asked. 'Why have you never said something?'

Veronica shrugged. 'No need to until now. I don't think you thought through having us at your mother's house, Florence.'

Florence hadn't thought about it at all, she had missed that particular part of the party's execution.

'Wot was the big deal that made you tell us your name was Jones anyway?' Orla asked, plucking some fluff off a long black velvet skirt – they'd been a mistake, thought Florence; by the end of the night they'd all looked like they'd been rolling around in sandpaper.

'There wasn't one, as it turned out,' Florence answered, 'I just needed to get away from my surname for a while, to find out who I was without it.'

'Amen to that,' Veronica said, standing up and stretching. 'I've still got three outstanding arrest warrants back in Tulsa.'

That, thought Florence, could actually be true.

'Anyway, we'd love to come to your party, Florence,' Veronica said, 'and meet all the Joneses – now, what do we think about the purple satin?'

Another mistake, Florence thought. She had felt like an overripe grape in it.

Orla yawned. 'Are we done yet?' she asked.

Not quite, thought Florence.

*

Isolde and Florence sat on the back deck, watching faraway lightning throw its spiky fingers across the sky. It was the night before the party, and Florence had just come back from making trays of blinis with Richard, who had slipped into the planning quietly, carrying a tray of canapés. Florence had gone to Kinsey earlier in the week to find him in the kitchen, Gilbert and Sullivan on the speakers, spooning teaspoons of mixture into tiny pastry cups. 'Mini quiches,' Richard had smiled at her. 'I've also made sausage rolls with a pepper glaze – they're in the freezer – and I thought perhaps some spring rolls. Do you have a dip preference?' Florence thought of all the times Richard had inserted himself into their daily lives like this, filling spaces before they realised they were empty. Or in this case, realising that if people were going to a party, they expected to be fed.

When she was younger, Florence had prickled with resentment at Richard's presence, shouting, 'You are not our father,' when she had come home from school to find him hanging pictures in the hallway. But all she'd felt when she saw Richard marching around the kitchen like a modern major general in a floral apron was a rushing gratitude.

'Thank you, Richard. I'm very new to this party thing. The last one I went to was at Amy Burton's. I was going to serve bowls of chips and lolly snakes,' she'd said.

He'd laughed, holding out a pair of oven-gloved hands for her to take.

'My pleasure, treasure,' he had smiled.

'Richard's been wonderful,' she told Isolde now. 'He's always been wonderful to us, hasn't he?'

'Yes,' Isolde said, 'because he's in love with Amanda.'

A long, spiky branch of lightning streaked across the sky, briefly illuminating Isolde's face as she said it. Did Isolde somehow time these things?

'No, he isn't, Issy,' Florence said, and Isolde rolled her eyes to half-mast.

'Yes, he is,' Isolde answered, 'always has been.'

'No, he isn't.'

'Yes, he is.'

'No, he isn't.'

Florence felt the familiar back and forth rhythm of her and Isolde's arguments, the two sisters serving their version of the same facts to each other, playing ping-pong with their words. Isolde, she knew, would never put her paddle down. Florence was exhausted already.

'Fine,' she said, putting up her hands. 'Can we talk about the party? The thing is, Issy, I feel like it's gotten away from me, and that I couldn't stop it now even if I wanted to, and I think I want to.'

Her week had been filled with updating the year's planting records for the Green Team, making paperbark Christmas cards with distracted classes from East Elm Primary and spooning beetroot jam onto blinis with Richard. She hadn't had time to think, and now that she did, she felt like the momentum was gathering without her.

'I haven't thought through the execution, Issy, I haven't thought about the execution at all,' she said.

Isolde put her arm around Florence. 'It's going to be fine,' she said. 'You are giving a party for your friend Albert to show him he's appreciated. Who wouldn't like that? I'd like that. I'd like someone to throw me a party just to say Isolde Marie-Louise Evangeline Saint Claire, we see you.

'That's all this party says, Florence, it says we see you, Albert Flowers, and not just because you're the size of a small lorry.'

Florence laughed and leant into Isolde, resting her head on her sister's shoulder.

Isolde lifted a hand to pat Florence's hair. 'This is just like Princess Diana speaking to her sisters the night before she married Prince Charles.'

'What?' said Florence.

'You know that story about how she had cold feet the night before she married him and went to her sisters for help?'

'No,' said Florence, 'I don't.' Sometimes trying to follow Isolde's conversation was like trying to follow one of those small silver balls ricocheting around inside pinball machines.

'Well, she was very nervous, and having second thoughts, and probably wishing she was marrying a stockbroker who wore red braces on his shirts, so she went to her sisters and told them she didn't think she could go through with it. And they said: "It's too late, Duch, your face is on the tea towels."'

Isolde stood up. 'Anyway, I'm off to bed. It really will be fine, Florence,' she said, turning to go inside.

Florence sat a little longer beneath the cracking sky and thought about what Isolde had said. She looked out at the lightning dancing across the darkness.

'I see you, Albert Flowers,' she said.

In bed that night, Florence thought about Princess Diana pacing about her room in Clarence House the night before her marriage, hearing the crowds outside calling out her name. Her sisters, Florence thought, should have spirited her away, thrown a blanket over her and legged it.

13

Albert walked up the driveway to Kinsey, stopping to admire a mango tree, three tyres swinging from its branches. A beauty, he thought, although he might take a look at the roots. They could be problematic one day, silently making their spreading claim beneath the house. Albert looked up at Kinsey, recognising the white and green gables from photos he had seen of it over the years. It was as charming as everyone said, but Albert knew that given the choice he'd save the tree and knock down the house.

He put his hand to his collar, shifting it a little from his neck. Walking towards the front steps, clutching his bottle of wine, Albert felt as if this was a first date and Lucas Saint Claire was going to come to the door and give him the once-over. Albert adjusted his collar again. He'd taken far more care than he usually did with his clothes, which was to say, he had ironed them. Silly to feel a bit shaky, it was only Florence and her family, a few of her friends, and Monty wearing one of his signature collection bow ties.

Albert looked down the length of the driveway. He'd hoped to arrive at the same time as someone else, so he could attach himself to them for the walk-in, as if he was joining in a quadrille. But nobody seemed to be around, and Albert couldn't loiter around the bottom of the steps any longer, pretending to examine a thriving Japanese windflower, although it was delightful, its pink flowers thrown like jewels across it.

Albert began climbing Kinsey's front stairs. He wondered if he had thought this through. What would he do with his hands when he had no drinks to serve? What would he talk about when he was not in charge of the bar banter? What if he couldn't get his words out? Albert faltered a little on the last step, then rang the doorbell.

The cherry-red door swung open before he had dropped his hand from the bell, and Florence stood behind it, holding out a flute of champagne, her smile stretching all the way to her earlobes.

He had never, he thought, seen it stretch so far. Florence almost looked like she was grimacing. 'Merry Christmas, Albert,' she said, passing him the flute. 'Come on in.'

Albert took the glass and stepped inside, passing Florence the bottle.

'Merry Christmas, Florence,' he said as she led him into the lounge room where people stood in knots talking and laughing, and something, thought Albert, was not quite right.

Then Florence put her hand lightly on his arm and raised her voice.

'Albert's here,' she shouted.

Then she raised her glass and shouted again, 'To Albert!' giving him a jolt.

The people in the lounge room stopped talking and laughing and turned their faces towards him.

'To Albert,' they echoed, raising their glasses.

Albert scanned the room, his eyes flicking across Florence to her sister, then Amanda Saint Claire in a floaty kaftan, a man beside her holding out a tray of blinis, Puck standing next to an astonishingly beautiful woman with red hair, and another one who looked like a drunk pixie. Laura Cox was standing with her parents and the Davenports, and Megan Stewart was raising her glass next to her mother Petra. Simon Bishop was smiling at him, his arm around Siobhan, her hands resting on a curved bump in full bloom. Natalie Bishop stood behind Siobhan, her hands on her daughter-in-law's shoulders. Monty and his wife Sharon, who was wearing some sort of flashing earrings dangling from her ears, were standing next to Victor, who looked like he'd leapt over the fence to get here, and Fiona Wilson was waving to him, for some reason out from behind the books at Savage Reader. And on either side of his sister Adelaide stood his parents. Georgina and Laurence Flowers. In Amanda Saint Claire's lounge room.

Off kilter. Albert felt very off kilter. He knew all these faces, or most of them, one way or the other, but he couldn't connect the dots between them. Or between them and Florence.

Why were they here, holding out their glasses to him, for what seemed like a very long time? Dots connected or not, clearly some sort of response was expected. Albert raised his glass. 'Thank you,' he said, 'although I'm really not sure what's going on.'

Everyone started laughing and someone – Simon Bishop? – called out, 'Good on you, Albert,' and then they all turned like clockwork figurines back into their previous positions. Albert stood, his own glass still raised, and he couldn't seem to bend his elbow to get it down again.

Albert felt Florence's hand rest in its crook.

'Come with me,' she said, her hand on his elbow guiding him to a small room off the hallway, gold records encased in glass frames on its walls.

They sat on a couch next to a low table where Lucas Saint Claire smiled winningly at him from a photo frame.

'I suppose you feel a bit sprung upon,' Florence said.

Albert supposed he did. He couldn't seem to get a hold of what he was feeling, but if he had to choose a frontrunner, it would be discombobulated. *What the hell*, he asked Lucas Saint Claire grinning at him from behind the glass, *is your daughter up to?*

Florence took a deep, inward breath, her words rushing out on the exhalation.

'This really is just Christmas drinks, Albert, but I thought you might like a night off from serving them for a change.'

Albert felt another jolt, this one down to his boots. He drained his glass as Florence kept talking, a red flush creeping across her face.

'I know about your Mobile Mixology business, Albert, and I know that I'm not really supposed to, but I do. And most of the people here are people you've poured a drink for at some stage or another, and all of them just want to say cheers to you. All you have to do is let them, just for the next couple of hours. You can interrogate me later, and I'll tell you everything I know about you, and everything you don't know about me, which is not a short list. But if we don't get back in there soon Amanda's going to start singing Jazz Cat and Veronica might start accidentally killing men by looking at them.'

Ah, the woman with the red hair, Albert thought.

As she spoke, Albert saw the flush in her cheeks, the tremor of the glass in her hand. Florence, who was frightened of nothing he knew of, who had once lazily stuck out an arm across his chest as they were walking down a track, stopped, said, 'Eastern Brown,' and then kept walking, was shaking.

Somehow that struck him as far more shocking than her knowing about his extracurricular activities. How she knew, and how much she knew, he had no idea, but for some reason she had gone to some lengths to get him, and all those other people standing outside the door, here. Albert didn't understand what that reason was and he still felt discombobulated, but Florence Saint Claire, the least likely person he knew to throw a party, was apparently throwing him one. At Kinsey. With her family. And his. With canapés. Albert looked at Florence's increasingly flushed face and decided that, for the next couple of hours at least, that would have to be all he needed to know. What had Florence said? 'You can interrogate me later, and I'll tell you everything

I know about you, and everything you don't know about me.' All he had to do was get through the next couple of hours to hear it.

'So, do we have a deal, Albert?' Florence said, standing up. 'Party now and shoot me later?'

Albert didn't want to be responsible for any more tremors.

'With bells on,' he said, and flinched at his words.

He followed Florence back inside to the lounge room where, once he quietened his own tremors and heard Isolde's whispered, 'Go with the flow, Albert Flowers,' as she passed him, he settled into the unexpected feeling of being among friends.

He patted Siobhan Bishop's baby bump, spoke to Victor about his hydrangeas, looked at some, but not too many, of the Davenports' photos from Greece, laughed at a very rude joke Laura Cox told, danced a little with Florence's friend Orla who he couldn't keep up with, commiserated with Megan Stewart about her disastrous twenty-first and the disastrous boyfriend who had caused it by kissing someone else during the speeches. Fiona Wilson handed him a card from Cat Morrison, which said: *I hope you have a wonderful night, Albert. I wish I could be there. If I still wore hats, I'd tip mine to you*, and someone called Richard kept giving him canapés.

At one stage he found himself outside on a small balcony with Simon Bishop. Simon had tapped his shoulder and said, 'Follow me, mate,' then winked and patted his shirt pocket meaningfully. Albert followed, thinking, *What's in there? A joint?* Was Simon Bishop going to try and give him some money? But it was a fat Cuban cigar Simon pulled from his pocket, passing it to Albert and pulling out another one for himself. 'I'm celebrating the baby, giving it up when it comes though, of course,' Simon said, tilting his head to one side, a brief flicker of a flame lighting the cigar's tip. Albert said thank you but he didn't smoke. And then he said, as if he and Simon Bishop were the sort of friends who said these things to each other, 'Wouldn't say no to a beer though.' Simon passed Albert his cigar, then darted back inside to get one.

He came back, holding two glasses, and exchanged one for the cigar. He took three quick puffs to relight it. 'I wanted to have a chat to you, in private' – *Don't say man to man*, Albert thought – 'man to man. I wanted to thank you for what you said to me at the wedding. I'm not sure if Sibby and I would even be having this baby if you hadn't made me pull my head in, so cheers for calling me a fucking idiot.'

They sat in companionable silence, the night air laced with spicy notes of Cuba. When they went back inside, Adelaide and Monty and Sharon Rollins were roaring with laughter at something Carl Davenport was saying, and his parents were deep in conversation with Natalie Bishop. *Merry Christmas, Mum*, Albert thought. He'd spoken to his parents earlier in the night, and both Laurence and Georgina seemed slightly bewildered to be inside Kinsey's whitewashed walls but determined to make some sort of go of it. It appeared to be paying off for his mother, who was nodding intently at something Natalie was saying – Georgina's days of patrolling her back fence might be over, Albert thought. He looked over to where Isolde was standing, tapping a microphone on a small raised stage he hadn't noticed on the way in.

'Good evening, everybody, my name is Isolde Saint Claire' – 'Go Issy!' someone shouted – 'and on behalf of my mother Amanda, my brother Puck, and my sister Florence, I'd like to welcome you all into our home. We do have some music here tonight.' Albert scanned the crowd for Florence, so he could meet her eyes and roll his at the impending entrance of Amanda Saint Claire and her Jazz Cat. 'So please welcome to this very small stage, hastily constructed by our very good friend Richard, the one and only Miss Suki and her glorious Nightshades.'

Orla and Veronica stepped out from behind a folding silk screen Albert also hadn't noticed, and took their places behind two standing microphones, a space between them. Then another woman stepped out and filled it. 'Good evening, everybody,' she said. 'I am Miss Suki, and these are my Nightshades, and we're going to take you down to a little place by the water we like to call Swingtown, don't we ladies?'

'Uh-huh,' Orla and Veronica said together, leaning in close to their microphones.

'And when we get to Swingtown, what do we like to do, Nightshades?' the woman asked, and Veronica answered: 'We like to. Cause. A. Ruckus.'

Albert peered at the women in their floor-length silver gowns and matching silver gloves – Orla, the one who looked like a slightly inebriated sprite; Veronica, the one who could apparently kill a man by raising an eyebrow at him; and the woman in the middle who was talking in Florence's voice but had someone else's face. Albert peered closer at Miss Suki, and as he did, she lifted her eyes to meet his, and beneath the layers, the painted-on lips, the coloured-in cheeks and the black, heavy lashes, was Florence. Albert drew his breath in sharply, a jolt that went all the way beneath his ribs.

Monty Rollins sidled up to him and said quietly, 'She's very good, wonderful pipes, as they say in the business. Sharon and I have had the pleasure of watching Florence, or should I say Miss Suki, perform several times.'

Albert nodded. Had they? Why hadn't he? Why hadn't Florence introduced him to Miss Suki? And why was she wearing so much makeup? If it weren't for her eyes, Albert would never have found her in there.

Monty continued in a low voice, 'Of course, we couldn't let her know we'd seen her. Florence likes to keep that part of her life mum. I don't understand it myself, but perhaps you might.'

They both kept their eyes on the stage as Monty spoke, Albert's trained on Miss Suki, who was Florence but with embellishments. At first he could only see Miss Suki beneath her cherry bob, the chalky mask on her skin, the black beauty spot painted high on one cheekbone; it was difficult to get past her. But the more he watched, the more Florence emerged from Miss Suki's skin: Florence striding ahead of him along the melaleuca track; Florence looking up at him from a seed catalogue; Florence telling off a woman who had pushed in front of Abigail Trenton in the borrowing line, saying, 'How about I push you, would you like that?' until Monty had stepped between them, and Florence had received a handwritten warning from him about codes of behaviour. By the time the set had finished, Florence was all he could see when the women took their bows, Orla turning to throw a kiss to the audience.

Everyone stood clapping and cheering, and Albert wondered if he wasn't going a little bit mad. He felt strangely as if he had heard the three women sing before, but he couldn't place where, like siren songs far out at sea.

The whole evening seemed conjured up somehow. Kinsey, like some suburban myth at the end of its driveway, an entire roomful of people turning to raise their glasses to him, Amanda Saint Claire floating by in her kaftan, Simon Bishop waving his cigar on the balcony, his mother asking the caterer for his blini recipe, and now Florence appearing in some strange glittery costume she didn't belong in. Surely this incarnation of Miss Suki would be at the top of Florence's list of promised revelations.

Monty had said he'd seen Florence perform before, and it was clear from their performance the three women hadn't just cobbled the act together. They had been wonderful. Florence had been astonishing.

Albert looked at all the people she had gathered from his own other life: the Davenports, Fiona Wilson, the Bishops, the Stewarts, Addie, his parents. Florence the Conjurer. And now, Florence the Cabaret Artist. The party seemed to be winding down; people were searching for handbags and keys, and thanking Amanda and the man he thought was the caterer standing beside her. Simon Bishop was putting a pea-green coat on his wife's shoulders, and Fiona Wilson was kissing Isolde on both cheeks. Albert was exhausted just looking at them. It had been a wonderful, if very strange evening, but now he couldn't wait for everyone to leave. He looked for Florence and her Nightshades, but they hadn't reappeared; probably somewhere upstairs, he thought, stripping away all those layers.

Albert thought he would wait for Florence, thank all the Saint Claires for their hospitality, make his goodbyes, and go for a very long walk – and he would ask Florence the Conjurer to come with him.

He felt a hand on his shoulder as Adelaide appeared beside him. 'Mum and Dad want to say goodbye,' she told him, 'and I have been sent over as an emissary.' Albert nodded, and saw his parents hovering by the front door. Why must they send Addie? Why could they never meet him halfway?

Albert smiled at his mother as he approached her, and Laurence Flowers put out his hand. 'Terrific night, Albert,' he said, 'we really enjoyed ourselves,' and Georgina Flowers echoed, 'We really did, I can't remember when I last had such a lovely evening,' and raised her hand to his cheek. Albert raised his own to touch the back of her palm briefly. Another jolt. The feel of his mother's skin as she leaned into his ear. 'Lasagne,' she said, 'your favourite meal is lasagne.' Then she patted his cheek and turned towards the door.

He walked his parents to the car, and as he turned back towards Kinsey, the front door opened and most of the party tumbled out of it. Monty stumbling a little on the steps, and Puck, sandwiched between Orla and Veronica. Megan Stewart and Adelaide emerged, their arms linked.

'We're all going to the pub,' Orla told him. 'Do you want to come? No? Come on then, Puck, my little midsummer night's dream. Let's see what you get for Christmas.'

Isolde appeared, cradling a man who looked wholly delighted to be there beneath her arm. 'Oh hi Albert,' she said, as if she had just come upon him on her parents' driveway and hadn't just been at a party where he was the unlikely guest of honour. 'This is Lance,' she said, and then whispered in his ear as she passed, 'I'm going with the flow too.'

Albert stood on Kinsey's front porch, thanking people for coming, feeling like an imposter on Lucas Saint Claire's doorstep, until everyone had left, calling out 'Merry Christmas!' down the driveway, and Victor loudly joking about how he would need to take a taxi home. Everyone except Florence, Amanda and Richard, who was not the caterer, he had eventually realised, but the Saint Claires' manager, and so clearly in love with Florence's mother, Albert wondered why Florence had never mentioned it. Among other things.

'Are you about to do a runner?'

Florence stood in the doorway, her face bare, no longer shrouded by Miss Suki.

'No,' he smiled, 'but I was going to go for a walk, if you want to come along?'

Florence shook her head. 'I would, but I've got a small party to clean up.'

Albert felt a shot of embarrassment at his cheeks. 'See,' he wanted to tell her 'I am no good at this. I was going to leave without lifting a finger to help you. I am woefully out of practice at parties. I've never been to one I haven't worked at.'

Instead, he looked at Florence's bare face and said, 'Then we'll do it together.'

*

Florence opened the music room door. She and Albert had cleaned up the flotsam and jetsam from the party downstairs: empty bottles and glasses, bowls half full of nuts, a Rudolph the Red Nose Reindeer earring from under the couch, its nose still half-heartedly flashing – 'Sharon,' she and Albert had laughed. They had cleared the lounge and begun on the kitchen, scraping soggy corn chips into the bin and putting the empty bottles in the recycling box. They had stacked the dishwasher, and when that was full, Albert had washed up by hand, Florence drying the dishes beside him and flicking him with her tea towel. When they were younger, she and Puck and Isolde had done this every night in Kinsey's kitchen, and Florence had been unable to resist the urge to do it again, her fingers twitching at the tea towel's corners from the moment she picked it up. Watching Albert dodging and twitching away from its flicking edges, Florence had thought that this could most certainly be called a lark.

Richard had come in to say goodnight, and to let them know Amanda had gone to bed, and not to move a muscle, he would let himself out.

'Doesn't he live here?' Albert had asked when Richard had gone. Florence had answered, 'No, why would he?' and Albert had told her the same ridiculous theory Isolde had about Richard and her mother. They had spoken about Monty's unexpectedly fluid dancing, Puck in animated conversation with Orla, and Florence's delight at spying Isolde and Lance Bueller entwined on one of the upstairs couches. She hadn't invited Lance, which meant either Puck or Isolde had. Either way, Isolde had finally noticed that Mercy Jones's long-time roadie had left adolescence behind.

They had spoken about Albert's mother fluttering around 'Call Me Natalie' Bishop like a moth to a flame. Albert had started a long story about how moths were not really attracted to flames, and Florence had told him she already knew, and flicked him with her tea towel again. When they had finished in the kitchen, she had asked Albert if he would like a glass of whiskey in the music room. It had seemed the right place for the conversation they were about to have; just her, Albert and the grey and white ringtail possums scurrying along the telegraph lines.

The music room was quiet and shadowy when she and Albert walked in, and it was time, she knew, to stop larking about.

She led Albert to the window seat.

'Here goes nothing,' she said silently to Lucas, somewhere in the shadows.

'This is where my dad did all his practice,' she said, 'and this is where I'd sit and listen to him.'

'I'm sorry about your father, Florence,' Albert said.

'I'm sorry about your brother, Albert,' she answered evenly.

And then she told him, as promised, what she knew. How she had gone to Avalon where the Milky Way was hiding in another sky, dressed as Miss Suki, in a tuxedo. How she had seen Albert behind the bar and heard the words of Oscar Bishop's friends.

How she had thought, fleetingly, of killing them. She told him about meeting Sadie Bishop at the bottom of Avalon's garden, and then Adelaide in a puff of smoke outside the library. She told him again that she was sorry Hamish had died, because she understood he was spectacular. And then she asked him if he had a photo of his brother. She felt sure that Albert carried his brother with him somewhere besides his memory.

Albert reached into his jeans pocket and pulled out a leather wallet. From behind one of its thin sleeves, he took out a folded strip of photographic paper and passed it to her.

It was from an instant photo booth, the type they used to have dotted around shopping centres like mushrooms. She and Isolde had loved them, pulling across the short curtain to sit smooshed together on a stool, pulling a series of cartoonish faces. There would be some sort of beeping sound to let the sitters know the camera was about to go off, but it still surprised her and Isolde every time. They always looked vaguely dazed in each shot. Dazed and delighted, and a little unhinged.

Florence carefully unfolded the strip in her hand.

Two boys. One in his early teens – Hamish – and the other still a boy – Albert. Both with sandy blond hair, Albert taller and with broader shoulders, but obviously younger. Both staring at the camera, their faces caught in that same look of surprise she and Isolde always wore, even though these boys also knew what was coming. Except, she supposed, they didn't. She flicked her eyes down the vertical squares of the strip. They were smiling. Then laughing. Then pulling faces, Albert with his tongue stuck out to the side of his mouth, and Hamish with his eyes crossed and his teeth bared. Then she looked at the last square on the strip. Hamish and Albert with their arms looped around each other in headlocks, holding each other in vice-like grips of tenderness. Florence handed the strip of photos back to Albert.

'He looks like you,' she said.

Albert smiled. 'Only smaller. People used to think I was his older brother. Sometimes we used to let them keep thinking that, just for fun. Or Hamish would send me to buy tickets for movies he couldn't get into. Once, I got us a six-pack of beer. I think I was about thirteen, the guy at the bottle shop didn't even ask me for ID. We snuck it into the house and Hamish drank them in his room. I remember Hamish playing *The Blues Brothers* soundtrack really loudly and Mum banging on the door and telling us to keep it down. Hamish hid the bottles under his pillow.' Albert started to laugh, and Florence did too. She could see them, two blond boys dancing in a bedroom, all hormones and beer and music.

Albert drained his glass and set it on a coaster.

'I was always a big boy, Florence, and people expected me to do all the things that big boys are meant to do. Play football, or row, or just go around demolishing things. And I didn't want to do any of that. Mostly I wanted to be left alone, you know?' Florence knew. 'My parents didn't know what to do with me. Mum was always pushing me out the door to make friends. I wanted to shout at her that I didn't know how to, and why couldn't she see I didn't want to. I was fine the way I was. Until I wasn't.'

Florence shut her eyes briefly, seeing herself in her room at Kinsey, reading her books on her bed and wishing that she could just stay there, tucked under her quilt while the adults downstairs discussed what on earth to do with her.

'I didn't actually know there was anything different about me until other people started pointing it out. At school the other kids started shoving into me in the hallways, or flicking rubbers at me in class. They'd kick at the back of my chair during lessons, because they knew I wouldn't kick back. I just didn't have it in me. I didn't want to kick anyone. Everything would have been all right,' he sighed, 'if I'd only played rugby.'

Their eyes met and they both started laughing again at the idea that if Albert had just popped in a mouthguard and barrelled his way through high school, everything would have been all right.

Florence uncurled her feet from under her. They had been sitting at the window seat for quite a while and her limbs felt restless. She had wanted to move them but didn't want Albert to take it as a sign that she was restless also.

But Albert shifted too, standing up to refresh their glasses.

'First time I've poured you a drink,' he smiled as he handed Florence hers.

Florence smiled back. 'Monty tells me you make an excellent Tequila Bon Bon.'

They clinked glasses. Florence looked out the window, where the sky still held on to its inky blackness. It had not yet given way to its lighter colours, but she knew it would soon enough and that she and Albert would witness it. It was that sort of night.

The sort of night where Albert Flowers could tell you, as he did now, that the reason he could make an excellent Tequila Bon Bon, or any other drink you might be partial to, was because he became a mobile mixologist. How Hamish had died and left him exactly the right amount of money to buy the business which had helped him get his words out. How he was sorry he hadn't, however, found the right ones to tell her about it.

'So,' he said, 'that's me. Weird kid. Big boy. Stutter. Brother I wish was here but isn't. Moonlighting bar attendant. Imaginary friends. I think that just about covers it.'

He met Florence's eyes. 'Your turn, Miss Suki.'

Florence wasn't sure where to begin. With music, she supposed. She began to go through her own back catalogue, which began with the Saint Claire Swingers, and ended with Miss Suki. In between, she told him about the *Jonathan Hammond Christmas Show*, and the boy in the yellow jacket, and how much she hated Jazz Cat. Florence told Albert about her own dead family member, Lucas Saint Claire, who had also eclipsed every person in every room he strolled into. How she had carried his death like stones in her pocket until a blue feather had floated from Leticia Pepsi's fingers. How she had prickled inside from longing to sing again, and Miss Suki had sprung from that longing.

Albert had been quiet during the telling. Florence was painting pictures on the music room's walls. He could see everything she said in her slow, steady voice. No rushing words now, no hastening to fill in the spaces between them.

'So,' she echoed Albert's closing statement, 'that's me.' Then she added, 'I'm a bit of a mess, Albert.'

'I'm a lot of a mess, Florence,' he answered.

'I don't think you are quite as messy as me,' she smiled. 'May I remind you I was a child star.'

'I was anything but,' he countered.

'I froze on stage.'

'I froze off it.'

'When I was little, I used to dig holes and sit in them, like a mole.'

'When I was little, I sent away for a shrinking kit from some dodgy comic book ad.'

'I thought I murdered my father.'

'I talk to my dead brother, mostly in his tennis whites.'

'I talk to my dead father, in fact he's possibly here right now.'

'I have imaginary friends called Jeremy and Lydia.'

'I hate Lydia, by the way.'

Albert smiled, and then continued. 'I pretended to have parties to go to when I was working at them.'

'I pretended to attend a hydroponics course when I was really singing in nightclubs.'

'I talk to plants.'

'So do I.'

'I think they can hear me.'

'I know they can.'

'I have an entire, made-up persona called "Albert Flowers, Mobile Mixologist".'

'I have an entire, made-up persona called Miss Suki.'

This felt good. *We are larking about*, Florence thought joyously.

'I threw a party recently where I didn't know any of the guests.' She smiled. 'I think I win.'

Albert laughed. 'How about we say we both win? How about we say that you and I are both as messy and weird and fucked-up as each other?'

He poured a last tumbler of whiskey, spiced with the heavy notes of Kip's mea culpa.

'To you, Florence Miss Suki Saint Claire,' Albert said.

Florence smiled. 'And to you, Albert "Mobile Mixologist" Flowers.' They clinked glasses, two frauds together on a velvet window seat.

*

'And now we have a very special surprise for all of you. Not seen together for many years, and here to perform their number one hit, "Santa Was A Jazz Cat", please welcome to the stage the Saint Claire Swingers!'

Beneath her feet, Florence felt the audience's roar before she heard it. She felt Isolde pressing her body into her back, her breath sharp and quick in Florence's ear. She saw Puck's hands drumming on his thighs, his head down, the starter at the gate. Then, from behind her, her mother's voice. 'Maximum wattage!' Amanda Saint Claire commanded as the stage lights dimmed, then bathed the floor in colour.

Puck walked out first, keeping his head down, and ducked behind the drum kit, then Isolde, smiling and waving at the crowd in the Domain like a homecoming queen. Florence followed in her wake, feeling the pull of her family. Then all three Saint Claire children turned their heads to where Amanda Saint Claire strode out, casting her light like shards of glass across the stage. Florence watched her mother stand in front of her microphone and run her eyes over the crowd, holding them still and silent in her gaze. Then she threw her arms out wide. 'Well, Hello 2000!' Amanda Saint Claire said, and the waves began rolling in.

Puck tapped his sticks together three times and Amanda began to sing in her low, throaty voice '*On Christmas Eve when the lights are low . . .*' and Florence stepped towards her microphone, curling her fingers around it. In the crowd, women whispered to each other that they had once had the most enormous crush on Lucas Saint Claire, and look at Amanda, the wife, still so gorgeous. And the children! So grown-up! And so brave, singing without their father.

From the stage, Florence heard her cue and started swinging. In an area close to the front of the stage, reserved for family and friends of the artists, Florence saw Orla, her eyes set only on Puck, and Veronica waving at her, and Victor smiling next to Monty and Sharon, who was wearing a cat's ears headband on her head. Florence saw Richard, his hands clapping in time to Jazz Cat, his eyes only on her mother, and for a brief moment she saw Amanda Saint Claire's eyes travel to his. Isolde was only partly right. It wasn't a one-sided affair.

Florence relaxed into the song, thinking about the last time she had sung in front of an audience with her family. This time there was no creeping flush on her cheeks, no boy in a yellow jacket to mock her. But there was, with one arm around his sister Adelaide, Albert Flowers in a sports coat, smiling at Florence, maximum wattage.

Then Lamanda's purr quietened to a slow growl, the musicians played out the closing notes of Jazz Cat and Puck lifted his hands from the drum kit.

The Domain's audience erupted as Amanda Saint Claire drew her arms out again and brought her children into them, as the Saint Claire Swingers bowed out.

'Well that was magnificent,' said one of the hosts, strolling onto the stage, and the other one answered, 'I wouldn't be surprised if Lucas Saint Claire was looking down on us all right now! What a way to welcome in the New Year, ladies and gentlemen. And it is time to welcome it. Are you ready? Let's count down together. Ten, nine, eight, seven, six . . .'

*

The sky was still spraying showers of light over the audience as they began pouring out of the Domain, one man making his way through the throng in the opposite direction, going against the tide. When he reached the front of the stage he raised his hand and tipped a grey felt hat from his head. Then he turned back towards the crowd and walked away, whistling.

In the Mount Bell State Forest, a breeze nudged The Comanche Dragon from its hiding place, lifting its wings as it rode the air currents under the watchful eyes of the mighty King Kong and landed exactly where it was meant to.

ACKNOWLEDGEMENTS

Thank you to Cate Paterson from Pan Macmillan for her unwavering support, steady hand, wise words, and much treasured friendship. Thank you to the whole team at Pan Macmillan, especially Brianne Collins for her deft editing, and cheering me on from the sidelines! Such a joy to work with. And from Pan Macmillan also, the wonderful Charlotte Ree who stepped in, stepped up, and is the best publicist an author could hope for. Also makes excellent Nutella brownies. Thanks to Anita Davidson for her unflagging support of my work.

Thanks to Julia Stiles, for her always clever suggestions, gently offered. We'll have that glass of champagne one day!

Thank you to my agent Catherine Drayton for believing in my stories.

Thank you to Claire Bickle for much needed advice on all things botanical.

My colleagues and friends, past and present at News Ltd, for words of support and love in the trenches. Thanks especially to all the team at *Q Weekend* and also *U on Sunday*, and to Robert 'Crash' Craddock, Dennis Atkins, Michael McKenna, Elissa Lawrence, and Jane Armitstead.

One of my favourite quotes is 'Be bold and mighty forces will come to your aid'. Here are a few of my mightiest forces. To the lovely Susan Johnson for making every day I worked with her a delight. To Matthew Condon, fellow author, for encouraging me to become one myself. To Liane Moriarty, who makes words sing, and is an all-round very good egg!

To Dame Quentin Bryce. Icon. Feminist. Bookworm. Hankie giver.

To Trent Dalton, who is always kind in word and deed. Thank you, Trent, for reading my book while you are possibly the busiest boy in the universe. Chancer. Journeyman. Gentleman.

There would be no book at all without Andrea, Pauline, Rebecca, Kirsten, Alison, Meg, Susan, Vanessa, Nicola, Justine, Emma, Patricia, Kate, Julie, Karen, Holly, Trish, Nuwani, Amber, Achini, Anthea, Zoy, Sally, Marina, Louise, Marg, and Marleni, because all of these women helped, in some way, to complete this book you are holding. And please forgive me if I have omitted someone.

Thanks to my family, and John's, for ongoing and appreciated support.

And thank you to John, lovely, stalwart friend and husband, for keeping me upright all these years, and for all the tea!

Thank you to Max and Tallulah for keeping me on my toes! You are, always have been, and always will be my best kind of beautiful.